Einar Falur Ingólfsson

Arnaldur Indriðason was born in 1961. He worked at an Icelandic newspaper, first as a journalist and then for many years as a film reviewer. He won the Glass Key Award for Best Nordic Crime Novel for both *Jar City* and *Silence of the Grave,* and in 2005 *Silence of the Grave* also won the CWA Gold Dagger Award for best crime novel of the year. Indriðason lives in Iceland, and he and J. K. Rowling are the only authors to simultaneously hold the top three spots on the Icelandic bestseller list.

Also by Arnaldur Indriðason
in English translation

Jar City
Silence of the Grave
The Draining Lake

Voices

Arnaldur Indriðason

Translated from the Icelandic by
Bernard Scudder

Picador
Thomas Dunne Books
St. Martin's Minotaur
New York

But when winter comes,
where will I find
the flowers, the sunshine,
the shadows of the earth?
The walls stand
speechless and cold,
the weathervanes
rattle in the wind.

From 'At the Middle of Life' by Friedrich Hölderlin
(translated by James Mitchell)

Voices

At last the moment arrived. The curtain went up, the auditorium unfolded; he felt glorious seeing all the people watching him and his shyness vanished in an instant. He saw some of his schoolmates and teachers, and the headmaster who seemed to nod approvingly at him. But most of them were strangers. All these people had come to listen to him and his beautiful voice, which had commanded attention, even outside Iceland.

The murmuring in the auditorium gradually died down and all eyes focused on him in silent expectation.

He saw his father sitting in the middle of the front row in his black horn-rimmed glasses, his legs crossed, and holding his hat on his knees. He saw him watching through the thick lenses and smiling encouragingly; this was the big moment in their lives. From now on, nothing would ever be the same.

The choirmaster raised his arms. Silence descended upon the auditorium.

And he began to sing with the clear, sweet voice that his father had described as divine.

FIRST DAY

1

Elínborg was waiting for them at the hotel.

A large Christmas tree stood in the lobby and there were decorations, fir branches and glittering baubles all around. 'Silent night, holy night', over an invisible sound system. A large shuttle coach stood in front of the hotel and a group approached the reception desk. Tourists who were planning to spend Christmas and the New Year in Iceland because it seemed to them like an adventurous and exciting country. Although they had only just landed, many had apparently already bought traditional Icelandic sweaters, and they checked into the exotic land of winter. Erlendur brushed the sleet off his raincoat. Sigurdur Óli looked around the lobby and caught sight of Elínborg by the lifts. He tugged at Erlendur and they walked over to her. She had examined the scene. The first police officers to arrive there had made sure that it would remain untouched.

The hotel manager had asked them not to cause a fracas. Used that phrase when he rang. This was a hotel and hotels thrive on their reputations, and he asked them to take that into account. So there were no sirens outside, nor uniformed policemen bursting in through the lobby. The manager said that at all costs they should avoid arousing fear among the guests.

Iceland mustn't be too exciting, too much of an adventure.

Now he was standing next to Elínborg and greeted Erlendur and

Sigurdur Óli with a handshake. He was so fat that his suit hardly encompassed his body. His jacket was done up across the stomach by one button that was on the verge of giving up. The top of his trousers was hidden beneath a huge paunch that bulged out of his jacket and the man sweated so furiously that he could never put away the large white handkerchief with which he mopped his forehead and the back of his neck at regular intervals. The white collar of his shirt was soaked in perspiration. Erlendur shook his clammy hand.

'Thank you,' the hotel manager said, puffing like a grampus. In his twenty years of managing the hotel he had never encountered anything like this.

'In the middle of the Christmas rush,' he groaned. 'I can't understand how this could happen! How could it happen?' he repeated, leaving them in no doubt as to how totally perplexed he was.

'Is he up or down?' Erlendur asked.

'Up or down?' the fat manager puffed. 'Do you mean whether he's gone to heaven?'

'Yes,' Erlendur said. 'That's exactly what we need to know ...'

'Shall we take the lift upstairs?' Sigurdur Óli asked.

'No,' the manager said, casting an irritated look at Erlendur. 'He's down here in the basement. He's got a little room there. We didn't want to chuck him out. And then you get this for your troubles.'

'Why would you have wanted to chuck him out?' Erlendur asked.

The hotel manager looked at him but did not reply.

They walked slowly down the stairs beside the lift. The manager went first. Going down the stairs was a strain for him and Erlendur wondered how he would get back up.

Apart from Erlendur, they had agreed to show a certain amount of consideration, to try to approach the hotel as discreetly as possible. Three police cars were parked at the back, with an ambulance. Police officers and paramedics had gone in through the back door. The

6

district medical officer was on his way. He would certify the death and call out a van to transport the body.

They walked down a long corridor with the panting manager leading the way. Plain-clothes policemen greeted them. The corridor grew darker the further they walked, because the light bulbs on the ceiling had blown and no one had bothered to change them. Eventually, in the darkness, they reached the door, which opened onto a little room. It was more like a storage space than a dwelling, but there was a narrow bed inside, a small desk and a tattered mat on the dirty tiled floor. There was a little window up near the ceiling.

The man was sitting on the bed, leaning against the wall. He was wearing a bright red Santa suit and still had the Santa cap on his head, but it had slipped down over his eyes. A large artificial Santa beard hid his face. He had undone the thick belt around his waist and unbuttoned his jacket. Beneath it he was wearing only a white vest. There was a fatal wound to his heart. Although there were other wounds on the body, the stabbing through the heart had finished him off. His hands had slash marks on them, as if he had tried to fight off the assailant. His trousers were down round his ankles. A condom hung from his penis.

'Rudolph the red-nosed reindeer,' Sigurdur Óli warbled, looking down at the body.

Elínborg hushed him.

In the room was a small wardrobe and the door was open. It contained folded trousers and sweaters, ironed shirts, underwear and socks. A uniform hung on a coat-hanger, navy blue with golden epaulettes and shiny brass buttons. A pair of smartly-polished black leather shoes stood beside the cupboard.

Newspapers and magazines were strewn over the floor. Beside the bed was a small table and lamp. On the table was a single book: *A History of the Vienna Boys' Choir*.

'Did he live here, this man?' Erlendur asked as he surveyed the scene. He and Elínborg had entered the room. Sigurdur Óli and the hotel manager were standing outside. It was too small for them all inside.

'We let him stay here,' the manager said awkwardly, mopping the sweat from his brow. 'He's been working for us for donkey's years. Since before my time. As a doorman.'

'Was the door open when he was found?' Sigurdur Óli asked, trying to be formal, as if to compensate for his little ditty.

'I asked her to wait for you,' the manager said. 'The girl who found him. She's in the staff coffee room. Gave her quite a shock, poor thing, as you can imagine.' The manager avoided looking into the room.

Erlendur walked up to the body and peered at the wound to the heart. He had no idea what kind of blade had killed the man. He looked up. Above the bed was an old, faded poster for a Shirley Temple film, sellotaped at the corners. Erlendur didn't know the film. It was called *The Little Princess*. The poster was the only decoration in the room.

'Who's that?' Sigurdur Óli asked from the doorway as he looked at the poster.

'It says on it,' Erlendur said. 'Shirley Temple.'

'Who's that then? Is she dead?'

'Who's Shirley Temple?' Elínborg was astonished at Sigurdur Óli's ignorance. 'Don't you know who she was? Didn't you study in America?'

'Was she a Hollywood star?' Sigurdur Óli asked, still looking at the poster.

'She was a child star,' Erlendur said curtly. 'So she's dead in a sense anyway.'

'Eh?' Sigurdur Óli said, failing to grasp the remark.

'A child star,' Elínborg said. 'I think she's still alive. I don't remember. I think she's something with the United Nations.'

It dawned on Erlendur that there were no other personal effects in the room. He looked around but could see no bookshelf, CDs or computer, no radio or television. Only a desk, chair, wardrobe and bed with a scruffy pillow and dirty duvet cover. The little room reminded him of a prison cell.

He went out into the corridor and peered into the darkness at the far end, and could make out a faint smell of burning, as if someone had been playing with matches there or possibly lighting their way.

'What's down there?' he asked the manager.

'Nothing,' he replied and looked up at the ceiling. 'Just the end of the corridor. A couple of bulbs have gone. I'll have that fixed.'

'How long had he lived here, this man?' Erlendur asked as he went back into the room.

'I don't know, since before my time.'

'So he was here when you became the manager?'

'Yes.'

'Are you telling me he lived in this hole for twenty years?'

'Yes.'

Elínborg looked at the condom.

'At least he practised safe sex,' she said.

'Not safe enough,' Sigurdur Óli said.

At that point the district medical officer arrived, accompanied by a member of the hotel staff who then went back along the corridor. The medical officer was very fat too, although nowhere near a match for the hotel manager. When he squeezed into the room, Elínborg darted back out for air.

'Hello, Erlendur,' the medical officer said.

'What does it look like?' Erlendur asked.

'Heart attack, but I need a better look,' replied the medical officer, who was known for his appalling sense of humour.

Erlendur looked out at Sigurdur Óli and Elínborg, who were grinning from ear to ear.

'Do you know when it happened?' Erlendur asked.

'Can't be very long ago. Some time during the last two hours. He's hardly begun to go cold. Have you located his reindeer?'

Erlendur groaned.

The medical officer lifted his hand from the body.

'I'll sign the certificate,' he said. 'You send it to the mortuary and they'll open him up there. They say that orgasm is a kind of moment of death,' he added, looking down at the body. 'So he had a double.'

'A double?' Erlendur didn't understand him.

'Orgasm, I mean,' the medical officer said. 'You'll take photographs, won't you?'

'Yes,' Erlendur said.

'They'll look nice in his family album.'

'He doesn't appear to have any family,' Erlendur said and looked around the room again. 'So you're done for the time being?' he asked, eager to put an end to the wisecracks.

The district medical officer nodded, squeezed back out of the room and went down the corridor.

'Won't we have to close down the hotel?' Elínborg asked, and noticed the manager gasp at her question. 'Stop all traffic in and out. Question everyone staying here and all the staff? Close the airports. Stop ships leaving port …'

'For God's sake,' the manager groaned, squeezing his handkerchief with an imploring look at Erlendur. 'It's only the doorman!'

Mary and Joseph would never have been given a room here, Erlendur thought to himself.

'This … this … filth has nothing to do with my guests,' the manager spluttered with indignation. 'They're tourists, almost all of them, and regional people, businessmen and the like. No one who has anything to do with the doorman. No one. This is one of the largest hotels in Reykjavík. It's packed over the holidays. You can't just close it down! You just can't!'

'We could, but we won't,' Erlendur said, trying to calm the manager down. 'We'll need to question some of the guests and most of the staff, I expect.'

'Thank God,' the manager sighed, regaining his composure.

'What was the man's name?'

'Gudlaugur,' the manager said. 'I think he's around fifty. And you're right about his family, I don't think he has any.'

'Who visited him?'

'I haven't got a clue,' the manager puffed.

'Has anything unusual happened at the hotel involving this man?'

'No.'

'Theft?'

'No. Nothing's happened.'

'Complaints?'

'No.'

'He hasn't become embroiled in anything that could explain this?'

'Not as far as I know.'

'Was he involved in any conflicts with anyone at this hotel?'

'Not that I know of.'

'Outside the hotel?'

'Not that I know of but I don't know him very well. Didn't,' the manager corrected himself.

'Not after twenty years?'

'No, not really. He wasn't very sociable, I don't think. Kept himself to himself as much as he could.'

'Do you think a hotel is the right place for a man like him?'

'Me? I don't know ... He was always very polite and there were never really any complaints about him.'

'Never really?'

'No, there were never any complaints about him. He wasn't a bad worker really.'

'Where's the staff coffee room?' Erlendur asked.

'I'll show you.' The hotel manager mopped his brow, relieved that they would not close the hotel.

'Did he have guests?' Erlendur asked.

'What?' the manager said.

'Guests,' Erlendur repeated. 'It looks like someone who knew him was here, don't you think?'

The manager looked at the body and his eyes dwelled on the condom.

'I don't know anything about his girlfriends,' he said. 'Nothing at all.'

'You don't know very much about this man,' Erlendur said.

'He's a doorman here,' the manager said, and felt that Erlendur should accept that by way of explanation.

They left the room. The forensics team went in with their equipment and more officers followed them. It was difficult for them all to squeeze their way past the manager. Erlendur asked them to examine the corridor carefully and the dark alcove further down. Sigurdur Óli and Elínborg stood inside the little room observing the body.

'I wouldn't like to be found like that,' Sigurdur Óli said.

'It's no concern of his any more,' Elínborg said.

'No, probably not,' Sigurdur Óli said.

'Is there anything in it?' Elínborg asked as she took out a little bag of salted peanuts. She was always nibbling at things. Sigurdur Óli thought it was because of nerves.

'In it?' Sigurdur Óli said.

She nodded in the direction of the body. After staring at her for a moment, Sigurdur Óli realised what she meant. He hesitated, then knelt down by the body and stared at the condom.

'No,' he said. 'It's empty.'

'So she killed him before his orgasm,' Elínborg said. 'The doctor thought—'

'She?' Sigurdur Óli said.

'Yes, isn't that obvious?' Elínborg said, emptying a handful of peanuts into her mouth. She offered some to Sigurdur Óli, who declined. 'Isn't there something tarty about it? He's had a woman in here,' she said. 'Hasn't he?'

'That's the simplest theory,' Sigurdur Óli said, standing up.

'You don't think so?' Elínborg said.

'I don't know. I don't have the faintest idea.'

2

The staff coffee room had little in common with the hotel's splendid lobby and well-appointed rooms. There were no Christmas decorations, no Christmas carols, only a few shabby kitchen tables and chairs, linoleum on the floor, torn in one place, and in one corner stood a kitchenette with cupboards, a coffee machine and a refrigerator. It was as if no one ever tidied up there. There were coffee stains on the tables and dirty cups all around. The ancient coffee machine was switched on and burped water.

Several hotel employees were sitting in a semicircle around a young girl who was still traumatised after finding the body. She had been crying and black mascara was smudged down her cheeks. She looked up when Erlendur entered with the hotel manager.

'Here she is,' the manager said as if she were guilty of intruding upon the sanctity of Christmas, and shooed the other staff out. Erlendur ushered him out after them, saying he wanted to talk to the girl in private. The manager looked at him in surprise but did not protest, muttering about having plenty of other things to do. Erlendur closed the door behind him.

The girl wiped the mascara off her cheeks and looked at Erlendur, uncertain what to expect. Erlendur smiled, pulled up a chair and sat facing her. She was around the same age as his own daughter, in her early twenties, nervous and still in shock from what she had seen. Her hair was black and she was slim, dressed in the hotel chambermaid's uniform, a light blue coat. A name tag was attached to her breast pocket. Ösp.

'Have you been working here long?' Erlendur asked.

'Almost a year,' Ösp said in a low voice. She looked at him. He did not give the impression that he would give her a hard time. With a snuffle she straightened up in her chair. Finding the body had clearly had a strong effect on her. She trembled slightly. Her name Ösp – meaning aspen – suited her, Erlendur thought to himself. She was like a twig in the wind.

'And do you like working here?' Erlendur asked.

'No,' she said.

'So why do you?'

'You have to work.'

'What's so bad about it?'

She looked at him as if he did not need to ask.

'I change the beds,' she said. 'Clean the toilets. Vacuum. But it's still better than a supermarket.'

'What about the people?'

'The manager's a creep.'

'He's like a fire hydrant with a leak.'

Ösp smiled.

'And some of the guests think you're only here for them to grope.'

'Why did you go down to the basement?' Erlendur asked.

'To fetch Santa. The kids were waiting for him.'

'Which kids?'

'At the Christmas ball. We have a Christmas party for the staff. For their children and any kids who are staying at the hotel, and he was playing Santa. When he didn't show up I was sent to fetch him.'

'That can't have been pleasant.'

'I've never seen a dead body before. And that condom.' Ösp tried to drive the image out of her mind.

'Did he have any girlfriends at the hotel?'

'None that I know of.'

'Do you know about any contacts of his outside the hotel?'

'I don't know anything about that man, though I've seen more of him than I should of.'

'Should have,' Erlendur corrected her.

'What?'

'You're supposed to say "should have", not "should of".'

She gave him a pitying look.

'Do you think it matters?'

'Yes, I do,' Erlendur said.

He shook his head, a remote expression on his face.

'Was the door open when you found him?'

Ösp thought.

'No, I opened it. I knocked and got no reply, so I waited and was just going to leave when it occurred to me to open the door. I thought it was locked but then it suddenly opened and he was sitting there naked with a rubber on his ...'

'Why did you think it would be locked?' Erlendur hurried to say. 'The door.'

'I just did. I knew it was his room.'

'Did you see anyone when you went down to fetch him?'

'No, no one.'

'So he'd got ready for the Christmas party, but someone came down and disturbed him. He was wearing his Santa suit.'

Ösp shrugged.

'Who did his bed?'

'What do you mean?'

'Who changed the linen? It hasn't been done for a long time.'

'I don't know. He must have done it himself.'

'You must have been shocked.'

'It was a revolting sight,' Ösp said.

'I know,' Erlendur said. 'You should try to forget it as quickly as possible. If you can. Was he a good Santa?'

The girl looked at him.

'What?' Erlendur said.

'I don't believe in Santa.'

The lady who organised the Christmas party was smartly dressed, short and, Erlendur thought, around thirty. She said she was the hotel's marketing and PR manager, but Erlendur could not have been less interested; most of the people he met these days were marketing-somethings. She had an office on the second floor and Erlendur found her on the phone there. The media had got wind of an incident at the hotel and Erlendur imagined she was telling lies to a reporter. The conversation came to a very abrupt end. The woman slammed down the phone with the words that she had absolutely no comment to make.

Erlendur introduced himself, shook her dry hand and asked her when she had last spoken to the, aahemm, man in the basement. He did not know whether to say doorman or Santa, he had forgotten his name. He felt he could hardly say Santa.

'Gulli?' she said, solving the problem. 'It was just this morning, to remind him of the Christmas party. I met him by the revolving doors. He was working. He was a doorman here as you perhaps know. And more than a doorman, a caretaker really. Mended things and all that.'

'Easy-going?'

'Pardon?'

'Helpful, easy-going, didn't need much nagging?'

'I don't know. Does that matter? He never did anything for me. Or rather, I never needed his help.'

'Why was he playing Santa? Was he fond of children? Funny? Fun?'

'That goes back before I started here. I've been working here for three years and this is the third Christmas party I've organised. He was the Santa the other two times and before that too. He was OK. As Santa. The kids liked him.'

Gudlaugur's death did not seem to have had the slightest effect on the woman. It was none of her business. All that the murder did was to disturb the marketing and PR for a while. Erlendur wondered how people could be so insensitive and boring.

'But what sort of person was he?'

'I don't know. I never got to know him. He was a doorman here. And the Santa. That was really the only time I ever spoke to him. When he was the Santa.'

'What happened to the Christmas party? When you found out that Santa was dead?'

'We called it off. Nothing else for it. Also out of respect for him,' she added, as if to show a hint of feeling at last. It was futile. Erlendur could tell that she could not care less about the body in the basement.

'Who knew this man best?' he asked. 'Here at the hotel, I mean.'

'I don't know. Try talking to the head of reception. The doorman worked for him.'

The telephone on her desk rang and she answered it. She gave Erlendur a look, implying that he was in her way, and he stood up and walked out, thinking that she could not go on telling lies over the phone for ever.

The reception manager had no time to deal with Erlendur. Tourists swarmed around the front desk and even though three other employees were helping to check them in, they could hardly handle the crowd. Erlendur watched them looking at passports, handing over key cards, smiling and moving on to the next guest. The crowd stretched back to the revolving doors. Through them Erlendur saw yet another tourist shuttle stop outside the hotel.

Policemen, most of them in plain clothes, were all over the building questioning the staff. A makeshift incident centre had been set up in the staff coffee room in the basement, from where the investigation was managed.

Erlendur contemplated the Christmas decorations in the lobby. A sentimental Christmas tune was playing over the sound system. He walked over to the large restaurant to one side of the lobby. The first guests were lining up around a splendid Christmas buffet. He walked past the table and admired the herring, smoked lamb, cold ham, ox tongue and all the trimmings, and the delicious desserts, ice cream, cream cakes and chocolate mousse, or whatever it was.

Erlendur's mouth watered. He had eaten almost nothing all day.

He looked all around and, almost too fast to be seen, popped a bite of spicy ox tongue into his mouth. He did not think anyone had noticed, and his heart leaped when he heard a sharp voice behind him.

'No, listen, that's not on. You mustn't do that!'

Erlendur turned round and a man wearing a large chef's hat walked up to him glaring.

'What's that supposed to mean, picking at the food? What kind of manners do you call that?'

'Take it easy,' Erlendur said, reaching for a plate. He began piling an assortment of delicacies onto the plate as if he had always intended to have the buffet.

'Did you know Santa Claus?' he asked to change the subject from the ox tongue.

'Santa Claus?' the cook said. 'What Santa Claus? And please don't put your fingers on the food. It's not—'

'Gudlaugur,' Erlendur interrupted him. 'Did you know him? He was a doorman and jack of all trades here, I'm told.'

'You mean Gulli?'

'Yes, Gulli.' Erlendur repeated his nickname as he put a generous slice of cold ham on his plate and a dash of yoghurt sauce over it. He wondered whether to call in Elínborg to appraise the buffet; she was a gourmet and had been assembling a book of recipes for many years.

'No, I … what do you mean by "did I know him"?' the cook asked.

'You haven't heard?'

'What? Is something wrong?'

'He's dead. Murdered. Hasn't word got around yet?'

'Murdered?' the cook groaned. 'Murdered! What, here? Who are you?'

'In his little room. Down in the basement. I'm from the police.'

Erlendur went on choosing goodies to put on his plate. The cook had forgotten the ox tongue.

'How was he murdered?'

'The least said the better.'

'At the hotel?'

'Yes.'

The cook looked all around.

'I don't believe it,' he said. 'Won't there be hell to pay?'

'Yes,' Erlendur said. 'There will be hell to pay.'

He knew that the hotel would never be able to shake off the murder. It would never wipe away the smear. After this it would always be known as the hotel where Santa was found dead with a condom on his penis.

'Did you know him?' Erlendur asked. 'Gulli?'

'No, hardly at all. He was a doorman here and fixed all sorts of stuff.'

'Fixed?'

'Yes, mended. I didn't know him at all.'

'Do you know who knew him best here?'

'No,' the cook said. 'I don't know anything about the man. Who could have murdered him? Here? At the hotel? My God!'

Erlendur could tell that he was more worried about the hotel than about the murdered man. He considered telling him that the murder might boost the occupancy rate. That's the way people think these days. They could even advertise the hotel as a murder scene. Develop crime-based tourism. But he could not be bothered. He wanted to sit down with his plate and eat the food. Have a moment's peace.

Sigurdur Óli turned up out of nowhere.

'Did you find anything?' Erlendur asked.

'No,' Sigurdur Óli said, looking at the cook, who hurried off to the kitchen with the news. 'Are you eating now?' he added with indignation.

'Oh, don't give me any crap. There was a compromising situation.'

'That man owned nothing, or if he did, he didn't keep it in his room,' Sigurdur Óli said. 'Elínborg found a couple of old records in his wardrobe. That was the lot. Shouldn't we shut down the hotel?'

'Shut down the hotel, what kind of nonsense is that?' Erlendur said. 'How are you going to go about shutting down this hotel? And how long do you plan to do that for? Are you going to send a search team into every room?'

'No, but the murderer could be one of the guests. We can't ignore that.'

'That's absolutely uncertain. There are two possibilities. Either he's at the hotel, a guest or an employee, or he's nothing to do with the hotel. What we need to do is to talk to all the staff and everyone who checks out over the next couple of days, especially those who check out earlier than they had planned, although I doubt that the person who did it would try to draw attention to himself like that.'

'No, right. I was thinking about the condom,' Sigurdur Óli said.

Erlendur looked for a vacant table, found one and sat down. Sigurdur Óli sat down with him and looked at the heaped plate, and his mouth began watering too.

'Well, if it's a woman she's still of child-bearing age, isn't she? Because of the condom.'

'Yes, that would have been the case twenty years ago,' Erlendur said, savouring the lightly smoked ham. 'Nowadays a condom's more than just a contraceptive. It's protection against bloody everything, chlamydia, Aids ...'

'The condom might also tell us that he wasn't very well acquainted with the ... the person who was in his room. That it must have been a quickie. If he'd known the person well he may not have used a condom.'

'We must remember that the condom doesn't rule out that he was with a man,' Erlendur said.

'What kind of implement could it be? The murder weapon?'

'We'll see what comes out of the autopsy. Obviously there's no problem getting hold of a knife at this hotel, if it was someone from here who attacked him.'

'Is that nice?' Sigurdur Óli asked. He had been watching Erlendur devouring the food and was sorely tempted to get some for himself but was afraid of causing even more of a scandal: two cops investigating a murder at a hotel, who sat down at the buffet as if nothing had happened.

'I forgot to check whether there was anything in it,' Erlendur said between bites.

'Do you think you ought to be eating at the murder scene?'

'This is a hotel.'

'Yes, but ...'

'I told you, I ran into a compromising situation. This was the only way to get out of it. Was there anything in it? The condom?'

'Empty,' Sigurdur Óli said.

'The medical officer thought he'd had an orgasm. Twice in fact, but I didn't really catch how he came to that conclusion.'

'I don't know anyone who can work out what he's talking about.'

'So the murder was committed in full swing.'

'Yes. Something happened when everything was hunky dory.'

'If everything was hunky dory, why take along a knife?'

'Maybe it was part of the game.'

'What game?'

'Sex has become much more complex than just the old missionary position,' Sigurdur Óli said. 'So it could be anyone?'

'Anyone,' Erlendur said. 'Why do they always talk about the missionary position? What's the mission?'

'I don't know.' Sigurdur Óli sighed. Sometimes Erlendur asked questions that irritated him because they were so simple but at the same time so infinitely complicated and dull.

'Is it something from Africa?'

'Or Catholicism,' Sigurdur Óli said.

'Why missionary?'

'I don't know.'

'The condom doesn't rule out either sex,' Erlendur said. 'Let's establish that. The condom doesn't rule out anything. Did you ask the manager why he wanted rid of Santa Claus?'

'No, did he want rid of Santa?'

'He mentioned it without any explanation. We have to find out what he meant.'

'I'll jot that down,' said Sigurdur Óli, who always carried around a notepad and pencil.

'And then there's one group that uses condoms more than other people.'

'Really?' Sigurdur Óli said, his face one huge question mark.

'Prostitutes.'

'Prostitutes?' Sigurdur Óli repeated. 'Hookers? Do you think there are any here?'

Erlendur nodded.

'They do a lot of missionary work at hotels.'

Sigurdur Óli stood up and dawdled in front of Erlendur, who had finished his plate and was eyeing up the buffet again.

'Ehmmm, where will you be spending Christmas?' Sigurdur Óli asked awkwardly.

'Christmas?' Erlendur said. 'I'll be ... what do you mean, where will I be spending Christmas? Where should I spend Christmas? What business of yours is that?'

Sigurdur Óli hesitated, then took the plunge.

'Bergthóra was wondering if you'd be on your own.'

'Eva Lind has some plans. What did Bergthóra mean? That I should visit you?'

'I don't know,' Sigurdur Óli said. 'Women! Who ever understands them?' Then he sauntered away from the table and down to the basement.

Elínborg was standing in front of the murdered man's room, watching the forensics team at work, when Sigurdur Óli came walking down the dim corridor.

'Where's Erlendur?' she asked, throttling her little bag of peanuts.

'At the buffet,' Sigurdur Óli said peevishly.

A preliminary test made that evening revealed that the condom was covered with saliva.

3

Forensics contacted Erlendur as soon as the biopsy results were available. He was still at the hotel. For a while the scene of the crime looked like a photographer's studio. Flashes lit up the dim corridor at regular intervals. The body was photographed from all angles, along with everything found in Gudlaugur's room. The corpse was then transported to the morgue on Barónsstígur where the postmortem would be performed. Forensics had combed the doorman's room for fingerprints and found many sets, which would be checked against the police records. All the hotel staff were to be fingerprinted and the forensics team's discovery also meant that saliva samples would have to be taken.

'What about the guests?' Elínborg asked. 'Won't we have to do the same with them?'

She yearned to get home and regretted the question; she wanted to finish her shift. Elínborg took Christmas very seriously and missed her family. She hung up fir branches and decorations all around her home. She baked delicious cookies, which she stored in her Tupperware boxes, carefully labelled by variety. Her Christmas roast was legendary, even outside her extended family. The main course every Christmas was a Swedish-style leg of pork, which she kept outside on the balcony to marinate for twelve days, and tended it just as carefully as if it had been the baby Jesus in swaddling clothes.

'I think we have to assume, initially, that the murderer is an Icelander,' Erlendur said. 'Let's keep the guests in reserve. The hotel is filling up for Christmas now and few people are checking out. We'll talk to the ones who do, take saliva samples, even fingerprints. We can't prevent them from leaving the country. They would have to be prime suspects for us to do that. And we need a list of the foreigners staying at the hotel at the time of the murder, we'll forget about the ones who check in afterwards. Let's try to keep it simple.'

'But what if it isn't that simple?' Elínborg asked.

'I don't think any of the guests know there was a murder,' said Sigurdur Óli, who wanted to get home too. Bergthóra, his partner, had phoned him towards evening and asked if he was on his way. It was exactly the right time now and she was waiting for him, she had said. Sigurdur Óli knew immediately what she meant by 'the right time'. They were trying to have a baby but nothing was happening and he had told Erlendur that they were beginning to talk about IVF.

'Don't you have to give them a jarful?' Erlendur asked.

'A jarful?' Sigurdur Óli said.

'In the mornings?'

Sigurdur Óli looked at Erlendur until he realised what he meant.

'I should never have told you,' he growled.

Erlendur sipped his foul-tasting coffee. The three of them were sitting by themselves in the staff coffee room in the basement. All the commotion was over, the police officers and forensics team had left, the room was sealed off. Erlendur was in no hurry. He had no one to go to, only his gloomy apartment in a block of flats. Christmas meant nothing to him. He had a few days holiday owing and nothing to do with them. Perhaps his daughter would visit him and they would boil smoked lamb. Sometimes her brother came with her. And Erlendur sat and read, which he always did anyway.

'You ought to get yourselves home,' he said. 'I'm going to potter around a little longer. Find out whether I can't talk to that head of reception who never has the time.'

Elínborg and Sigurdur Óli stood up.

'Will you be OK?' Elínborg asked. 'Why don't you just go home? Christmas is coming and—'

'What's with you and Sigurdur Óli? Why don't you leave me in peace?'

'It's Christmas,' Elínborg said with a sigh. Dithered. Then she said, 'Forget it.' She and Sigurdur Óli turned round and left the coffee room.

Erlendur sat for a good while, sunk in thought. He pondered Sigurdur Óli's question about where he was going to spend Christmas, and mulled over Elínborg's thoughtfulness. He saw an image of his flat, the armchair, the battered old television set and the books lining the walls.

Sometimes he bought a bottle of Chartreuse at Christmas and had a glass beside him while he read about ordeals and death in the days when people travelled everywhere on foot and Christmas could be the most treacherous time of the year. Determined to visit their loved ones, people would battle with the forces of nature, go astray and perish; for those awaiting them back home, Christmas turned from a celebration of salvation to a nightmare. The bodies of some travellers were found. Others were not. They were never found.

These were Erlendur's Christmas carols.

The head of reception had taken off his hotel jacket and was putting on his raincoat when Erlendur located him in the cloakroom. He said he was exhausted and wanted to get home to his family like everyone else. He had heard about the murder, yes, terrible, but did not know how he could be of assistance.

'I understand you knew him better than most people at the hotel,' Erlendur said.

'No, I don't think that's right,' the head of reception said as he wrapped a thick scarf around his neck. 'Who told you that?'

'He worked for you, didn't he?' Erlendur replied, ignoring the question.

'Worked for me, yes, probably. He was a doorman, I'm in charge of the reception, the check-in, as you may know. Do you know how long the shops are open tonight?'

He gave the impression of not being particularly interested in Erlendur and his questions, which irritated the detective. And it irritated him that no one seemed to care in the slightest about the fate the man in the basement had met.

'Round the clock, I don't know. Who could have wanted to stab your doorman in the chest?'

'Mine? He wasn't my doorman. He was the hotel's doorman.'

'And why did he have his trousers round his ankles and a condom on his todger? Who was with him? Who normally came to visit him? Who were his friends at the hotel? Who were his friends outside the hotel? Who were his enemies? Why was he living at this hotel? What was the deal? What are you hiding? Why can't you answer me like a decent human being?'

'Hey, I, what…?' The man fell silent. 'I just want to get home,' he said eventually. 'I don't know the answers to all those questions. Christmas is coming. Can we talk tomorrow? I haven't had a moment's rest all day.'

Erlendur looked at him.

'We'll talk tomorrow,' he said. As he left the cloakroom he suddenly remembered the question that had been vexing him ever since he met the hotel manager. He turned round. The man was on his way out through the door when Erlendur called to him.

'Why did you want to get rid of him?'

'What?'

'You wanted to get rid of him. Santa. Why?'

The reception manager hesitated.

'He'd been sacked.'

Erlendur found the hotel manager sitting down to a meal. He was at a large table in the kitchen, wearing a chef's apron and devouring the contents of the half-empty trays that had been brought in from the buffet.

'You can't imagine how I love eating,' he said, wiping his mouth, when he noticed Erlendur staring at him. 'In peace,' he added.

'I know exactly what you mean,' Erlendur said.

They were alone in the large, polished kitchen. Erlendur could only admire him. He ate quickly, but deftly and without greed. There was something almost elegant about the motions of his hands. One bite after another disappeared inside him, smoothly and with a visible passion.

He was calmer now that the body had been removed from the hotel and the police had gone, along with the reporters who had been standing outside the hotel; the police had ordered them to stay out, the entire building was deemed a crime scene. The hotel was returning to business as normal. Very few tourists knew about the body in the basement, but many noticed the police activity and asked about it. The manager instructed his staff to say something about an old man and a heart attack.

'I know what you're thinking. You think I'm a pig, don't you?' he said, pausing to take a sip of red wine. His little finger darted out, the size of a cocktail sausage.

'No, but I do understand why you want to run a hotel,' Erlendur said. Then he lost his patience. 'You're killing yourself, you know that,' he said brashly.

'I weigh 180 kilos,' the manager said. 'Farmed pigs don't get much heavier. I've always been fat. Never known otherwise. Never been on a diet. I've never been able to think of changing my lifestyle, as they say. I feel good. Better than you, from the look of things,' he added.

Erlendur remembered hearing that fat people were supposed to be jollier than skinny people. He did not believe it himself.

'Better than me?' he said with a hint of a smile. 'You're the last person to judge. Why did you sack the doorman?'

The manager had resumed eating and some time passed before he put down his knife and fork. Erlendur waited patiently. He could see the manager weighing up the best answer, how to phrase it, given that he had found out about the dismissal.

'We haven't been doing too well,' he said eventually. 'We're over-booked in the summer and there's always plenty of traffic over Christmas and the New Year, but then come dead periods that can be damned difficult. The owners said we had to cut back. Lay off staff. I didn't think it was necessary to have a full-time doorman all year round.'

'But I'm told he was much more than just a doorman. Santa Claus, for example. A jack of all trades. Mended things. More like a care-taker.'

The manager had gone back to feeding his face yet again and another break in their conversation ensued. Erlendur looked around. After taking down their names and addresses, the police had allowed the staff who had finished their shifts to go home; it had still not been established who was the last person to talk to the victim, nor what happened on the last day of his life. No one had noticed anything unusual about Santa. No one had seen anybody go down to the base-ment. No one knew of him ever having visitors there. Only a couple of people knew that he lived there permanently, that the little room was his home, and apparently they wanted to know as little as pos-sible about him. Very few said they knew him and he did not seem to have had any friends at the hotel. Nor did the employees know about any friends of his outside it.

A real Lone Wolf, Erlendur thought to himself.

'No one is indispensable,' the manager said, his sausage-like finger protruding again he took another sip of red wine. 'Of course, firing people is never fun, but we can't afford to have a doorman all year. That's why he was sacked. No other reason. And there wasn't really much door-manning to do. He put on his uniform when film stars or foreign dignitaries came, and he threw out undesirables.'

'Did he take it badly? Being sacked?'

'He understood, I think.'

'Are any knives missing from the kitchen?' Erlendur asked.

'I don't know. We lose knives and forks and glasses worth hundreds of thousands of krónur every year. And towels and … Do you think he was stabbed with a knife from the kitchen?'

'I don't know.'

Erlendur watched the manager eat.

'He worked here for twenty years and no one knew him. Don't you find that unusual?'

'Employees come and go,' the manager shrugged. 'There's a high staff turnover in this business. I think people knew about him, but who knows who? Don't ask me. I don't know anyone here that well.'

'You've stayed put through all these staff changes.'

'I'm difficult to move.'

'Why did you talk about chucking him out?'

'Did I say that?'

'Yes.'

'Then it was just a turn of phrase. I didn't mean anything by it.'

'But you'd sacked him and were going to chuck him out,' Erlendur said. 'Then someone comes along and kills him. It hasn't exactly been going well for him recently.'

The manager acted as though Erlendur was not even there while he filled himself with cakes and mousse with his delicate, gourmandising motions, trying to savour the treats.

'Why was he still here if you'd sacked him?'

'He was supposed to leave at the end of last month. I'd been hurrying him along, but didn't pressure him. I should have. Then I'd have avoided this nonsense.'

Erlendur watched the manager scoffing his food, and said nothing. Maybe it was the buffet. Maybe the gloomy block of flats. Maybe the time of year. The microwave dinner waiting for him at home. The lonely Christmas. Erlendur did not know. Somehow the question just came out. Before he knew it.

'A room?' the manager said, as if not understanding what Erlendur meant.

'It doesn't have to be anything special,' Erlendur said.

'You mean for you?'

'A single room is fine,' Erlendur said.

'We're fully booked. Unfortunately.' The hotel manager stared at Erlendur. He didn't want to have the detective over him day and night.

'The head of reception said there was a vacant room,' Erlendur lied, more firmly now. 'He said it was no problem if I just talked to you.'

The manager stared at him. Looked down at his unfinished mousse. Then he pushed the plate away, his appetite ruined.

It was cold in the room. Erlendur stood gazing out of the window, but saw nothing apart from his own reflection in the glass. He hadn't looked that man in the face for some time and he noticed in the darkness how he was ageing. Snowflakes fell cautiously to the ground, as if the heavens had split open and their dust was being strewn over the world.

A little book of verse that he owned suddenly entered his mind, exceptionally elegant translations of poems by Hölderlin. He let his mind wander through them until he stopped at a line that he knew applied to the man looking back at him from the window.

The walls stand speechless and cold, the weathervanes rattle in the wind.

4

He was falling asleep when he heard a tap on his door and a voice whispering his name.

He knew at once who it was. When he opened the door he saw his daughter, Eva Lind, standing in the corridor. They looked each other in the eye, she smiled at him and slipped past him into the room. He closed the door. She sat down at the little desk and took out a packet of cigarettes.

'I don't think you're allowed to smoke in here,' said Erlendur, who had obeyed the smoke-free policy.

'Yeah, yeah,' Eva Lind said, fishing a cigarette out of the packet. 'Why's it so cold in here?'

'I think the radiator's broken.'

Erlendur sat down on the side of the bed. Dressed only in his underpants, he pulled the quilt over his head and shoulders and wore it like a wrap.

'What are you doing?' Eva Lind asked.

'I'm cold,' Erlendur said.

'I mean, the hotel room, why don't you just go home?' She inhaled deep into her lungs, almost a third of the cigarette frizzled away, and then she exhaled, filling the room with smoke.

'I don't know. I don't ...' Erlendur stopped.

'Feel like getting yourself home?'

'Somehow it didn't seem right. A man was murdered in this hotel today, have you heard?'

'Santa Claus, wasn't it? Was he murdered?'

'The doorman. He was supposed to play Santa for the children in the hotel. How are you doing?'

'Great,' Eva Lind said.

'Still at work?'

'Yes.'

Erlendur watched her. She looked better. She was still as skinny as ever but the rings under her beautiful blue eyes had faded and her cheeks were not so sunken. He didn't think she had touched drugs for almost eight months. Not since she had a miscarriage and lay in a coma at the hospital, halfway between this world and the next. When she was discharged from the hospital she moved in with him and got herself a steady job for the first time in two years. For the past few months she had been renting a room in town.

'How did you find out where I was?' Erlendur asked.

'I couldn't get you on your mobile so I called the station and was told you had checked in to the hotel. What's going on? Why don't you go home?'

'I don't really know what to say,' Erlendur said. 'Christmas is a funny time.'

'Yeah,' Eva Lind said, and they fell silent.

'Heard anything from your brother?' Erlendur asked.

'Sindri's still working out of town,' Eva Lind said, and the cigarette hissed as it burned down to the filter. Ash dropped to the floor. She looked for an ashtray but couldn't see one, so she stood the cigarette up on end on the desk to let it burn out.

'And your mother?' Erlendur said. It was always the same questions, and the answers were generally the same as well.

'OK. Slaving away as usual.'

Erlendur said nothing. Eva Lind watched the blue cigarette smoke curling up from the desk.

'I don't know if I can hold out any longer,' she said, staring at the smoke.

Erlendur looked up from beneath his quilt.

There was a knock on the door and they exchanged looks of surprise. Eva stood up and opened the door. A member of staff was standing in the corridor, dressed in his hotel jacket. He said he worked at reception.

'Smoking is prohibited here,' was the first thing he said when he looked inside the room.

'I asked her to put it out,' Erlendur said, sitting in his underpants under the quilt. 'She's never listened to me.'

'And it's prohibited to have girls in the rooms too,' the man said. 'Because of what happened.'

Eva Lind gave a faint smile and looked over at her father. Erlendur looked up at his daughter and then at the employee.

'We were told a girl had come up here,' he continued. 'That's not allowed. You'll have to leave. Now.'

He stood in the doorway, waiting for Eva Lind to accompany him. Erlendur stood up, still with the quilt over his shoulders, and walked over to the man.

'She's my daughter,' he said.

'Of course,' the man from the reception said, as if that was none of his business.

'Seriously,' Eva Lind said.

The man looked at each of them in turn.

'I don't want any trouble,' he said.

'Bugger off then and leave us in peace,' Eva Lind said.

He stood looking at Eva Lind and at Erlendur in his underpants beneath the quilt, and did not budge.

'There's something wrong with the radiator in here,' Erlendur said. 'It doesn't heat up.'

'She'll have to come with me,' the man said.

Eva Lind looked at her father and shrugged.

'We'll talk later,' she said. 'I'm not taking this bullshit.'

'What do you mean, you can't hold out any longer?' Erlendur said.

'We'll talk later,' Eva said, and went out of the door.

The man smiled at Erlendur.

'Are you going to do something about the radiator in here?' Erlendur asked.

'I'll notify maintenance,' he said, and closed the door.

Erlendur sat back down on the edge of the bed. Eva Lind and Sindri Snaer were the fruit of a failed marriage that had come to an end more than two decades ago. Erlendur had had virtually no contact with his children after the divorce. His ex-wife, Halldóra, made sure of that. She felt betrayed and used the children to get her own back on him. Erlendur resigned himself to it. Ever since, he had regretted not insisting on his right to see his children. Regretted leaving it all up to Halldóra. When they grew older they tracked him down for themselves. His daughter was doing drugs by then. His son had already been through rehab for alcoholism.

He knew what Eva meant when she said she didn't know whether she could hold out. She had not been through treatment. Not been to any institution for help with her problem. She had tackled it herself, alone. Had always been reticent, spiteful and headstrong when the question of her lifestyle arose. Even when pregnant she had not managed to kick the drug habit. She made attempts, and gave up for a while, but lacked the resolve to quit for good. She tried, and Erlendur knew that she did so in complete earnestness, but it was too much and she always slipped back into her old ways. He didn't know what made her so dependent on drugs that she gave them priority over everything else in life. Didn't know the root of her self-destruction, but realised that in some way he had failed her. That in some way he was also to blame for the situation she was in.

He had sat by Eva's bedside at the hospital when she was in a coma, talking to her because the doctor said she might hear his voice and even sense his presence. A few days later she came round and the first thing she asked was to see her father. She was so frail that she could hardly speak. When he visited her she was asleep and he sat beside her and waited for her to wake up.

At last, when she opened her eyes and saw him, she seemed to try to smile, but she started to cry and he stood up and hugged her. She trembled in his arms and he tried to calm her, laid her back on the pillow and wiped the tears from her eyes.

'Where have you been all these long days?' he said, stroking her cheek and trying to give a smile of encouragement.

'Where's the baby?' she asked.

'Didn't they tell you what happened?'

'I lost it. They didn't tell me where it is. I haven't been allowed to see it. They don't trust me …'

'I came very close to losing you.'

'Where is it?'

Erlendur had been to see the baby when it lay still-born in the operating theatre, a little girl who might have been given the name Audur.

'Do you want to see the baby?' he asked.

'Forgive me,' Eva said in a low voice.

'For what?'

'The way I am. The way the baby …'

'I don't need to forgive the way you are, Eva. You shouldn't apologise for the way you are.'

'Yes, I should.'

'Your fate isn't in your own hands alone.'

'Would you …?'

Eva Lind stopped talking and lay on the bed, exhausted. Erlendur waited in silence while she mustered her strength. A long time passed. Eventually she looked at her father.

'Will you help me bury her?' she said.

'Of course,' he said.

'I want to see her,' Eva said.

'Do you think …?'

'I want to see her,' she repeated. 'Please. Let me see her.'

After a moment's hesitation Erlendur went to the mortuary and came back with the body of the girl whom in his mind he called Audur because he did not want her to be anonymous. He carried the body along the hospital corridor in a white towel because Eva was too weak to move, and he brought it to her in intensive care. Eva held her baby, looked at it, then looked up at her father.

'It's my fault,' she said in a low voice.

Erlendur thought she was about to burst into tears and was surprised when she did not. There was an air of calm about her that veiled the repulsion she felt towards herself.

'Feel free to have a cry,' he said.

Eva looked at him.

'I don't deserve to cry,' she said.

She sat in a wheelchair in Fossvogur cemetery and watched the vicar strewing the three spadefuls of soil over the coffin, with an expression of unflinching toughness. Only with difficulty could she stand, but she pushed Erlendur away when he moved to help her. She made the sign of the cross over her daughter's grave and her lips quivered; Erlendur couldn't tell whether through fighting back the tears or mouthing a silent prayer.

It was a beautiful spring day, the sun was glittering on the surface of the water in the bay and down in Nauthólsvík people could be seen strolling in the fine weather. Halldóra stood some distance away and Sindri Snaer by the edge of the grave, far from his father. They could hardly have stood further apart; a disparate group with nothing in common except the misery of their lives. Erlendur reflected that the family hadn't been all together for almost a quarter of a century. He looked over at Halldóra, who avoided looking his way. He did not speak to her, nor she to him.

Eva Lind slumped back into the wheelchair and Erlendur attended to her and heard her groan.

'Fuck life.'

Erlendur snapped out of his thoughts when he remembered something that the man from the reception had said which he wanted to insist on an explanation for. He stood up, went into the corridor and saw the man disappearing into the lift. Eva was nowhere to be seen. He called out to the man who held the lift door, stepped back out and sized up Erlendur as he stood in front of him, barefoot, in his underpants with the quilt still draped over him.

'What did you mean when you said "Because of what happened"?' Erlendur asked.

'Because of what happened?' the man repeated with a puzzled expression.

'You said I couldn't have the girl in my room because of what happened.'

'Yes.'

'You mean what happened to Santa in the basement.'

'Yes. What do you know about …?'

Erlendur looked down at his underpants and hesitated for a moment.

'I'm taking part in the investigation,' he said. 'The police investigation.'

The man looked at him, unable to conceal an expression of disbelief.

'Why did you make that connection?' Erlendur hurried to say.

'I don't follow,' the man said, dithering in front of him.

'So if Santa hadn't been killed it would be all right to have a girl in the room. That was the way you said it. You see what I mean?'

'No,' the man said. 'Did I say "Because of what happened"? I don't remember that.'

'You said just that. The girl wasn't allowed to be in the room because of what happened. You thought my daughter was a ...' Erlendur tried to put it delicately but failed. 'You thought my daughter was a tart and you came to throw her out because Santa got murdered. If that hadn't happened it would have been all right to have a girl in the room. Do you allow girls in the rooms? When everything's all right?'

The man looked at Erlendur.

'What do you mean by girls?'

'Tarts,' Erlendur said. 'Do tarts hang around the hotel, nipping into the rooms, and you ignore it apart from now because of what happened? What did Santa have to do with that? Was he connected with it somehow?'

'I haven't a clue what you're talking about,' the man said.

Erlendur changed tack.

'I can understand that you want to exercise caution when there's been a murder at the hotel. You don't want to draw attention to anything unusual or abnormal even if it's innocent, and there's nothing to say about that. People can do what they want and pay for it for all I care. What I need to know is whether Santa was connected with prostitution at this hotel.'

'I don't know anything about any prostitution,' the man said. 'As you saw, we keep a lookout for girls who go to rooms on their own. Was that really your daughter?'

'Yes,' Erlendur said.

'She told me to fuck off.'

'That's her.'

Erlendur closed the door to his room behind him, lay down on the bed and soon fell asleep, dreaming that the heavens were strewn over him, and that he heard the sound of weathervanes rattling in the wind.

SECOND DAY

5

The reception manager had not yet arrived for work when Erlendur went down to the lobby and asked for him. He had given no explanation for his absence, nor phoned in sick or to say he needed the day off to run some errands. A lady in her thirties who worked at reception told Erlendur that it was certainly unusual for the reception manager not to turn up on time, always such a punctual man, and incomprehensible of him not to get in touch if he needed time off.

She told Erlendur this in between pauses while a biotechnician from the National Hospital took a swab of her saliva. Three biotechnicians were collecting samples from the hotel staff. Another group went to the homes of the employees who were not at work. Soon the biotechnicians would have DNA from the hotel's entire staff to compare with the saliva on Santa's condom.

Detectives interrogated the staff about their acquaintanceship with Gudlaugur and the whereabouts of each and every one of them the previous afternoon. The entire Reykjavík CID took part in the murder investigation while information and evidence were being collected.

'What about people who've recently left or worked here a year ago or whatever, and knew Santa?' Sigurdur Óli asked. He sat down beside Erlendur in the dining room and watched him partake of herring and ryebread, cold ham, toast and piping hot coffee.

'Let's see what we discover from this for starters,' Erlendur said, slurping his coffee. 'Have you found out anything about this Gudlaugur?'

'Not much. There doesn't seem to be a lot to say about him. He was forty-eight, single, no children. He'd been working here for the past twenty years or so. I understand he lived in that little room down in the basement for years. It was only supposed to be a temporary solution at the time, that fat manager implied. But he says he's not familiar with the matter. Told us to talk to the previous manager. He was the one who made the deal with Santa. Fatso reckoned Gudlaugur had lost the place he was renting and was allowed to keep his stuff in the room, and he just never left.'

Sigurdur Óli paused, then said: 'Elínborg told me you stayed at the hotel last night.'

'I can hardly recommend it. The room's cold and the staff never give you a moment's peace. But the food's good. Where is Elínborg?'

The dining room was busy and the hotel guests made a din as they indulged in the breakfast spread. Most of them were tourists wearing traditional Icelandic sweaters, hiking boots and thick winter clothing, even though they were going no further than the city centre, ten minutes' walk away. The waiters made sure their coffee cups were refilled and their used plates taken away. Christmas songs were playing softly over the sound system.

'The main hearing starts today. You knew that, didn't you?' Sigurdur Óli asked.

'Yes.'

'Elínborg's down there. How do you think it will turn out?'

'I suppose it will be a couple of months, suspended. Always the same with those bloody judges.'

'Surely he won't be allowed to keep the boy.'

'I don't know,' Erlendur said.

'The bastard,' Sigurdur Óli said. 'They ought to put him in the stocks in the town square.'

Elínborg had been in charge of the investigation. An eight-year-old boy had been committed to hospital after being seriously assaulted. No one had been able to get a word out of him about the attack. The initial theory was that older children had set on him outside the school and beaten him up so badly that he suffered a broken arm, fractured cheekbone and two loose upper teeth. He crawled home in a terrible state. His father notified the police when he got back from work shortly afterwards. An ambulance took the boy to hospital.

The boy was an only child. His mother was in the Kleppur mental hospital when the incident took place. He lived with his father, who owned and ran an internet company, in a big and beautiful two-storey house with a commanding view of the city in Breidholt suburb. Naturally, the father was distressed after the assault and talked about taking vengeance on the boys who had hurt his son so horrifically. He insisted that Elínborg bring them to justice.

Elínborg might never have found out the truth had they not lived in a two-storey house with the boy's room upstairs.

'She identifies with it in a bad way,' Sigurdur Óli said. 'Elínborg has a boy the same age.'

'You shouldn't let that influence you too much,' Erlendur said vacantly.

'Says who?'

The peaceful atmosphere of the breakfast buffet was disturbed by a noise from the kitchen. All the guests looked up, then at each other. A loud-voiced man was ranting about something or other. Erlendur and Sigurdur Óli stood up and went into the kitchen. The voice belonged to the head chef who had caught Erlendur when he nibbled at the ox tongue. He was raging at a biotechnician who wanted to take a saliva sample from him.

' ... and bugger off out of here with your bloody swabs!' the chef shouted at a woman of fifty who had a little sampling box open on the table. She went on insisting politely in spite of his fury, which did not soothe his temper. When he saw Erlendur and Sigurdur Óli his rage was redoubled.

'Are you mad?' he shouted. 'Do you think I was down there with Gulli putting a condom on his dick? Are you lot mental? Fucking idiots! No way. No bloody way. I don't give a monkey's what you say! You can stick me in jail and throw away the key but I'm not taking part in this bloody fiasco! Just get that straight! Fucking idiots!'

The chef strode out of the kitchen, swollen with righteous male indignation which was rather undermined, however, by his chimney-like white hat, and Erlendur began to smile. He looked at the bio-technician who smiled back and started to laugh. The tension in the kitchen eased. The cooks and waiters who had gathered round roared with laughter.

'You having trouble?' Erlendur asked the biotechnician.

'No, not at all,' she said. 'Everyone's very understanding really. He's the first one to make a scene about it.'

She smiled, and Erlendur thought her smile was pretty. She was roughly the same height as him, with thick, blond hair, cut short, and was wearing a colourful knitted cardigan buttoned down the front. Under the cardigan was a white blouse. She was wearing jeans and elegant black leather shoes.

'My name's Erlendur,' he said, almost instinctively, and held out his hand.

She became a little flustered.

'Yes,' she said, shaking his hand. 'I'm Valgerdur.'

'Valgerdur?' he repeated. He did not see a wedding ring.

Erlendur's mobile phone rang in his pocket.

'Excuse me,' he said, answering the phone. He heard an old, familiar voice asking for him.

'Is that you?' the voice asked.

'Yes, it's me,' Erlendur said.

'I'll never get the hang of these mobile phones,' the voice said. 'Where are you? Are you at the hotel? Maybe you're rushing off somewhere. Or in a lift.'

'I'm at the hotel.' Erlendur put his hand over the mouthpiece and asked Valgerdur to wait a moment, then went back into the dining room and out to the lobby. It was Marion Briem on the phone.

'Are you sleeping at the hotel?' Marion asked. 'Is something wrong? Why don't you go home?'

Marion Briem had worked for the old Police Investigation Department when that institution was still around, and had been Erlendur's mentor. Was already there when Erlendur joined and had taught him the detective's craft. Marion sometimes phoned Erlendur and complained that he never visited. Erlendur had never really liked his former boss and felt no particular urge to reappraise his feelings in Marion's old age. Perhaps because they were too similar. Perhaps because in Marion he saw his own future and wanted to avoid it. Marion lived a lonely life and hated being old.

'Why are you phoning?' Erlendur asked.

'Some people still keep me in the picture, even if you don't,' Marion said.

Erlendur was about to put a swift end to the conversation, but stopped himself. Marion had assisted him before, without being asked. He mustn't be rude.

'Can I help you with anything?' Erlendur asked.

'Give me the man's name. I might find something you've over-looked.'

'You never give up.'

'I'm bored,' Marion said. 'You can't imagine how bored I am. I retired almost ten years ago and I can tell you, every day in this hell is like an eternity. Like a thousand years, every single day.'

'There are plenty of things for senior citizens to do,' Erlendur said. 'Have you tried bingo?'

'Bingo!' Marion roared.

Erlendur passed on Gudlaugur's name. He briefed Marion on the case and then said goodbye. His phone rang almost immediately afterwards.

'Yes,' Erlendur said.

'We found a note in the man's room,' a voice said over the phone. It was the head of forensics.

'A note?'

'It says: Henry 18.30.'

'Henry? Wait a minute, when did the girl find Santa?'

'It was about seven.'

'So this Henry could have been in his room when he was killed?'

'I don't know. And there's another thing.'

'Go on.'

'Santa could have owned the condom himself. There was a packet of them in the pocket of his doorman's uniform. It's a packet of ten and three are missing.'

'Anything else?'

'No, just a wallet with a five-hundred-króna note, an old ID card and a supermarket receipt dated the day before yesterday. Oh yes, and a key ring with two keys on it.'

'What sort of keys?'

'One looks like a house key, but the other could be to a locker or something like that. It looks much smaller.'

They said goodbye and Erlendur looked around for the biotechnician, but she was gone.

Two guests at the hotel were named Henry. Henry Bartlet, American, and Henry Wapshott, British. The latter did not answer when his room was dialled, but Bartlett was in and showed surprise when it emerged that the Icelandic police wanted to talk to him. The hotel manager's story about the old man's heart attack had clearly got around.

Erlendur took Sigurdur Óli with him to meet Henry Bartlet; Sigurdur Óli had studied criminology in the US and was rather proud of the fact. He spoke the language like a native and although Erlendur had a particular dislike for the American drawl, he put up with it.

On the way up to Bartlett's floor, Sigurdur Óli told Erlendur that they had talked to most of the hotel employees who were on duty when Gudlaugur was attacked. All had alibis and named people to corroborate their stories.

Bartlet was about thirty, a stockbroker from Colorado. He and his wife had seen a programme about Iceland on American breakfast television some years before and were enchanted by the dramatic scenery and the Blue Lagoon – they had since been there three times. They had decided to make a dream come true and spend Christmas and the New Year in the distant land of winter. The beautiful landscape enthralled them, but they found the prices exorbitant at the restaurants and bars in the city.

Sigurdur Óli nodded. To him, America was paradise on earth. He was impressed on meeting the couple and discussing baseball and American Christmas preparations with them, until Erlendur had had enough and gave him a prod.

Sigurdur Óli explained the death of the doorman and told them about the note in his room. Mr and Mrs Henry Bartlet stared at the detectives as if they had suddenly been transported to a different planet.

'You didn't know the doorman, did you?' Sigurdur Óli said when he saw their expressions of astonishment.

'A murder?' Henry groaned. 'At this hotel?'

'Oh my God,' his wife said and sat down on the double bed.

Sigurdur Óli decided not to mention the condom. He explained how the note implied that Gudlaugur had arranged to meet a man called Henry, but they did not know what day, whether the meeting had taken place or whether it was supposed to be after two days, a week, ten days.

Henry Bartlet and his wife flatly denied all knowledge of the doorman. They hadn't even noticed him when they arrived at the hotel four days before. Erlendur and Sigurdur Óli's questions had clearly upset them.

'Jesus,' Henry said. 'A murder!'

'You have murders in Iceland?' his wife – Cindy, she had told Sigurdur Óli her name when they greeted each other – asked, glancing over at the Icelandair brochure on the bedside table.

'Rarely,' he said, trying to smile.

'This Henry character is not necessarily a guest at the hotel,' Sigurdur Óli said while they waited for the lift back down. 'He doesn't even have to be a foreigner. There *are* Icelanders by the name of Henry.'

6

Sigurdur Óli had located the former hotel manager, so he said good-bye to Erlendur when they got to the lobby and went off to meet him. Erlendur asked for the head of reception but he had still not turned up for work and had not phoned in. Henry Wapshott had left the key card to his room at reception early that morning without anyone noticing him. He had spent almost a week at the hotel and was expected to stay for two more days. Erlendur asked to be notified as soon as Wapshott reappeared.

The hotel manager plodded past Erlendur.

'I hope you're not disturbing my guests,' he said.

Erlendur took him to one side.

'What are the rules about prostitution at this hotel?' Erlendur asked straight out as they stood next to the Christmas tree in the lobby.

'Prostitution? What are you talking about?' The hotel manager heaved a deep sigh and wiped his neck with a scruffy handkerchief.

Erlendur looked at him in anticipation.

'Don't you go mixing up any bloody nonsense in all this,' the manager said.

'Was the doorman involved with tarts?'

'Come off it,' the manager said. 'There are no tar— no prostitutes at this hotel.'

'There are prostitutes at all hotels.'

'Really?' the manager said. 'Are you talking from experience?'

Erlendur didn't answer him.

'Are you saying that the doorman was a pimp?' the manager said in a shocked tone. 'I've never heard such rubbish in my life. This isn't a strip joint. This is one of the largest hotels in Reykjavík!'

'No women in the bars or lobby who stalk the men? Go up to their rooms with them?'

The manager hesitated. He acted as though he wanted to avoid antagonising Erlendur.

'This is a big hotel,' he said eventually. 'We can't keep an eye on everything that goes on. If it's straightforward prostitution and there's no question about it, we try to prevent it, but it's a difficult matter to deal with. Otherwise the guests are free to do what they like in their rooms.'

'Tourists and businessmen, regional people, isn't that how you described the guests?'

'Yes, and much more besides, of course. But this isn't a doss-house. It's a quality establishment and as a rule the guests can easily afford the accommodation. Nothing smutty goes on here and for God's sake don't go spreading that kind of rumour around. The competition is tough enough as it is; it's terrible to shake off a murder.'

The hotel manager paused.

'Are you going to continue sleeping at this hotel?' he asked. 'Isn't that highly irregular?'

'The only thing that's irregular is the dead Santa Claus in your basement.' Erlendur smiled.

He saw the biotechnician from the kitchen leaving the bar on the ground floor with her sampling kit in her hand. With a nod to the manager he walked over to her. She had her back to him and was walking towards the cloakroom by the side door.

'How's it going?' Erlendur asked.

She turned and recognised him at once, but kept walking.

'Is it you who's in charge of the investigation?' she asked, going into the cloakroom where she took a coat from a hanger. She asked Erlendur to hold her sampling kit.

'They let me tag along,' Erlendur said.

'Not everyone was pleased with the idea of saliva samples,' she said, 'and I don't just mean the chef.'

'Above all we were eliminating the staff from our enquiries, I thought you were told to give that explanation.'

'Didn't work. Got any others?'

'That's an old Icelandic name, Valgerdur, isn't it?' Erlendur said, without answering her question. She smiled.

'So you're not allowed to talk about the investigation?'

'No.'

'Do you mind? Valgerdur being an old name, I mean?'

'Me? No, I ...' Erlendur stammered.

'Was there anything in particular?' Valgerdur said, reaching out for her bag. She smiled at this man standing in front of her in a cardigan buttoned up under a tattered jacket with worn elbows, looking at her with sorrowful eyes. They were of a similar age, but she looked ten years younger.

Without completely realising it, Erlendur blurted it out. There was something about this woman.

And he saw no wedding ring.

'I was wondering if I could invite you to the buffet here tonight, it's delicious.'

He said this without knowing a thing about her, as if he had no chance of a reply in the affirmative, but he said it all the same and now he waited, thinking to himself that she would probably start laughing, was probably married with four children, a big house and a summer chalet, confirmation parties and graduation parties and had married off her oldest child and was waiting to grow old in peace with her beloved husband.

'Thank you,' she said. 'It's nice of you to ask. But … unfortunately. I can't. Thanks all the same.'

She took her sampling kit from him, hesitated for a moment and looked at him, then walked away and out of the hotel. Erlendur was left behind in the cloakroom, half stunned. He hadn't asked a woman out for years. His mobile starting ringing in his jacket pocket and he eventually took it out, absent-mindedly, and answered. It was Elínborg.

'He's entering the courtroom,' she almost whispered into the telephone.

'Pardon?' Erlendur said.

'The father, he's coming in with his two lawyers. That's the minimum it will take to whitewash him.'

'Is anyone there?' Erlendur asked.

'Very few. It looks like the boy's mother's family, and the press are here too.'

'How's he looking?'

'Unruffled as usual, in a suit and tie like he's going out to dinner. He doesn't have a shred of conscience.'

'Not true,' Erlendur said. 'He definitely has a conscience.'

Erlendur had gone to the hospital with Elínborg to talk to the boy as soon as the doctors gave permission. By then he had undergone surgery and was in a ward with other children. There were children's drawings around the walls, toys in their beds, parents by their bedsides, tired after sleepless nights, endlessly worried about their children.

Elínborg sat down beside him. The bandaging around the boy's head left little of his face visible apart from his mouth and his eyes, which looked full of suspicion at the police officers. His arm was in a plaster cast, suspended by a small hook. The dressings after his operation were hidden by his quilt. They had managed to save his spleen.

The doctor said they could talk to the boy, but whether the boy would talk to them was a different matter.

Elínborg started by talking about herself, who she was and what she did in the police, and how she wanted to catch the people who did this to him. Erlendur stood at a distance, watching. The boy stared at Elínborg. She knew that she was only supposed to talk to him in the presence of one of his parents. Elínborg and Erlendur had arranged to meet the father at the hospital but half an hour had gone by and he hadn't turned up.

'Who was it?' Elínborg said at last when she thought it was time to get to the point.

The boy looked at her but said nothing.

'Who did this to you? It's all right to tell me. They won't attack you again. I promise.'

The boy cast a glance at Erlendur.

'Was it the boys from your school?' Elínborg asked. 'The big boys. We've found out that two of the suspects are known troublemakers. They've beaten up boys like you before, but not so violently. They say they didn't do anything to you but we know they were at the school at the time you were attacked.'

Silently, the boy watched Elínborg tell her story. She had gone to the school and talked to the headmaster and teachers, then gone to the homes of the two boys to find out about their backgrounds, where she heard them deny doing anything to him. The father of one of them was in prison.

The paediatrician entered the room. He told them that the boy needed to rest and they would have to come back later. Elínborg nodded and they took their leave.

Erlendur also accompanied Elínborg to meet the boy's father at his house later the same day. The father's explanation for not being able to go to the hospital was that he had to take part in an important conference call with his colleagues in Germany and the US. 'It came up unexpectedly,' he told them. When he finally managed to get away they had left the hospital.

While he was saying this the winter sun started to shine in through the lounge window, illuminating the marble floor and the carpet on the stairs. Elínborg was standing and listening when she noticed the stain on the stair carpet and another on the stair above it.

Little stains, almost invisible had it not been for the winter sun pouring in.

Stains that had been almost cleansed from the carpet and on first impression seemed to be part of the texture of the material.

Stains that turned out to be little footprints.

'Are you there?' Elínborg said over the telephone. 'Erlendur? Are you there?'

Erlendur came back to his senses.

'Let me know when he leaves,' he said, and they rang off.

The head waiter at the hotel was aged about forty, thin as a rake, wearing a black suit and shiny black patent leather shoes. He was in an alcove off the dining room, checking the reservations for that evening. When Erlendur introduced himself and asked whether he might disturb him for a moment, the head waiter looked up from his dog-eared reservations book to reveal a thin black moustache, dark stubble that he obviously needed to shave twice a day, a brownish complexion and brown eyes.

'I didn't know Gulli in the slightest,' said the man, whose name was Rósant. 'Terrible what happened to him. Are you getting anywhere?'

'Nowhere at all,' Erlendur said curtly. His mind was on the biotechnician and the father who beat up his son, and he was thinking about his daughter, Eva Lind, who said she could not hold out any longer. Although he knew what that meant, he hoped he was wrong. 'Busy around Christmas,' Erlendur said, 'aren't you?'

'We're trying to make the most of the season. Trying to fill the dining room three times for each buffet, which can be very difficult because some people think that when they've paid it's like a take-away. The murder in the basement doesn't help.'

'No,' Erlendur said without any interest. 'So you haven't been working here long if you didn't know Gudlaugur.'

'Two years. But I didn't have much contact with him.'

'Who do you think knew him best among the hotel staff?'

'I just don't know,' the head waiter said, stroking his black moustache with his index finger. 'I don't know anything about the man. The cleaners, maybe. When do we hear about the saliva tests?'

'Hear what?'

'Who was with him. Isn't it a DNA test?'

'Yes,' Erlendur said.

'Do you have to send it abroad?'

Erlendur nodded.

'Do you know whether anyone visited him in the basement? People from outside the hotel?'

'There's so much traffic here. Hotels are like that. People are like ants, in and out, up and down, never a moment's peace. At catering college we were told that a hotel isn't a building or rooms or service, but people. A hotel's just people. Nothing else. Our job is to make them feel good. Feel at home. Hotels are like that.'

'I'll try to remember that,' Erlendur said, and thanked him.

He checked whether Henry Wapshott had returned to the hotel, but he was still out. However, the head of reception was back at work and he greeted Erlendur. Yet another coach had pulled up outside, full of tourists, who swarmed into the lobby, and he gave Erlendur an awkward smile and shrugged, as if it was not his fault they couldn't talk and their business would have to wait.

7

Gudlaugur Egilsson joined the hotel in 1982, at the age of twenty-eight. He had held various jobs before, most recently as a nightwatchman at the Ministry for Foreign Affairs. When it was decided to employ a full-time doorman at the hotel, he got the job. Tourism was booming then. The hotel had expanded and was taking on more staff. The previous hotel manager couldn't remember exactly why Gudlaugur was selected, but he didn't recall there having been many applicants.

He made a good impression on the hotel manager. With his gentle-manly manner, polite and service-minded, he turned out to be a fine employee. He had no family, neither a wife nor children, which caused the manager some concern, because family men often proved to be more loyal. In other respects Gudlaugur did not say much about himself and his past.

Shortly after joining the staff he went to see the manager and asked if there was a room at the hotel for him to use while he was finding himself a new place to live. After losing his room at short notice he was on the street. He pointed out that there was a little room at the far end of the basement corridor where he could stay until he found a place of his own. They went down to inspect the room. All kinds of rubbish had been stored away in it and Gudlaugur said he knew of a place where it could all be kept, although most of it deserved to be thrown out anyway.

So in the end Gudlaugur, then a doorman and later a Santa Claus, moved into the little room where he would stay for the rest of his life. The hotel manager thought he would be there for a couple of weeks at the very most. Gudlaugur spoke in those terms and the room was not the sort of place anyone would want to live permanently. But Gudlaugur demurred about finding himself proper living quarters and soon it was taken for granted that he lived at the hotel, especially after his job developed more towards caretaking than being a straightforward doorman. As time wore on it was seen as a convenient arrangement to have him on call round the clock, lest something went wrong and a handyman was needed.

'Shortly after Gudlaugur moved into the room, the old manager left,' said Sigurdur Óli, who was up in Erlendur's room describing his meeting. It was well into the afternoon and beginning to get dark.

'Do you know why?' Erlendur asked. He was stretched out on the bed, staring up at the ceiling. 'The hotel had just been expanded, loads of new staff recruited and he leaves shortly afterwards. Don't you find that strange?'

'I didn't go into that. I'll find out what he says if you think it's of the slightest importance. He didn't know Gudlaugur had played Santa Claus. That started after his day and he was really shocked to hear that he was found murdered in the basement.'

Sigurdur Óli looked around the bare room.

'Are you going to spend Christmas here?'

Erlendur didn't answer.

'Why don't you get yourself off home?'

Silence.

'The invitation still stands.'

'Thank you, and give my regards to Bergthóra,' Erlendur said, deep in thought.

'What's the name of the game anyway?'

'It's none of your business, if the game ... actually has a name.'

'I'm off home, anyway,' Sigurdur Óli said.

'How's it going with starting a family?'

'Not too well.'

'Is it your problem or just a coincidence between the two of you?'

'I don't know. We haven't had ourselves checked. But Bergthóra's started talking about it.'

'Do you want children anyway?'

'Yes. I don't know. I don't know what I want.'

'What's the time?'

'Just gone half past six.'

'Go home,' Erlendur said. 'I'm going to check out our other Henry.'

Henry Wapshott had returned to the hotel but was not in his room. Erlendur had reception call him, went up to the floor he was staying on and knocked on his door, but met no response. He wondered whether to get the manager to open the room for him, but first he would need a search warrant from a magistrate, which could take well into the night, besides which it was altogether uncertain whether Henry Wapshott was in fact the Henry whom Gudlaugur was supposed to meet at 18.30.

Erlendur was standing in the corridor weighing up the options when a man probably in his early sixties came around the corner and walked in his direction. He was wearing a shabby tweed jacket, khaki trousers and a blue shirt with a bright red tie; he was balding, with his dark hair fondly combed right across the patch.

'Is it you?' he asked in English when he reached Erlendur. 'I was told someone was asking after me. An Icelander. Are you a collector? Did you want to see me?'

'Is your name Wapshott?' Erlendur asked. 'Henry Wapshott?' His English was not good. These days he could understand the language reasonably well, but spoke it badly. Global crime had forced the police force to organise special English courses, which Erlendur had attended and enjoyed. He was beginning to read books in English.

'My name's Henry Wapshott,' the man said. 'What do you want to see me about?'

'Maybe we shouldn't stand out here in the corridor,' Erlendur said. 'Can we go in your room? Or ...?'

Wapshott looked at the door, then back at Erlendur.

'Maybe we should go down to the lobby,' he said. 'What is it you want to see me about? Who are you?'

'Let's go downstairs,' Erlendur said.

Hesitantly, Henry Wapshott followed him to the lift. When they were down in the lobby Erlendur went to the smokers' table and seats to one side of the dining room, and they sat down. A waitress appeared at once. Guests were beginning to sit down to the buffet, which Erlendur found no less tempting than the day before. They ordered coffee.

'It's very odd,' Wapshott said. 'I was supposed to meet someone at precisely this spot half an hour ago, but the man never came. I didn't get any message from him, and then you're standing right outside my door and you bring me down here.'

'What man were you going to meet?'

'He's an Icelander. Works at this hotel. His name's Gudlaugur.'

'And you were going to meet him here at half past six today?'

'Right,' Wapshott said. 'What ...? Who are you?'

Erlendur told him he was from the police, described Gudlaugur's death and how they had found a note in his room referring to a meeting with a man called Henry, who was clearly him. The police wanted to know why they were going to meet. Erlendur did not mention his suspicion that Wapshott may well have been in the room when Santa was murdered. He just mentioned that Gudlaugur had worked at the hotel for twenty years.

Wapshott stared at Erlendur while he gave this account, shaking his head in disbelief as if he failed to grasp the full implications of what he was being told.

'Is he dead?'

'Yes.'

'Murdered?'

'Yes.'

'Oh my God,' Wapshott groaned.

'How did you know Gudlaugur?' Erlendur asked.

Wapshott seemed rather remote, so he repeated the question.

'I've known him for years,' Wapshott said eventually, smiling to reveal small, tobacco-stained teeth, some of the lower ones with black crests. Erlendur thought he must be a pipe smoker.

'When did you first meet?' Erlendur asked.

'We've never met,' Wapshott said. 'I've never seen him. I was going to meet him for the first time today. That's why I came to Iceland.'

'You came to Iceland to meet him?'

'Yes, among other things.'

'So how did you know him? If you never met, what kind of relationship did you have?'

'There was no relationship,' Wapshott said.

'I don't understand.'

'There's never been any "relationship",' Wapshott repeated, putting the final word in quotation marks with his fingers.

'What then?' Erlendur asked.

'Only one-sided worship,' Wapshott said. 'On my part.'

Erlendur asked him to repeat the last words. He could not understand how this man, who had come all the way from England and had never met Gudlaugur, could worship him. A hotel doorman. A man who lived in a dingy little room in a hotel basement and was found dead with his trousers round his ankles and a knife wound through his heart. One-sided worship of a man who played Father Christmas at children's parties.

'I don't know what you're talking about,' Erlendur said. Then he remembered that, in the corridor upstairs, Wapshott had asked him if he was a collector. 'Why did you want to know if I was a collector?' he asked. 'What did you mean?'

'I thought you were a record collector,' Wapshott said. 'Like me.'

'What kind of record collector? Records? You mean ...?'

'I collect old records,' Wapshott said. 'Old gramophone records. LPs, EPs, singles. That's how I know Gudlaugur. I was going to meet him here just now and was looking forward to it, so you must understand it's quite a shock for me to hear that he's dead. Murdered! Who could have wanted to murder him?'

His surprise seemed genuine.

'Did you meet him last night maybe?' Erlendur asked.

At first, Wapshott didn't realise what Erlendur meant, until it dawned on him and he stared at the detective.

'Are you implying ... do you think I'm lying to you? Am I ...? Are you saying I'm a suspect? Do you think I had something to do with his death?'

Erlendur watched him, saying nothing.

'How absurd!' Wapshott raised his voice. 'I've been looking forward to meeting that man for a long time. For years. You can't be serious.'

'Where were you around this time last night?' Erlendur asked.

'In town,' Wapshott said. 'I was in town. I was at a collectors' shop on the high street, then I had dinner at an Indian restaurant not far away.'

'You've been at the hotel for a few days. Why didn't you meet Gudlaugur before?'

'But ... weren't you just saying that he's dead? What do you mean?'

'Didn't you want to meet him as soon as you checked in? You looked forward to meeting him, you said. Why did you wait so long?'

'He decided the time and venue. Oh my God, what have I got myself into?'

'How did you contact him? And what did you mean by "one-sided worship"?'

Henry Wapshott looked at him.

'I mean—' Wapshott began, but Erlendur didn't allow him to complete the sentence.

'Did you know he worked at this hotel?'

'Yes.'

'How?'

'I'd found out. I make a point of researching my subjects. For collection purposes.'

'And that's why you stayed at this hotel?'

'Yes.'

'Were you buying records from him?' Erlendur continued. 'Is that how you knew each other? Two collectors, the same interest?'

'As I said, I didn't know him, but I was going to meet him in person.'

'What do you mean?'

'You haven't got the faintest idea who he was, have you?' Wapshott said, surprised that Erlendur had never heard of Gudlaugur Egilsson.

'He was a caretaker or a doorman and a Father Christmas,' Erlendur said. 'Is there anything else I need to know?'

'Do you know my specialist field?' Wapshott replied. 'I'm not sure how much you know about collecting in general or record collecting in particular, but most collectors specialise in a certain field. People can be rather eccentric about it. It's incredible what people can be bothered to collect. I've heard of a man who has sick bags from every airline in the world. I also know a woman who collects hair from Barbie dolls.'

Wapshott looked at Erlendur.

'Do you know what I specialise in?'

Erlendur shook his head. He was not completely convinced that he had understood the part about airline sick bags. And what was all that about Barbie dolls?

'I specialise in boys' choirs.'

'Boys' choirs?'

'Not only boys' choirs. My special interest is choirboys.'

Erlendur hesitated, unsure whether he had misunderstood.

'Choirboys?'

'Yes.'

'You collect records of choirboys?'

'I do. Of course I collect other records, but choirboys are – how should I put it? – my passion.'

'How does Gudlaugur fit in with all this?'

Henry Wapshott smiled. He stretched out for a black leather brief-case that he had with him. Opening it, he took out the sleeve of a 45 single.

He took his glasses out of his breast pocket and Erlendur noticed that he dropped a white piece of paper onto the floor. Erlendur reached for it and saw the name *Brenner's* printed on it in green.

'Thank you. A serviette from a hotel in Germany,' Wapshott said. 'Collecting is an obsession,' he added apologetically.

Erlendur nodded.

'I was going to ask him to autograph this sleeve for me,' Wapshott said, handing it to Erlendur.

On the front of the sleeve was the name 'GUDLAUGUR EGILSSON' in a little arc of golden letters, with a black-and-white photograph of a young boy, hardly more than twelve years old, slightly freckled, his hair carefully smoothed down, who smiled at Erlendur.

'He had a marvellously sensitive voice,' Wapshott said. 'Then along comes puberty and ...' He shrugged in resignation. There was a hint of sadness and regret in his tone. 'I'm astonished you haven't heard of him or don't know who he was, if you're investigating his death. He must have been a household name in his day. According to my sources, he could be described as a well-known child star.'

Erlendur looked up from the album sleeve, at Wapshott.

'A child star?'

'He performed on two records, singing solo and with church choirs. He must have been quite a name in this country. In his day.'

'A child star,' Erlendur repeated. 'You mean like Shirley Temple? That kind of child star?'

'Probably, by your standards, I mean here in Iceland, a small country off the beaten track. He must have been pretty famous even if everyone seems to have forgotten him now. Shirley Temple was of course ...'

'The Little Princess,' Erlendur muttered to himself.

'Pardon?'

'I didn't know he was a child star.'

'It was ages ago.'

'And? He made records?'

'Yes.'

'That you collect?'

'I'm trying to acquire copies. I specialise in choirboys like him. He was a unique boy soprano.'

'Choirboy?' Erlendur said almost to himself. He recalled the poster of *The Little Princess* and was about to ask Wapshott in more detail about the child star Gudlaugur, when someone disturbed him.

'So here you are,' Erlendur heard someone say above him. Valgerdur was standing behind him, smiling. She no longer carried her sampling kit. She was wearing a thin, black, knee-length leather coat with a beautiful red sweater underneath, and she had put on her make-up so carefully that it hardly showed. 'Does the invitation still stand?' she asked.

Erlendur leaped to his feet. But Wapshott had already stood up.

'Sorry,' Erlendur said, 'I didn't realise ... Of course.' He smiled. 'Of course.'

8

They moved to the bar next to the dining room when they had eaten their fill of the buffet and drunk coffee afterwards. Erlendur bought them drinks and they sat down at a booth well inside the bar. She said she couldn't stay long, from which Erlendur read polite caution. Not that he was planning to invite her up to his room – the thought didn't even cross his mind and she knew that – but he felt a sense of insecurity about her and the same kind of barriers he encountered from people who were sent to him for interrogation. Perhaps she didn't know herself what she was doing.

Talking to a detective intrigued her and she wanted to know everything about his job, the crimes and how he went about catching criminals. Erlendur told her that it was mostly boring administrative work.

'But crimes have become more vicious,' she said. 'You read it in the papers. Nastier crimes.'

'I don't know,' Erlendur said. 'Crimes are always nasty.'

'You're always hearing stories about the drug world; debt collectors attacking kids who owe money for their dope, and if the kids can't pay, their families are attacked instead.'

'Yes,' said Erlendur, who sometimes worried about Eva Lind for precisely that reason. 'It's quite a changed world. More brutal.'

They fell silent.

Erlendur tried to find a topic of conversation but he had no idea how to approach women. The ones he associated with could not prepare him for what might be called a romantic evening like this. He and Elínborg were good friends and colleagues, and there was a fondness between them that had been formed by years of collaboration and shared experience. Eva Lind was his child and a constant source of worry. Halldóra was the woman he married a whole generation before, then divorced and whose hatred he earned for doing so. These were the only women in his life apart from the occasional one-night stands that never brought anything more than disappointment and awkwardness.

'What about you?' he asked. 'Why did you change your mind?'

'I don't know,' she said. 'I haven't had an invitation like that for ages. What made you think to ask me out?'

'No idea. It slipped out over the buffet. I haven't done this for a long time either.'

They both smiled.

He told her about Eva Lind and his son, Sindri Snaer, and she told him she had two sons, also both grown up. He had the feeling that she didn't want to talk too much about herself and her circumstances, and he liked that. He didn't want to poke his nose into her life.

'Are you getting anywhere with the man who was murdered?'

'No, not really. The man I was talking to in the lobby ...'

'Did I interrupt you? I didn't know he was connected with the investigation.'

'That's all right,' Erlendur said. 'He collects records, vinyl that is, and it turns out that the man in the basement was a child star. Years ago.'

'A child star?'

'He made records.'

'I can imagine that's difficult, being a child star,' Valgerdur said. 'Just a kid with all kinds of dreams and expectations that rarely come to anything. What do you think happens after that?'

'You shut yourself up in a basement room and hope no one remembers you.'

'You think so?'

'I don't know. Someone might remember him.'

'Do you think that's connected with his murder?'

'What?'

'Being a child star.'

Erlendur tried to say as little as possible about the investigation without appearing standoffish. He hadn't had time to ponder this question and didn't know whether it made any difference.

'We don't know yet,' he said. 'But we'll find out.'

They stopped talking.

'So you weren't a child star,' Valgerdur then said.

'No,' Erlendur said. 'Devoid of talent in all fields.'

'Same here,' Valgerdur said. 'I still draw like a three-year-old.'

'What do you do when you're not at work?' she asked after a short silence.

Unprepared for this question, Erlendur dithered until she began to smile.

'I didn't mean to invade your privacy,' she said when he gave no answer.

'No, it's … I'm not accustomed to talking about myself,' Erlendur said.

He could not claim to play golf or any other sport. At one time he had been interested in boxing, but that had waned. He never went to the cinema and rarely watched television. Travelled alone around Iceland in the summer, but had done less of that in recent years. What did he do when he wasn't at work? He didn't know the answer himself. Most of the time he was just on his own.

'I read a lot,' he said suddenly.

'And what do you read?' she asked.

Once more he hesitated, and she smiled again.

'Is it that difficult?' she said.

'About deaths and ordeals,' he said. 'Death in the mountains. People who freeze to death outdoors. There are whole series of books about that. Used to be popular, once.'

'Deaths and ordeals?' she said.

'And plenty of other things, of course. I read a lot. History. Local history. Chronicles.'

'Everything that's old and gone,' she said.

He nodded.

'But why deaths? People who freeze to death? Isn't that awful to read?'

Erlendur smiled to himself.

'You ought to be in the police force,' he said.

In that short part of an evening she had penetrated a place in his mind that was carefully fenced off, even to himself. He did not want to talk about it. Eva Lind knew about it but was not entirely familiar with it and did not link it in particular with his interest in accounts of deaths. He sat in silence for a long time.

'It comes with age,' he said finally, regretting the lie immediately. 'What about you? What do you do when you've finished sticking cotton wool buds in people's mouths?'

He tried to rewind and make a joke but the bond between them had been tarnished and it was his fault.

'I really haven't had time for anything other than work,' she said, realising that she had unwittingly struck a nerve. She became awkward and he sensed that.

'I think we ought to do this again soon,' he said to wind things up. The lie was too much for him.

'Definitely,' she said. 'To tell you the truth I was very hesitant but I don't regret it. I want you to know that.'

'Nor do I,' he said.

'Good,' she said. 'Thank you for everything. Thanks for the

Drambuie,' she added as she finished her liqueur. He had also ordered a Drambuie for himself to keep her company, but hadn't touched it.

Erlendur lay stretched out on the bed in his hotel room looking up at the ceiling. It was still cold in the room and he was wearing his clothes. Outside, it was snowing. It was a soft, warm and pretty snow that fell gently to the ground and melted instantaneously. Not cold, hard and merciless like the snow that caused death and destruction.

'What are those stains?' Elínborg asked the father.

'Stains?' he said. 'What stains?'

'On the carpet,' Erlendur said. He and Elínborg had just returned from seeing the boy in hospital. The winter sun lit up the stair carpet that led to the floor where the boy's room was.

'I don't see any stains,' the father said, bending down to scrutinise the carpet.

'They're quite clear in this light,' Elínborg said as she looked at the sun through the lounge window. The sun was low and pierced the eyes. To her, the creamy marble tiles on the floor looked as if they were aflame. Close by the stairway stood a beautiful drinks cabinet. It contained spirits, expensive liqueurs, red and white wines rested forward onto their necks in racks. There were two glass windows in the cabinet and Erlendur noticed a smudge on one of them. On the side of the cabinet facing the staircase, a little drip had been spilt, measuring roughly a centimetre and a half. Elínborg put her finger on the drip and it was sticky.

'Did anything happen by this cabinet?' Erlendur asked.

The father looked at him.

'What are you talking about?'

'It's like something's been splashed on it. You've cleaned it recently.'

'No,' the father said. 'Not recently.'

73

'Those marks on the staircase,' Elínborg said. 'They look like a child's footprints to me.'

'I can't see any footprints on the staircase,' the father said. 'Just now you were talking about stains. Now they're footprints. What are you implying?'

'Were you at home when your son was assaulted?'

The father said nothing.

'The attack took place at the school,' Elínborg went on. 'School was over for the day but he was playing football and when he set off home they attacked him. That's what we think happened. He hasn't been able to talk to you, nor to us. I don't think he wants to. Doesn't dare. Maybe because the boys said they would kill him if he told the police. Maybe because someone else said they would kill him if he talked to us.'

'Where's all this leading?'

'Why did you come home early from work that day? You came home around noon. He crawled home and up to his room, and shortly afterwards you arrived and called the police and an ambulance.'

Elínborg had already been wondering what the father was doing at home in the middle of a weekday, but had not asked him until now.

'No one saw him on his way home from school,' Erlendur said.

'You're not implying that I attacked ... that I attacked my own boy like that? Surely you're not implying that?'

'Do you mind if we take a sample from the carpet?'

'I think you ought to get out of here,' the father said.

'I'm not implying anything,' Erlendur said. 'Eventually the boy will say what happened. Maybe not now and maybe not after a week or a month, maybe not after one year, but he will in the end.'

'Out,' the father said, enraged and indignant by now. 'Don't you dare ... don't you dare start ... You leave. Get out. Out!'

Elínborg went straight to the hospital and into the children's ward. The boy was asleep in his bed with his arm suspended from the hook.

She sat down beside him and waited for him to wake up. After she had stayed by the bedside for fifteen minutes the boy stirred and noticed the tired-looking policewoman, but the sad-eyed man in the woollen cardigan who had been with her earlier that day was nowhere to be seen now. Their eyes met and Elínborg did her utmost to smile.

'Was it your dad?'

She went back to the father's house when night had fallen, with a search warrant and forensics experts. They examined the marks on the carpet. They examined the marble floor and the drinks cabinet. They took samples. They swept up tiny grains from the marble. They plucked at the spilt drop on the cabinet. They went upstairs to the boy's room and took samples from the head of his bed. They went to the laundry room and looked at the cloths and towels. They examined the dirty laundry. They opened the vacuum cleaner. They took samples from the broom. They went out to the dustbin and rummaged around in the rubbish. They found a pair of the boy's socks in the bin.

The father was standing in the kitchen. He dialled a lawyer, his friend, as soon as the forensics team appeared. The lawyer came round promptly and looked at the warrant from the magistrate. He advised his client not to talk to the police.

Erlendur and Elínborg watched the forensics team at work. Elínborg glared at the father, who shook his head and looked away.

'I don't understand what you want,' he said. 'I don't get it.'

The boy had not said it was his father. When Elínborg asked him, his only response was that his eyes filled with tears.

The head of forensics phoned two days later.

'It's about the stains on the stair carpet,' he said.

'Yes,' Elínborg said.

'Drambuie.'

'Drambuie? The liqueur?'

'There are traces of it all over the sitting room and a trail on the carpet up to the boy's room.

Erlendur was still staring at the ceiling when he heard a knock on the door. He got to his feet, opened the door and Eva Lind darted into his room. Erlendur looked along the corridor, then closed the door behind her.

'No one saw me,' Eva said. 'It would make things easier if you could be arsed to go home. I can't suss out what you're playing at.'

'I'll get myself home,' Erlendur said. 'Don't worry about that. What are you doing here? Do you need anything?'

'Do I need a special reason to want to see you?' Eva said. She sat down at the desk and took out a packet of cigarettes. She threw a plastic bag onto the floor and nodded towards it. 'I brought you some clothes,' she said. 'If you plan to hang around at this hotel you'll need to change.'

'Thank you,' Erlendur said. He sat down on the bed facing her and borrowed a cigarette from her. Eva lit them both.

'It's nice to see you,' he said, exhaling.

'How's it going with Santa?'

'Bit by bit. What's new with you?'

'Nothing.'

'Have you seen your mother?'

'Yes. Same as usual. Nothing happens in her life. Work and television and sleep. Work, television, sleep. Work, television, sleep. Is that it? All that awaits you? Am I staying clean so I can slave away until I croak? And just look at you! Hanging round in a hotel room like a dickhead instead of getting your arse back home!'

Erlendur inhaled the smoke and blew it out through his nose.

'I didn't mean to—'

'No, I know,' Eva interrupted him.

'Are you giving in?' he said. 'When you came yesterday ...'

76

'I don't know if I can stand it.'

'Stand what?'

'This fucking life!'

They sat smoking, and the minutes passed.

'Do you sometimes think about the baby?' Erlendur asked at last. Eva was seven months' pregnant when she miscarried, and sank into a deep depression when she moved in with him after leaving hospital. Erlendur knew that she had nowhere near shaken it off. She blamed herself for the baby's death. The night that it happened she called him for help and he found her lying in her own blood outside the National Hospital after collapsing on her way to the maternity ward. She came within a hair's breadth of losing her life.

'This fucking life!' she said again, and stubbed out her cigarette on the desktop.

The telephone on the bedside table rang when Eva Lind had left and Erlendur had gone to bed. It was Marion Briem.

'Do you know what time it is?' Erlendur asked, looking at his watch. It was past midnight.

'No,' Marion said. 'I was thinking about the saliva.'

'The saliva on the condom?' Erlendur said, too lethargic to lose his temper.

'Of course they'll find it out for themselves, but it might not do any harm to mention cortisol.'

'I've still got to talk to forensics, they'll surely tell us something about the cortisol.'

'You can work a few things out from that. See what was going on in that basement room.'

'I know, Marion. Anything else?'

'I just wanted to remind you about the cortisol.'

'Goodnight, Marion.'

'Goodnight.'

THIRD DAY

9

Erlendur, Sigurdur Óli and Elínborg held a meeting early the following morning. They sat at a little round table to one side of the dining room and had breakfast from the buffet. It had snowed during the night, then turned warmer and the streets were clear. The weathermen were forecasting a green Christmas. Long queues of cars built up at every junction and the city swarmed with people.

'This Wapshott,' Sigurdur Óli said. 'Who is he?'

Much ado about nothing, Erlendur thought to himself as he sipped his coffee and looked out of the window. Odd places, hotels. He found staying at a hotel a welcome change but it was accompanied by the strange experience of having someone go into his room when he was not in it to tidy everything up. In the morning he left his room and the next time he returned someone had been in and restored it to normal: made the bed, changed the towels, put fresh soap on the sink. He was aware of the presence of the person who put his room back in order but saw no one, did not know who tidied up his life.

When he went downstairs in the morning he asked reception not to have his room cleaned any more.

Wapshott was going to meet him again later that morning and tell him more about his record collecting and Gudlaugur Egilsson's singing career. They had shaken hands on parting when Valgerdur interrupted them the previous evening. Wapshott had stood to attention, waiting for Erlendur to introduce him to the woman, but when nothing of the sort happened he had held out his hand, introduced himself and bowed. Then he'd asked to be excused; he was tired and hungry and was going up to his room to deal with some business before dining and going to bed.

They did not see him come down to the dining room where they were eating, and talked about how he might have ordered a meal by room service. Valgerdur mentioned that he looked tired.

Erlendur had accompanied her to the cloakroom and helped her put on her smart leather coat, then walked with her to the revolving doors where they stood for a moment before she went out into the falling snow. When he lay on his bed, after Eva Lind had left, Valgerdur's smile accompanied him into sleep, along with the faint scent of perfume that lingered on his hand from when they had said their goodbyes.

'Erlendur?' Sigurdur Óli said. 'Hello! Wapshott, who is he?'

'All I know is that he's a British record collector,' Erlendur said, after telling them about his meeting with him. 'And he's leaving the hotel tomorrow. You ought to phone the UK and get some details on him. We're going to meet before noon and I'll get some more out of him.'

'A choirboy?' Elínborg said. 'Who could have wanted to kill a choirboy?'

'Naturally, he wasn't a choirboy any longer,' Sigurdur Óli said.

'He was famous once,' Erlendur said. 'Released some records that are clearly rare collectors' items today. Henry Wapshott comes up here from the UK on account of them, on account of him. He specialises in choirboys and boys' choirs from all over the world.'

'The only one I've heard of is the Vienna Boys' Choir,' Sigurdur Óli said.

'Specialises in choirboys,' Elínborg said. 'What kind of man collects records of choirboys? Shouldn't we give that some thought? Isn't there something odd about that?'

Erlendur and Sigurdur Óli looked at her.

'What do you mean?' Erlendur asked.

'What?' Elínborg's expression turned to one of astonishment.

'Do you think there's something odd about collecting records?'

'Not records, but choirboys,' Elínborg said. 'Recordings of choir-boys. There's a huge difference there, I reckon. Don't you see anything pervy about that?' She looked at them both in turn.

'I haven't got a dirty mind like you,' Sigurdur Óli said, looking at Erlendur.

'Dirty mind! Did I imagine seeing Santa Claus with his trousers down in a little basement room and a condom on his willy? Did I need a dirty mind for that? Then a man who worships Santa, but only when he was twelve years old or so, just so happens to be staying at the same hotel and comes over from the UK to meet him? Are you two plugged in?'

'Are you putting this in a sexual context?' Erlendur asked.

Elínborg rolled her eyes.

'You're like a couple of monks!'

'He's just a record collector,' Sigurdur Óli said. 'As Erlendur said, some people collect airline sick bags. What's their sex life like, according to your theories?'

'I can't believe how blind you two are! Or frustrated. Why are men always so frustrated?'

'Oh, don't you start,' Sigurdur Óli said. 'Why do women always talk about how frustrated men are? As if women aren't frustrated with all their stuff, "Oh, I can't find my lipstick" ...'

'Blind, frustrated old monks,' Elínborg said.

'What does being a collector mean?' Erlendur asked. 'Why do people collect certain objects to have around them and why do they see one item as being more valuable than others?'

'Some items are more valuable than others,' Sigurdur Óli said.

'They must be looking for something unique,' Erlendur said.

'Something no one else has. Isn't that the ultimate goal? Owning a treasure that no one else in the whole wide world has?'

'Aren't they often pretty strange characters?' Elínborg said.

'Strange?'

'Loners. Aren't they? Weirdos?'

'You found some records in Gudlaugur's cupboard,' Erlendur said to her. 'What did you do with them? Did you look at them at all?'

'I just saw them in the cupboard,' Elínborg said. 'Didn't touch them and they're still there if you want to take a look.'

'How does a collector like Wapshott make contact with a man like Gudlaugur?' Elínborg continued. 'How did he hear about him? Are there intermediaries? What does he know about recordings of Icelandic choirboys in the 1960s? A boy soloist singing up here in Iceland more than thirty years ago?'

'Magazines?' Sigurdur Óli suggested. 'The Internet? Over the phone? Through other collectors?'

'Do we know anything else about Gudlaugur?' Erlendur asked.

'He had a sister,' Sigurdur Óli said. 'And a father who's still alive. They were informed of his death, of course. The sister identified him.'

'We should definitely take a saliva sample from Wapshott,' Elínborg said.

'Yes, I'll see to that,' Erlendur said.

Sigurdur Óli began gathering information about Henry Wapshott; Elínborg undertook to arrange a meeting with Gudlaugur's father and sister, and Erlendur headed down to the doorman's room in the basement. Walking past reception, he remembered that he still had to talk to the manager about his absence from work. He decided to do it later.

He found the records in Gudlaugur's cupboard. Two singles. One sleeve read: *Gudlaugur sings Schubert's 'Ave Maria'*. It was the same record that Henry Wapshott had shown him. The other showed the boy standing in front of a small choir. The choirmaster, a young man, stood to one side. *Gudlaugur Egilsson sings solo* was printed in large letters across the sleeve.

On the back was a brief account of the child prodigy.

Gudlaugur Egilsson has commanded much-deserved attention with Hafnarfjördur Children's Choir and this twelve-year-old singer definitely has a bright future ahead. On his second recording, he sings with unique expression in his beautiful boy soprano under the direction of Gabríel Hermannsson, choirmaster of Hafnarfjördur Children's Choir. This record is a must for all lovers of good music. Gudlaugur Egilsson proves beyond all doubt that he is a singer in a class of his own. He is currently preparing for a tour of Scandinavia.

A child star, Erlendur thought as he looked at the film poster for *The Little Princess* with Shirley Temple. What are you doing here? he asked the poster. Why did he keep you?

He took out his mobile.

'Marion,' he said when the call was answered.

'Is that you, Erlendur?'

'Anything new?'

'Did you know that Gudlaugur made song recordings when he was a child?'

'I've just found that out,' Erlendur said.

'The record company went bankrupt about twenty years ago and there's not a trace of it left. A man by the name of Gunnar Hansson owned and ran it. The name was GH Records. He released a bit of hippy stuff but it all went down the plughole.'

'Do you know what happened to the stock?'

'The stock?' Marion Briem said.

'The records.'

'They must have gone towards paying off his debts. Isn't that usually the case? I spoke to his family, two sons. The company never released much and I drew a total blank at first when I asked about it. The sons hadn't heard it mentioned for decades. Gunnar died in the mid-eighties and all he left behind was a trail of debts.'

'There's a man staying here at the hotel who collects choral music, choirboys. He was planning to meet Gudlaugur but nothing came of it. I was wondering whether his records might be worth something. How can I find out?'

'Find some collectors and talk to them,' Marion said. 'Do you want me to?'

'Then there's another thing. Could you locate a man called Gabríel Hermannsson who was a choirmaster in Hafnarfjördur in the sixties? You're bound to find him in the phone directory if he's still alive. He may have taught Gudlaugur. I've got a record sleeve here, there's a photo of him and he looks to me as if he was in his twenties then. Of course, if he's dead then it stops there.'

'That's generally the rule.'

'What?'

'If you're dead, it stops.'

'Quite.' Erlendur hesitated. 'What are you talking about death for?'

'No reason.'

'Everything's all right, isn't it?'

'Thanks for throwing some morsels my way,' Marion said.

'Wasn't that what you wanted? To spend your wretched old age delving into obscurities?'

'It absolutely makes my day,' Marion said. 'Have you checked about the cortisol in the saliva?'

'I'll look into it,' Erlendur said and rang off.

*

The head of reception had a little room of his own in the lobby beside the reception desk and was doing some paperwork when Erlendur walked in and closed the door behind him. The man stood up and began to protest, saying he couldn't spare the time to talk, he was on his way to a meeting, but Erlendur sat down and folded his arms.

'What are you running away from?' he asked.

'What do you mean?'

'You didn't come to work yesterday, in the hotel's peak season. You acted like a fugitive when I spoke to you the evening the doorman was murdered. You're all jittery now. To my mind you're top of the list of suspects. I'm told you knew Gudlaugur better than anyone else at this hotel. You deny it – say you don't know a thing about him. I think you're lying. You were his boss. You ought to be a little more cooperative. It's no joke spending Christmas in custody.'

The man stared at Erlendur without knowing what to do, then slowly sat back down in his chair.

'You haven't got anything on me,' he said. 'It's nonsense to think I did that to Gudlaugur. That I was in his room and ... I mean with the condom and all that.'

Erlendur was concerned by how the details of the case appeared to have leaked and how the staff were wallowing in them. In the kitchen, the chef knew precisely why they were collecting saliva samples. The reception manager could picture the scene in the doorman's room. Maybe the hotel manager had blurted it all out, maybe the girl who found the body, maybe police officers.

'Where were you yesterday?' Erlendur asked.

'Off sick,' the reception manager said. 'I was at home all morning.'

'You didn't tell anyone. Did you go to the doctor? Did he give you a note? Can I talk to him? What's his name.'

'I didn't go to the doctor. I stayed in bed. I'm better now.' He forced out a cough. Erlendur smiled. This man was the worst liar he had ever encountered.

'Why these lies?'

'You haven't got a thing on me,' the manager said. 'All you can do is threaten me. I want you to leave me alone.'

'I could talk to your wife too,' Erlendur said. 'Ask her if she brought you a cup of tea in bed yesterday.'

'You leave her out of it,' the manager said, and suddenly there was a tougher, more serious tone to his voice. He went red in the face.

'I'm not going to leave her out of it,' Erlendur said.

The manager glared at Erlendur.

'Don't talk to her,' he said.

'Why not? What are you hiding? You've become too mysterious to get rid of me.'

The man stared into space, then heaved a sigh.

'Leave me alone. It's nothing to do with Gudlaugur. These are personal problems I got myself into, which I'm trying to fix.'

'What are they?'

'I don't have to tell you anything about them.'

'Let me be the judge of that.'

'You can't force me.'

'As I said, I can make a request for custody, or I can simply talk to your wife.'

The man groaned. He looked at Erlendur.

'This won't go any further?'

'Not if it has nothing to do with Gudlaugur.'

'It's nothing to do with him.'

'All right then.'

'My wife received a phone call the day before yesterday,' the head of reception said. 'The same day you found Gudlaugur.'

On the phone, a woman whose voice the manager's wife did not recognise asked for him. This was in the middle of a weekday, but it was not uncommon for him to receive calls at home at such times. His acquaintances knew that he worked irregular hours. His wife, a doctor, worked shifts and the call woke her up: she was on duty that evening. The woman on the phone acted as though she knew the head of reception, but immediately took umbrage when his wife wanted to know who she was.

'Who are you?' she had asked. 'What are you calling here for?'

'He owes me money,' the voice on the phone said.

'She'd threatened that she would phone my house,' the reception manager told Erlendur.

'Who was it?'

He had gone out for a drink ten days before. His wife was at a medical conference in Sweden and he went out for a meal with three old friends. They had a lot of fun, went on a pub crawl after the restaurant and ended up at a popular nightspot in town. He lost his friends there, went to the bar and met some acquaintances from the hotel trade, stood by a small dance floor and watched the dancing. Although quite tipsy, he wasn't too drunk to make sensible decisions. That was why he couldn't understand it. He had never done anything like it before.

She approached him and, just like in a movie scene, held a cigarette between her fingers and asked him for a light. Although he didn't smoke, because of his job he made a point of always carrying a lighter. It was a habit from the days when people could smoke wherever they wanted. She started talking to him about something he had now forgotten, and asked if he was going to buy her a drink. He looked at her. But of course. They stood at the bar while he bought the drinks, then sat down at a little table when it became vacant. She was exceptionally attractive and flirted subtly with him. Unsure what was going on, he played along. Women didn't treat him like this as a rule. She sat up close to him and was forward and self-assured. When he stood up to fetch a second drink she stroked his thigh. He looked at her and she smiled. An enchanting, beautiful woman who knew what she wanted. She could have been ten years his junior.

Later that night she asked him to walk her home. She lived nearby. He was still unsure and hesitant, but excited as well. It was so strange for him that he might just as easily have been walking on the moon. In twenty-three years he had been faithful to his wife. Two or three times in all those years he'd perhaps had the chance to kiss another woman, but nothing like this had ever happened to him before.

'I lost the plot completely,' he told Erlendur. 'Part of me wanted to run home and forget the whole thing. Part of me wanted to go with the woman.'

'I bet I know which part that was,' Erlendur said.

They stood by the door to her flat, in the stairwell of a modern apartment block, and she put the key in the lock. Somehow even that act became voluptuous in her hands. The door opened and she moved close to him. 'Come inside with me,' she said, stroking his crotch.

He went inside with her. First she mixed drinks for them. He sat down on the sofa. She put on some music, came over to him with a glass in her hand and smiled, her beautiful white teeth shining behind the red lipstick. Then she sat beside him, put down her glass, grabbed the belt of his trousers and slowly unzipped his flies.

'I've never ... It was ... She could do the most incredible things,' the reception manager said.

Erlendur watched him without saying a word.

'I was going to sneak out in the morning, but she was one step ahead. My conscience was killing me, I felt like shit for betraying my wife and children. We've got three children. I was going to get out and forget about it. Never wanted to see that woman again. She was wide awake when I started creeping around the room in the dark.'

She sat up and switched on the beside lamp. 'Are you going?' she asked. He said he was. Claimed to be late. For an important meeting. Something of that sort.

'Did you enjoy it last night?' she asked.

Holding his trousers in his hands, he looked at her.

'It was amazing,' he said. 'But I just can't go on with this. I can't. Sorry.'

'I want eighty thousand krónur,' she said calmly, as if that was almost too obvious to mention.

He looked at her as if he had not heard what she said.

'Eighty thousand,' she repeated.

'What do you mean?'

'For the night,' she said.

'The night?' he said. 'What, are you selling yourself?'

'What do you think?' she said.

He didn't understand what she was talking about.

'Do you think you can get a woman like me for free?' she said.

Gradually it dawned on him what she meant.

'But you didn't say anything about that!'

'Did I need to say anything? Pay me eighty thousand and I might just let you come back home with me some other time.'

'I refused to pay,' the reception manager told Erlendur. 'Walked out. She went berserk. Called work and threatened to phone my wife if I didn't pay.'

'What are they called?' Erlendur said. 'A ... hustler? Was she one of them? Is that what you're saying?'

'I don't know what she was but she knew what she was doing and in the end she phoned home and told my wife what happened.'

'Why didn't you just pay her? Then you'd have been rid of her.'

'I'm not sure I would have been rid of her even if I had coughed up,' the manager said. 'My wife and I went through all this yesterday.

I described what happened just as I described it to you. We've been together for twenty-three years and although I have no excuse it was a trap, the way I see it. If that woman hadn't been after money it would never have happened.'

'So it was all her fault?'

'No, of course not, but … it was still a trap.'

They paused.

'Does that sort of thing go on at this hotel?' Erlendur asked. 'Prostitution?'

'No,' the reception manager said.

'It's not something you'd miss?'

'I was told you were asking about that. Nothing of that kind goes on here.'

'Quite,' Erlendur said.

'Are you going to keep schtum about this?'

'I need the woman's name if you have it. And her address. It won't go any further.'

The manager hesitated.

'Fucking bitch,' he said, slipping for an instant out of the role of the polite hotelier.

'Are you going to pay her?'

'That was one thing we agreed on, my wife and I. She's not getting a penny.'

'Do you think it could have been a prank?'

'A prank?' the manager said. 'I don't follow. What do you mean?'

'I mean, could someone want to harm you so badly that they would set you up? Someone you've quarrelled with?'

'The thought hadn't even crossed my mind. Are you suggesting that I've got enemies who would do something like that to me?'

'They needn't be enemies. Practical jokers, your friends.'

'No, my friends aren't like that. Besides, as a practical joke that would have been going a bit far – way beyond funny.'

'Was it you who fired Santa?'

'What do you mean?'

'Was it you who told him the news? Or did he receive a letter, or …?'

'I told him.'

'And how did he take it?'

'Not well. Understandably. He'd been working here for ages. Much longer than I have.'

'Do you think he could have been behind it, if anyone was?'

'Gudlaugur? No, I can't imagine that. Gudlaugur? Doing that sort of thing? I think not. He was really not the joking sort. Absolutely not.'

'Did you know Gudlaugur was a child star?'

'A child star? How?'

'He made records. A choirboy.'

'I didn't know that,' the manager said.

'Just one final thing,' Erlendur said, standing up.

'Yes?'

'Could you fix me up with a record player in my room?' Erlendur asked, and saw that the head of reception did not have the faintest idea what he was talking about.

When Erlendur went back into the lobby he saw the head of forensics coming up the stairs from the basement.

'How's it going with the saliva you found on the condom?' Erlendur asked. 'Have you checked the cortisol?'

'We're working on it. What do you claim to know about cortisol?'

'I know that too much of it in the saliva can prove dangerous.'

'Sigurdur Óli was asking about the murder weapon,' the head of forensics said. 'The pathologist doesn't think it's a particularly remarkable knife. Not very long, with a thin, serated edge.'

'So it's not a hunting knife or a carving knife?'

'No, it sounds to me like a fairly unremarkable instrument,' the head of forensics said. 'A pretty nondescript knife.'

10

Erlendur took the two records from Gudlaugur's room up to his own, then called the hospital and asked for Valgerdur. He was put through to her department. Another woman answered. He asked for Valgerdur again. The woman said, 'One moment, please,' and at last Valgerdur answered.

'Have you got any of those cotton wool buds left?' he asked.

'Is that Mr Deaths and Ordeals speaking?' she said.

Erlendur grinned.

'There's a tourist at the hotel we need to test.'

'Is it a rush job?'

'It will have to be done today.'

'Will you be there?'

'Yes.'

'I'm on my way.'

Erlendur rang off. Mr Deaths and Ordeals, he chuckled to himself. He was supposed to meet Henry Wapshott at the hotel bar. He went down, sat at the bar and waited. The waiter asked if he wanted anything, but he declined. Changed his mind and called out to him to bring a glass of water. He looked along the shelves of drinks behind the bar, rows of bottles in all colours of the rainbow, rows of liqueurs.

They had found powdered glass, too minute to be seen, on the marble floor of the lounge. Traces of Drambuie on the drinks cabinet, Drambuie on the boy's socks and on the staircase. They found fragments of glass in the broom and the vacuum cleaner. All the signs were that a bottle of liqueur had fallen onto the marble floor. The boy probably stepped in the puddle that it left, then ran straight up to his room. The marks on the staircase indicated that he ran rather than walked. Frightened little feet. They concluded that the boy broke the bottle, his father lost his temper and attacked him so brutally that he put him in hospital.

Elínborg had him taken to the police station on Hverfisgata for questioning, where she told him about the results of the forensic tests, the boy's reaction when he was asked whether his father had hit him, and her personal conviction that he was the culprit. Erlendur was present at the interrogation. She informed the father that he was in the legal position of being a suspect and was allowed to have a lawyer present. He should have one. The father protested his innocence and repeated that he was astonished to be under suspicion simply because a liqueur bottle had fallen onto his floor.

Erlendur switched on the tape recorder in the interrogation room.

'What we believe happened is this,' Elínborg said, acting as if reading aloud from a report; she tried to put her emotions to one side. 'The boy came home from school. It was just gone three o'clock. You came back shortly afterwards. We understand that you left work early that day. Maybe you were at home when it happened. For some reason the boy dropped a large bottle of Drambuie on the floor. Panicking, he ran up to his room. You flew into a rage, and more than that. You totally lost control of yourself and went up to the boy's room to punish him. It got out of hand and you beat your son so badly that you then had to call an ambulance.'

The father watched Elínborg without saying a word.

'You used a weapon that we have not managed to identify, a rounded or at least blunt instrument; possibly you banged him against the head of the bed. You persistently kicked him. Before calling an ambulance you tidied up in the lounge. You wiped up the liqueur with three towels, which you threw in the dustbin outside the house. You vacuum-cleaned the tiniest fragments of glass. You swept the marble floor as well and gave it a quick scrub. You washed the cabinet carefully. You took the boy's socks off and threw them in the dustbin. You used detergent on the stains on the stairs but did not manage to remove them completely.'

'You can't prove a thing, since it's rubbish anyway. The boy hasn't said anything. He hasn't said a word about who assaulted him. Why don't you try to find his classmates?'

'Why didn't you tell us about the liqueur?'

'It's nothing to do with this.'

'And the socks in the dustbin? The little footprints on the staircase?'

'A liqueur bottle did get broken, but I was the one who broke it. It happened two days before my boy was attacked. I was getting myself a drink when I dropped it on the floor and it smashed. Addi saw this and it made him jump. I told him to be careful where he walked, but by then he had trodden in the spillage and ran up the stairs to his room. This has nothing to do with him being attacked and I must say this scenario astonishes me. You haven't a shred of evidence! Has he said that I hit him? I doubt that. And he never will say it, because it wasn't me. I'd never do anything like this to him. Never.'

'Why didn't you tell us about it straight away?'

'Straight away?'

'When we found the stains. You didn't say anything about it then.'

'This is precisely what I thought would happen. I knew you'd link that accident with Addi getting beaten up. I didn't want to complicate matters. The boys at the school did it.'

'Your company's heading for bankruptcy,' Elínborg said. 'You've laid off twenty employees and expect to make more redundancies. I expect you're under a lot of strain. You're losing your house ...'

'That's just business,' he said.

'We have reason to believe you've used violence before.'

'Hey, wait a minute ...'

'We checked the medical reports. Twice in the past four years he has broken his finger.'

'Have you got kids? Kids are always having accidents. This is nonsense.'

'A paediatrician remarked on the broken finger the second time and informed the child welfare agency. It was the same finger. The agency sent people to your house. Examined the conditions. Found nothing of note. The paediatrician came and found needlemarks on the back of the boy's hand.'

The father said nothing.

Elínborg could not control herself.

'You bastard,' she hissed.

'I want to talk to my lawyer,' he said and looked away.

'I said, good morning!'

Erlendur returned to his senses and saw Henry Wapshott standing over him. Absorbed in his thoughts about the fleeing boy, he hadn't noticed Wapshott walk into the bar or heard his greeting.

He leaped to his feet and shook him by the hand. Wapshott was wearing the same clothes as the previous day. His hair was more unkempt and he looked tired. He ordered coffee, and so did Erlendur.

'We were talking about collectors,' Erlendur said.

'Yes,' Wapshott said, a wincing smile forming on his face. 'A bunch of loners, such as myself.'

'How does a collector like you in the UK find out that forty years ago there was a choirboy with a beautiful voice in Hafnarfjördur in Iceland?'

'Oh, much more than a beautiful voice,' Wapshott said. 'Much, much more than that. He had a unique voice, that boy.'

'How did you hear about Gudlaugur Egilsson?'

'Through people with the same interest as me. Record collectors specialise, as I believe I told you yesterday. If we take choral music, for example: collectors can be divided into those who collect only certain songs or certain arrangements, and others who collect certain choirs. Others still, like me, choirboys. Some collect only choirboys who recorded 78 rpm glass records, which they stopped manufacturing in the sixties. Others go in for 45 rpm singles, but only from one particular label. There are infinite types of specialisation. Some look for all the versions of a single song, let's say "Stormy Weather", which I'm sure you know. Just so you understand what's involved. I heard about Gudlaugur through a group or association of Japanese collectors who run a big website for trading. No one collects Western music on the scale of the Japanese. They go all over the world like Hoovers, buying up everything that's ever been released that they can get their hands on. Particularly Beatles and hippy music. They're renowned in the record markets, and the best thing of all is that they have money.'

Erlendur was wondering whether it was permitted to smoke at the bar and decided to give it a shot. Seeing that he was about to have a cigarette, Wapshott took out a crumpled packet of Chesterfields and Erlendur gave him a light.

'Do you think we can smoke here?' Wapshott asked.

'We'll find out,' Erlendur said.

'The Japanese had one copy of Gudlaugur's first single,' Wapshott said. 'The one I showed you last night. I bought it from them. Cost me a fortune but I don't regret it. When I asked about its background they said they'd bought it from a collector from Bergen in Norway at a record fair in Liverpool. I got in touch with the Norwegian collector and found out that he'd bought some records from the estate of a music publisher in Trondheim. He may have had the copy sent from

Iceland, possibly even by someone who wanted to promote the boy abroad.'

'A lot of research for an old record,' Erlendur said.

'Collectors are like genealogists. Part of the fun is tracing the origin. Since then I've tried to acquire more copies of his records, but it's very tough. He only made the two recordings.'

'You said the Japanese sold you your copy for a fortune. Are these records worth anything?'

'Only to collectors,' Wapshott said. 'And we're not talking about huge sums.'

'But big enough for you to come up here to Iceland to buy more. That's why you wanted to meet Gudlaugur. To find out if he had any copies.'

'I've been dealing with two or three Icelandic collectors for some time now. That goes back long before I became interested in Gudlaugur. Unfortunately, virtually none of his records are around any more. The Icelandic collectors couldn't locate any. I might have a copy on the way through the Internet from Germany. I came here to meet those collectors, to meet Gudlaugur because I adore his singing, and to go to record shops here and look at the market.'

'Do you make a living from this?'

'Hardly,' Wapshott said, chugging on his Chesterfield, his fingers yellow after decades of smoking. 'I came into an inheritance. Properties in Liverpool. I manage them, but most of my time goes on collecting records. You could call it a passion.'

'And you collect choirboys.'

'Yes.'

'Have you found anything interesting on this trip?'

'No. Nothing. There doesn't seem to be much interest in preserving anything here. It all has to be modern. Old stuff is rubbish. Nothing is worth keeping. People seem to treat records badly here.

They're just thrown away. From dead people's estates, for example. No one is called in to examine them. They're just driven off to the dump. For a long time I used to think that a company in Reykjavík called Sorpa was a collectors' society. It was always being mentioned in correspondence. It turned out to be a recycling plant that runs a second-hand outlet on the side. Collectors here find all kinds of valuables among the rubbish and sell them over the Internet for good money.'

'Is Iceland of special interest to collectors?' Erlendur asked. 'On its own.'

'The big plus about Iceland for collectors is the small size of the market. Only a few copies of each record are released and it doesn't take long for them to disappear and become lost. Like Gudlaugur's records.'

'It must be exciting to be a collector in a world where people hate everything old and useless. It must make you happy to think you're rescuing things of cultural value.'

'We're a few nutters who resist destruction,' Wapshott said.

'And you profit from it.'

'You can.'

'What happened to Gudlaugur Egilsson? What happened to the child star?'

'What happens to all child stars,' Wapshott said. 'He grew up. I don't know exactly what became of him, but he never sang as a teenager or adult. His career was short but beautiful, then he vanished into the crowd and stopped being unique. Nobody championed him any more and he surely missed it. You need strong nerves to withstand admiration and fame at such a young age, and even stronger nerves when people turn their backs on you.'

Wapshott looked at the clock that hung above the bar, then at his watch, and cleared his throat.

'I'm taking the evening flight to London and need to run a few errands before I set off. Was there anything else you wanted to know?'

Erlendur looked at him.

'No, I think that's all. I thought you were going to leave tomorrow.'

'If there's anything further I can help you with, here's my card,' Wapshott said as he took a card out of his breast pocket and handed it to Erlendur.

'It's changed,' Erlendur said. 'Your flight.'

'Because I didn't meet Gudlaugur,' Wapshott said. 'I've finished most of what I planned to do on this trip and I'll save myself the price of a night at the hotel.'

'There's just one thing,' Erlendur said.

'OK.'

'A biotechnician is coming here to take a saliva sample from you, if that's all right.'

'A saliva sample?'

'For the murder investigation.'

'Why saliva?'

'I can't tell you at the moment.'

'Am I a suspect?'

'We're taking samples from everyone who knew Gudlaugur. For the investigation. That says nothing about you.'

'I understand,' Wapshott said. 'Saliva! How queer.'

He smiled, and Erlendur stared at the teeth in his lower jaw, stained black from nicotine.

11

They entered the hotel through the revolving doors: he was old and frail and in a wheelchair; and she followed behind, short and slim, with a thin, hooked nose and tough, piercing eyes that scoured the lobby. The woman was in her fifties, dressed in a thick, brown winter coat and long leather boots, pushing him along in front of her. The man looked about eighty, white straggles of hair stood out from under the brim of his hat and his skinny face was deathly pale. He sat hunched up, white bony hands protruding from the sleeves of a black coat. He had a scarf around his neck and thick black horn-rimmed glasses that magnified his eyes like a fish's.

The woman pushed him to the check-in desk. The head of reception, who was leaving his office, watched them approach.

'Can I help you?' he asked when they reached the desk.

The man in the wheelchair ignored him, but the woman asked for a detective named Erlendur who she had been told was at work at the hotel. Leaving the bar with Wapshott, Erlendur had seen them enter. They caught his attention immediately. There was something reminiscent of death about them.

He wondered whether to ground Wapshott and stop him from going back to the UK for the time being, but could not think of a good enough reason to detain him. He was pondering who those people could be, the man with haddock eyes and the woman with the eagle's beak, when the head of reception saw him and waved to him. Erlendur was about to say goodbye to Wapshott, but suddenly he was gone.

'They're asking for you,' the head of reception said as Erlendur approached the check-in desk.

Erlendur walked behind the desk. The haddock's eyes stared at him from beneath the hat.

'Are you Erlendur?' the man in the wheelchair asked in an old and slurred voice.

'Do you want to talk to me?' Erlendur asked. The eagle's beak pointed up in the air.

'Are you in charge of the investigation into the death of Gudlaugur Egilsson at this hotel?' the woman asked.

Erlendur said he was.

'I'm his sister,' she said. 'And this is our father. Can we talk somewhere quiet?'

'Do you want me to help you with him?' Erlendur offered. She looked insulted and pushed the wheelchair along. They followed Erlendur into the bar and over to the table where he had been sitting with Wapshott. They were the only people inside. Even the waiter had disappeared. Erlendur did not know whether the bar was open before noon as a rule. Since the door was unlocked he assumed that it must be, but few people seemed to know about it.

The woman steered the wheelchair up to the table and locked the wheels. Then she sat down facing Erlendur.

'I was just on my way to see you,' Erlendur lied; he had intended to let Sigurdur Óli and Elínborg talk to Gudlaugur's family. He could not remember whether he had actually asked them to do so.

'We'd prefer not to have the police inside our house,' the woman said. 'That has never happened. A lady phoned us, presumably your colleague, I think she said her name was Elínborg. I asked who was in charge of the investigation and she told me you were one of them.

I was hoping we could get this over with and that you would then leave us in peace.'

There was no hint of sorrow in their demeanour. No mourning for a loved one. Only cold nastiness. They felt they had certain duties to dispatch, felt obliged to give a report to the police, but clearly had a repulsion against doing so and did not mind showing it. It didn't seem as if the corpse found in the hotel basement was any concern of theirs in the slightest. As if they were above that.

'You know the circumstances in which Gudlaugur was found,' Erlendur said.

'We know he was killed,' the old man said. 'We know he was stabbed.'

'Do you know who could have done it?'

'We don't have the faintest idea,' the woman said. 'We had no contact with him. We don't know who he associated with. Don't know his friends, nor his enemies if he had any.'

'When was the last time you saw him?'

Elínborg walked into the bar. She approached them and sat down beside Erlendur. He introduced her to them but they showed no reaction, both equally determined to allow none of this ruffle them.

'I suppose he must have been about twenty then,' the woman said. 'The last time we saw him.'

'Twenty?' Erlendur thought he must have misheard.

'As I said, there was no contact.'

'Why not?' Elínborg asked.

The woman did not even look at her.

'Isn't it enough for us to talk to you?' she asked Erlendur. 'Does this woman have to be here too?'

Erlendur looked at Elínborg. He seemed to cheer up slightly.

'You don't seem to be mourning his fate very much,' he said without answering her. 'Gudlaugur. Your brother,' he said, and looked at the woman again. 'Your son,' he said, and looked at the old man. 'Why?

Why haven't you seen him for thirty years? And as I told you, her name is Elínborg,' he added. 'If you have any more comments to make we'll take you down to the police station and continue there, and you can lodge a formal complaint. We've got a police car outside.'

The eagle's beak rose, offended. The haddock's eyes narrowed.

'He lived his own life,' she said. 'We lived ours. There's not much more to say about it. There was no contact. That's the way it was. We were happy with that. So was he.'

'Are you telling me that you last saw him in the mid-seventies?' Erlendur said.

'There was no contact,' she repeated.

'Not once in all that time? Not one phone call? Nothing?'

'No,' she said.

'Why not?'

'That's a family matter,' the old man said. 'Nothing to do with this. Not a bit. Over and done with. What more do you want to know?'

'Did you know he was working at this hotel?'

'We heard about him every so often,' the woman said. 'We knew he was a doorman here. Put on some stupid uniform and held the door open for the hotel guests. And I understand he used to play Santa Claus at Christmas parties.'

Erlendur's eyes were riveted to her. She said this as if Gudlaugur could not have humiliated his family more, except by being found murdered, half naked, in a hotel basement.

'We don't know much about him,' Erlendur said. 'He doesn't seem to have had many friends. He lived in a little room at this hotel. He seems to have been liked. People thought he was good with children. As you say, he played Santa at the hotel's Christmas parties. However, we've just heard that he was a promising singer. A young boy who made gramophone recordings, two of them I think, but of course you know more about that. I saw on a record sleeve that he was going to tour Scandinavia, and it sounded as if he had the world at his feet.

Then somehow that came to an end, apparently. No one knows that boy today apart from a few nutters who collect old records. What happened?'

The eagle's beak had lowered and the haddock's eyes dimmed while Erlendur was talking. The old man looked away from him and down at the table, and the woman, who still tried to retain her air of authority and pride, no longer appeared quite so self-assured.

'What happened?' Erlendur repeated, suddenly remembering that he had Gudlaugur's singles up in his room.

'Nothing happened,' the old man said. 'He lost his voice. He matured early and lost his voice at the age of twelve and that was the end of that.'

'Couldn't he sing afterwards?' Elínborg asked.

'His voice turned bad,' the old man said irritatedly. 'You couldn't teach him anything. And you couldn't do anything for him. He turned against singing. Rebellion and anger took hold of him and he opposed everything. Opposed me. Opposed his sister who tried to do her best for him. He attacked me and blamed me for it all.'

'If there isn't anything else,' the woman said with a look at Erlendur. 'Haven't we said enough? Haven't you had enough?'

'We didn't find much in Gudlaugur's room,' Erlendur said, pretending not to have heard her. 'We found some of his records and we found two keys.'

He had asked forensics to return the keys when they had been examined. Taking them out of his pocket, he placed them on the table. They dangled from a key ring with a miniature penknife. It was set in pink plastic and on one side was a picture of a pirate with a wooden leg, cutlass and patch over one eye, with the word PIRATE written in English underneath it.

After a quick glance at the keys the woman said she did not recognise them. The old man adjusted his glasses on his nose and looked at the keys, then shook his head.

'One is probably a front door key,' Erlendur said. 'The other looks like the key to a cupboard or locker of some kind.' He watched them but received no response, so he put the keys back in his pocket.

'Did you find his records?' the woman asked.

'Two,' Erlendur said. 'Did he make any more?'

'No, there weren't any more,' the old man said, glaring at Erlendur for an instant but quickly averting his gaze.

'Could we have the records?' the woman asked.

'I assume you'll inherit everything he left,' Erlendur replied. 'When we consider the investigation to be over you'll get everything he owned. He had no other family, did he? No children? We haven't been able to locate anything of that kind.'

'The last time I knew he was single,' the woman said. 'Can we help you any further?' she then asked, as if they had made a major contribution to the investigation by taking the trouble to call at the hotel.

'It wasn't his fault that he matured and lost his voice,' Erlendur said. He could stand their indifference and haughtiness no longer. A son had lost his life. A brother had been murdered. Yet it was as if nothing had happened. As if it was nothing to do with them. As if his life had long ago ceased to be part of their lives, because of something that was being kept from Erlendur.

The woman looked at Erlendur.

'If there wasn't anything else,' she said again, and released the brake on the wheelchair.

'We'll see,' Erlendur said.

'You don't think we show enough sympathy, do you?' she suddenly said.

'I don't think you show any sympathy,' Erlendur said. 'But that's no business of mine.'

'No,' the woman said. 'It's no business of yours.'

'But all the same, what I want to know is whether you had any

108

feelings towards the man. He was your brother.' Erlendur turned to the old man in the wheelchair. 'Your son.'

'He was a stranger to us,' the woman said, and stood up. The old man grimaced.

'Because he didn't live up to your expectations?' Erlendur rose to his feet as well. 'Because he failed you at the age of twelve. When he was a child. What did you do? Did you throw him out? Did you throw him out on the street?'

'How dare you talk to my father and me in that tone?' the woman said through clenched teeth. 'How dare you? Who appointed you the conscience of the world?'

'Who took your conscience away?' Erlendur snarled back.

She looked daggers at him. Then she seemed to give up. She jerked the wheelchair towards her, swung it away from the table and pushed it in front of her out of the bar. She strode across the lobby towards the revolving door. Over the sound system an Icelandic soprano was singing melancholically ... *O touch my harp, you heaven-born goddess* ... Erlendur and Elínborg set off after them and watched them leave the hotel, the woman holding her head high but the old man sunk even deeper into his wheelchair, nothing of him visible apart from his head nodding above the back.

... And others will little children e'er abide ...

12

When Erlendur went back to his room shortly after midday, the reception manager had set up a record player and two loudspeakers. The hotel had a few old turntables that had not been used for some time. Erlendur owned one himself so he quickly worked out how to operate it. He had never had a CD player and hadn't bought a record for years. He didn't listen to modern music. For a long time after hearing people at work talking about hip-hop he thought it was a variation on hopscotch.

Elínborg was on her way to Hafnarfjördur. Erlendur had told her to go there and find out where Gudlaugur attended school. He had intended to ask the father and sister but hadn't had the chance when their meeting came to its abrupt end. He would talk to them again later. In the meantime, he wanted Elínborg to locate people who knew Gudlaugur when he was a child star, to talk to his schoolmates. He wanted to know what effect his reputed fame had on the boy at such a young age. Also what his schoolmates had thought about it, and he wanted to know whether any remembered what happened when he lost his voice, and what became of him in the first few years afterwards. He was also wondering whether anyone knew of any enemies of Gudlaugur's from that time.

Outlining all this to Elínborg in the lobby, he noticed her irritation at having it all spelled out. She knew what the case involved and was quite capable of setting targets for herself.

'And you can buy yourself an ice cream on the way,' he added to tease her even more. With a few muttered curses about male chauvinist pigs, she went out of the door.

'How do I recognise this tourist?' said a voice behind him, and when he turned round he saw Valgerdur standing there, sampling kit in hand.

'Wapshott? You met him last night. He's the haggard old Brit with stained teeth who collects choirboys,' Erlendur said.

She smiled.

'Stained teeth?' she said. 'And collects choirboys?'

'It's a long, long story that I'll tell you some time. Any news about all those samples?'

He was strangely pleased to see her again. His heart almost skipped a beat when he heard her behind him. The gloom lifted from him for a moment and his voice became animated. He felt slightly breathless.

'I don't know how it's going,' she said. 'There's an incredible amount of samples.'

'I, er ...' Erlendur groped for an excuse for what had happened the previous night. 'I really seized up last night. Deaths and fatalities. I didn't quite tell you the truth when you asked about my interest in people dying in the wilds.'

'You don't have to tell me anything,' she said.

'Yes, I definitely do need to tell you,' Erlendur said. 'Is there any chance we could do that again?'

'Don't ...' She paused. 'Don't make an issue of it. It was great. Let's forget it. OK?'

'OK, if that's the way you want it,' Erlendur said, much against his wishes.

'Where is this Wapshott guy?'

Erlendur accompanied her to reception where she was given the number of his room. They shook hands and she walked over to the lift. He watched her. She waited for the lift without looking back. He wondered whether to pounce and was on the verge of doing so when the door opened and she stepped inside. She glanced at him the moment that the door closed, smiling an almost imperceptible smile.

Erlendur stood still for a moment and watched the number of the lift as it stopped on Wapshott's floor. Then he pressed the button and ordered it back. He could smell Valgerdur's perfume on the way up to his floor.

He put a recording of choirboy Gudlaugur Egilsson on the turntable and made sure the speed was set to 45 rpm. Then he stretched out on the bed. The record was brand new. It sounded as though it had never been played. Not a scratch or speck of dust on it. After a slight crackle at the beginning came the prelude, and finally a pure and celestial boy soprano started to sing 'Ave Maria'.

He stood alone in the passageway, carefully opened the door to his father's room and saw him sitting on the edge of the bed, staring into space in silent anguish. His father did not take part in the search. He had battled his way home to the farm after losing sight of his two sons on the moor in the storm that broke without warning. He had roamed around in the blizzard calling to them, unable to see a thing with the howling of the storm smothering his shouts. His desperation defied description. He had taken the boys along to help round up the sheep and bring them back to the folds. Winter had arrived but it seemed to be a fine day when they set off. But it was only a forecast and only an outlook. The storm came unannounced.

Erlendur approached his father and stopped by his side. He could not understand why he was sitting on the bed instead of joining the search party up on the moor. His brother had still not been found. He might be alive, though it was unlikely. Erlendur read the hopelessness in the faces of the exhausted men returning home to rest and eat before setting out again. They came from the villages and farms all around, everyone who was up to the task, bringing dogs and long sticks that they plunged into the snow. That was how they had found Erlendur. That was how they were going to find his brother.

They went up to the moor in teams of eight to ten, stabbing their sticks into the snow and shouting his brother's name. Two days had passed since they had found Erlendur and three days since the storm had split up the three travellers. The brothers had stayed together for a long time. They shouted into the blizzard and listened for their father's voice. Two years the elder, Erlendur led his brother by the hand, but their hands were numbed by the frost and Erlendur did not feel when he lost his grip. He thought he was still holding his brother's hand when he turned round and could not see him any longer. Much later he thought he remembered the hand slipping away from his, but that was an invention. He never actually felt it happen.

He was convinced that he would die at the age of ten in a seemingly incessant blizzard. It attacked him from all directions, tore him and cut him and blinded his sight, cold and harsh and merciless. In the end he fell down into the snow and tried to bury himself. Lay there thinking about his brother who was also dying on the moor.

A sharp jab in his shoulder woke him and suddenly a face he did not recognise appeared. He could not hear what the man said. He wanted to go on sleeping. He was heaved out of the snow and the men took turns carrying him down from the moor, although he remembered little of the journey home. He heard voices. He heard his mother nursing him. A doctor examined him. Frostbite on his feet and legs, but not very severe. He saw inside his father's room. Saw him sitting alone on the edge of the bed as if nothing that had happened had affected him.

Two days later, Erlendur was up and about again. He stood beside his father, helpless and afraid. Strange pangs of conscience had haunted him when he began to recover and regain his strength. Why him? Why him and not his brother? And if they had not found him, would they possibly have found his brother instead? He wanted to ask his father about this and wanted to ask why he was not taking part in the search. But he asked nothing. Just watched him, the deep lines etched into his face, his stubble, his eyes black with sorrow.

A long time elapsed and his father ignored him. Erlendur put his hand on his father's and asked whether it was his fault. That his brother was missing. Because he had not held him tightly enough, should have taken better care of him, should have had him by his side when he himself was found. He asked in a soft and hesitant voice but lost control of himself and began whimpering. His father bowed his head. Tears welled up in his eyes, he hugged Erlendur and started to weep as well, until his huge body shook and trembled in his son's arms.

All this passed through Erlendur's mind until the record began crackling again. He had not allowed himself these contemplations for a long time, but suddenly the memories unfolded within him and he once again felt the heavy sorrow that he knew would never be completely buried or forgotten.

Such was the power of the choirboy.

13

The telephone on the bedside table rang. He sat up, lifted the needle from the record and switched off the player. Valgerdur was calling. She told him that Henry Wapshott was not in his room. When she had the hotel staff call his room and look for him, he was nowhere to be found.

'He was going to wait around for the sample,' Erlendur said. 'Has he checked out of the hotel? I understand he had a flight booked for tonight.'

'I haven't asked about that,' Valgerdur said. 'I can't wait here much longer and ...'

'No, of course not, sorry,' Erlendur said. 'I'll send him to you when I find him. Sorry about that.'

'OK then, I'm off.'

Erlendur hesitated. Although he didn't know what to say, he didn't want to let her go immediately. The silence became prolonged and suddenly there was a knock on his door. He thought Eva Lind had come to visit him.

'I'd so like to meet you again,' he said, 'but I understand if you can't be bothered.'

Again there was a knock on the door, harder this time.

'I wanted to tell you the truth about that deaths and ordeals business,' Erlendur said. 'If you can be bothered to listen.'

'What do you mean?'

'Do you fancy that?'

He didn't know himself exactly what he meant. Why he wanted to tell this woman what he had never told anyone but his daughter before. Why he would not wind up the matter, get on with his life and let nothing disturb it, not now or ever.

Valgerdur did not answer immediately, and there was a third knock on the door. Erlendur put down the phone and opened the door without looking outside to see who was there; he assumed it could only be Eva. When he picked up the telephone again, Valgerdur had gone.

'Hello,' he said. 'Hello?' There was no reply.

After putting down the receiver again, he turned around. In his room stood a man he had never seen before. He was short, wearing a thick, dark blue winter coat and a scarf, with a blue peaked cap on his head. Drops of water glittered on his cap and coat where the snow had melted. He was fairly fat-faced with thick lips, and enormous, dark bags beneath small, tired eyes. He reminded Erlendur of photographs of the poet W. H. Auden. A drip hung from the end of his nose.

'Are you Erlendur?' he said.

'Yes.'

'I was told to come to this hotel and talk to you,' the man said. He took off his cap, tapped it against his coat and wiped the drip from his nose.

'Who told you that?' Erlendur asked.

'Someone by the name of Marion Briem. I don't know who that is. Something about the Gudlaugur Egilsson investigation and talking to everyone who knew him in the past. I used to know him and that Marion told me to talk to you about it.'

'Who are you?' Erlendur said, trying to recall where he had seen his face before.

'My name's Gabríel Hermannsson and I used to conduct the Hafnarfjördur Children's Choir once,' the man said. 'May I sit down on the bed? Those long corridors ...'

'Gabríel? Be my guest. Have a seat.' The man unbuttoned his coat and loosened his scarf. Erlendur picked up one of Gudlaugur's record sleeves and looked at the photograph of the Hafnarfjördur Children's Choir. The choirmaster stared cheerfully into the camera. 'Is this you?' he asked, handing him the sleeve.

Gabríel looked at the sleeve and nodded.

'Where did you get that?' he asked. 'Those records have been un-available for decades. I stupidly lost mine somehow or other. Lent it to someone. You should never lend anything.'

'It belonged to Gudlaugur,' Erlendur said.

'I'm only, what, twenty-eight there,' Gabríel said. 'When the photo was taken. Incredible how time flies.'

'What did Marion say to you?'

'Not much. I said what I knew about Gudlaugur and was told to talk to you. I was coming to Reykjavík anyway so I thought it would be ideal to use the opportunity.'

Gabríel hesitated.

'I couldn't quite tell from the voice,' he said, 'but I was wondering whether it was a man or a woman. Marion. I thought it would be rude to ask but I couldn't make up my mind. Normally you can tell from the voice. Funny name. Marion Briem.'

Erlendur discerned in his voice a note of interest, almost eagerness, as if it mattered to know.

'I've never thought about that,' Erlendur said. 'That name. Marion Briem. I was listening to this record,' he said, pointing to the sleeve. 'His voice has a strong effect, there's no denying that. Considering how young the lad was.'

'Gudlaugur was probably the best choirboy we ever had,' Gabríel said as he looked at the sleeve. 'In retrospect. I don't think we realised what we had in our hands until much later, maybe not even until only a few years ago.'

'When did you first get to know him?'

'His father brought him to me. The family lived in Hafnarfjördur then, and still do, I think. The mother died a little while later and he brought the children up entirely by himself: Gudlaugur and a girl who was some years older. The father knew that I'd just got back from studying music abroad. I taught music, private lessons and other things. I was appointed choirmaster when I managed to round up enough children to form a choir. It was mostly girls, as always, but we advertised specially for boys and Gudlaugur's father brought him to my house one day. He was ten at the time and had a wonderful voice. That wonderful voice. And he knew how to sing. I could tell straight away that his father made great demands on the boy and was strict with him. He said he'd taught him everything he knew about singing. I later found out that he was hard on the boy, punished him, kept him indoors when he wanted to go out and play. I don't think you could call it a good upbringing because so much was expected of him and he wasn't allowed to hang around with friends much. He was a classic example of parents taking control of their children and trying to turn them into what they want. I don't think Gudlaugur had a particularly happy childhood.'

Gabríel stopped.

'You've wondered about this quite a lot, haven't you?' Erlendur said.

'I just saw it happening.'

'What?'

'Strict discipline and unwavering demands can have an awful effect on children. I'm not talking about discipline when children are naughty and need restraint or guidance, that's a completely different matter. Of course children need discipline. I'm talking about when children aren't allowed to be children. When they're not allowed to enjoy being what they are and what they want to be, but are shaped and even broken to make them something different. Gudlaugur had this beautiful boy soprano and his father intended a big role for him in life. I'm not saying that he treated him badly in a conscious, calculated way, he just deprived him of his life. Robbed him of his childhood.'

Erlendur thought about his own father who did nothing but teach him good manners and show him affection. The single demand he made was to behave well and treat other people kindly. His father had never tried to turn him into anything he was not. Erlendur thought about the father who was awaiting sentence for a brutal assault on his own son, and he imagined Gudlaugur continually trying to live up to his father's expectations.

'Maybe we see this most clearly with religion,' Gabríel continued. 'Children who find themselves in certain religions are made to adopt their parents' faith and in effect live their parent's lives much more than their own. They never have the opportunity to be free, to step outside the world they're born into, to make independent decisions about their lives. Of course the children don't realise until much later, and some never do. But often when they are adolescents or grown-up, they say: "I don't want this any more", and conflicts can arise. Suddenly the child doesn't want to live its parents' life, and that can lead to great tragedy. You see it everywhere: the doctor who wants his child to be a doctor. The lawyer. The company director. The pilot. There are people all over the place who make impossible demands of their children.'

'Did that happen in Gudlaugur's case? Did he say, "This is where I draw the line"? Did he rebel?'

Gabríel waited before replying.

'Have you met Gudlaugur's father?' he asked.

'I spoke to him this morning,' Erlendur said. 'Him and his daughter. They're full of some kind of anger and antipathy and they clearly didn't have any warm feelings for Gudlaugur. They didn't shed a tear for him.'

'And was he in a wheelchair? The father?'

'Yes.'

'That happened several years afterwards,' Gabríel said.

'After what?'

'Several years after the performance. That dreadful performance just before the boy was due to tour Scandinavia. It had never happened before, a boy leaving Iceland to sing solo with choirs in Scandinavia. His father sent his first record to Norway, a record company there became interested and organised a concert tour with the aim of releasing his records in Scandinavia. His father once told me that his dream, *nota bene his* dream, not necessarily Gudlaugur's, was for the lad to sing with the Vienna Boys' Choir. And he could have, no question about it.'

'So what happened?'

'What always happens sooner or later with boy sopranos; nature intervened,' Gabríel said. 'At the worst imaginable time in the boy's life. It could have happened at a rehearsal, could have happened while he was alone at home. But it happened there and the poor child ...'

Gabríel looked at Erlendur.

'I was with him backstage. The children's choir was supposed to sing some songs and a crowd of local children were there, leading musicians from Reykjavík, even a couple of critics from the papers. The concert was widely advertised and his father was sitting in the middle of the front row, of course. The boy came to see me later, much later, when he'd left home, and told me how he felt on that fateful night, and since then I've often thought how a single incident can mark a person for life.'

*

Every seat in Hafnarfjördur cinema was occupied and the audience

120

was buzzing. He'd been to that charming building twice before to watch films and was enchanted by everything he saw: the beautiful lighting in the auditorium and the raised stage where plays were performed. His mother had taken him to *Gone with the Wind* and he had been with his father and sister to see a Walt Disney cartoon.

But these people had come not to watch the heroes of the silver screen, but to listen to him. Him singing with the voice that had already featured on two records. Instead of shyness, he was beset by uncertainty now. He had sung in public before, in the church in Hafnarfjördur and at school, in front of large audiences. Often he was shy and downright scared. Later he came to realise that he was sought-after by others, which helped him overcome his reticence. There was a reason that people came to hear him sing, a reason that people wanted to hear him, and it was nothing to be shy about. The reason was his voice and his singing. Nothing else. He was the star.

His father had shown him the advertisement in the newspaper: Iceland's best boy soprano is performing tonight. There was no one better. His father was beside himself with joy and much more excited than the boy himself. Talked about it for days on end. If only your mother could have lived to see you singing at that place, he said. That would have pleased her so much. It would have pleased her indescribably.

People in other countries were impressed with his singing and wanted him to perform there too. They wanted to release his records there. I knew it, his father said over and again. I knew it. He had worked hard on preparing the trip. The concert in Hafnarfjördur was the finishing touch to that work.

The stage manager showed him how to peep through into the auditorium to watch the audience taking their seats. He listened to the murmurings and saw people he knew he would never meet. He saw the choirmaster's wife sit down with their three children at the end of the third row. He saw several of his classmates with their parents, even some who had teased him, and he saw his father take his place in the middle of the front row, with his big sister beside him, staring up at the ceiling. His mother's family were there too, aunts he hardly knew, men holding their hats in their hands waiting for the curtain to open.

He wanted to make his father proud. He knew how much his father had sacrificed to make a successful singer of him, and now the fruits of that toil were going to be seen. It had cost relentless training. Complaining was futile. He had tried that and it made his father angry.

He trusted his father completely. That was the way it had always been. Even when he was singing in public against his own wishes. His father drove him on, encouraged him and had his own way in the end. It was torture for the boy the first time he sang for strangers: stage fright, bashfulness in front of all those people. But his father would not yield an inch, not even when the boy was bullied over his singing. The more he performed in public, at school and in church, the worse the boys and some girls too treated him, calling him names, even mocking his voice. He could not understand what motivated them.

He did not want to provoke his father's wrath. He was devastated after their mother died. She contracted leukaemia and it killed her within months. Their father was by her bedside day and night, accompanied her to the hospital and slept there while her life ebbed away. The last words he said before they left home for the concert were: Think about your mother. How proud she would have been of you.

The choir had taken up its position on the stage. All the girls in identical frocks paid for by the town council. The boys in white shirts and black trousers, just like he was wearing. They whispered together, excited at all the attention the choir was receiving, determined to do their best. Gabríel, the choirmaster, was talking to the stage manager.

The compère stubbed out a cigarette on the floor. Everything was ready. Soon it would be curtain up.

Gabríel called him over.

'Everything all right?' he asked.

'Yes. It's a packed house.'

'And they've all come to see you. Remember that. They've all come to see you and hear you sing and no one else, and you ought to be proud of that, pleased with yourself and not shy. Maybe you're a bit nervous now, but that will wear off as soon as you start singing. You know that.'

'Yes.'

'Shall we start then?'

He nodded.

Gabríel put his hand on the boy's shoulder.

'It's bound to be difficult for you to look all those people in the eye, but you only need to sing and everything will be all right.'

'Yes.'

'The compère doesn't come on until after the first song. We've rehearsed all this. You start singing and everything will be fine.'

Gabríel gave a sign to the stage manager. He gestured to the choir who immediately fell silent and lined up. Everything was in place. They were all ready.

The lights in the auditorium dimmed. The murmuring stopped. The curtain went up.

Think of your mother.

The last thought that crossed his mind before the auditorium opened up in front of him was his mother on her deathbed the final time he saw her, and for a second he lost his concentration. He was with his father, they were sitting together on one side of the bed, and she was so weak she could hardly keep her eyes open. She closed them and seemed to have fallen asleep, then opened them slowly, looked at him and tried to smile. They could not speak to each other any longer. When it was time to say goodbye they stood up, and he always regretted not having given her a farewell kiss, because this was the last time they were together. He simply stood up and walked out of the ward with his father, and the door closed behind them.

The curtain rose and he met his father's gaze. The auditorium vanished from his sight and all he could see was his father's glaring eyes.

Someone in the auditorium began laughing.

He came back to his senses. The choir had begun to sing and the choirmaster had given a sign, but he had missed it. Trying to gloss over the incident, the choirmaster took the choir through another round of the verse, and now he came in at the right place and had just started the song when something happened.

Something happened to his voice.

*

'It was a wolf,' Gabríel said, sitting in Erlendur's cold hotel room. 'There was a wolf in his voice, as the saying goes. Straight away in the first song, and then it was all over.'

14

Gabríel sat motionless on the bed, staring straight ahead, transported back to the stage at Hafnarfjördur cinema as the choir gradually fell silent. Gudlaugur, who could not understand what was happening to his voice, cleared his throat repeatedly and kept on trying to sing. His father got to his feet and his sister ran up onto the stage to make her brother stop. People whispered to each other at first, but soon the occasional half-smothered laugh broke out, gradually growing louder, and a few people whistled. Gabríel went to lead Gudlaugur off, but the boy stood as if nailed to the floor. The stage manager tried to bring down the curtain. The compère walked onto the stage with a cigarette in his hand, but did not know what to do. In the end Gabríel managed to move Gudlaugur and push him away. His sister was with him and shouted out to the audience not to laugh. His father was still standing in the same place in the front row, thunderstruck.

Gabríel came to earth and looked at Erlendur.

'I still shudder to think of it,' he said.

'A wolf in his voice?' Erlendur said. 'I'm not too well up on ...'

'It's an idiom for when your voice breaks. What happens is that the vocal cords stretch in puberty, but you go on using your voice in the same way and it shifts an octave lower. The result isn't pretty, you sort of yodel downwards. This is what ruins all boys' choirs. He could have had another two or three years, but Gudlaugur matured early.

His hormones started working prematurely and produced the most tragic night of his life.'

'You must have been a good friend of his, if you were the first person he went to later to discuss the whole affair.'

'You could say that. He regarded me as a confidant. Then that gradually ended, the way it does. I tried to help him as best I could and he continued singing with me. His father did not want to give up. He was going to make a singer out of his son. Talked about sending him to Italy or Germany. Even Britain. They've cultivated the most boy sopranos and have hundreds of fallen choral stars. Nothing is as short-lived as a child star.'

'But he never became a singer?'

'No. It was over. He had a reasonable adult voice, nothing special actually, but his interest was gone. All the work that had been put into singing, his whole childhood really, turned to dust that evening. His father took him to another teacher but nothing came of that. The spark had gone. He just played along for his father's sake, then he gave up for good. He told me he had never really wanted any of it. Being a singer and a choirboy and performing in public. It was all his father's wish.'

'You mentioned something before that happened some years later,' Erlendur said. 'Some years after the concert at the cinema. I thought it was connected with his father being in a wheelchair. Was I mistaken?'

'A rift gradually developed between them. Between Gudlaugur and his father. You described the way the old man behaved when he came to see you with his daughter. I don't know the whole story. Only a fragment of it.'

'But you give the impression that Gudlaugur and his sister were close.'

'There was no question about that,' Gabríel said. 'She often came to choir practice with him and was always there when he sang at school and in church. She was kind to him, but she was devoted to her father too. He had an incredibly strong character. He was unflinching and firm when he wanted his own way, but could be tender at other times. In the end she took her father's side. The boy was in rebellion. I can't explain what it was, but he ended up hating his father and blaming him for what happened. Not just up there on the stage but everything.'

Gabríel paused.

'One of the last times I talked to him, he said his father had robbed him of his childhood. Turned him into a freak.'

'A freak?'

'That was the word he used, but I didn't know any more than you what he meant by it. That was shortly after the accident.'

'Accident?'

'Yes.'

'What happened?'

'I suppose Gudlaugur would have been in his teens. He moved away from Hafnarfjördur afterwards. We really had no contact by then but I could well imagine that the accident was caused by his rebellion. The rage that had built up inside him.'

'Did he leave home after this accident?'

'Yes, so I understand.'

'What happened?'

'There was a high, steep staircase in their house. I went there once. It led upstairs from the hall. Wooden stairs with a narrow well. Apparently it began with an argument between Gudlaugur and his father, who had his study upstairs. They were at the top of the staircase and I'm told Gudlaugur pushed him and he fell down the stairs. It was quite a fall. He never walked again. Broke his back. Paralysed from the waist down.'

'Was it an accident? Do you know?'

'Gudlaugur alone knew that. And his father. They completely shut him out afterwards, the father and daughter. Cut off all contact and refused to have anything more to do with him. That might suggest he went for his father. That it wasn't a simple accident.'

'How do you know this? If you weren't in touch with those people?'

'It was the talk of the town that he'd pushed his father down the stairs. The police investigated the matter.'

Erlendur looked at the man.

'When was the last time you saw Gudlaugur?'

'It was just here at the hotel, by sheer coincidence. I didn't know where he was. I was out for dinner and caught a glimpse of him in his doorman's uniform. I didn't recognise him immediately. Such a long time had passed. This was five or six years ago. I went up to him and asked if he remembered me, and we chatted a little.'

'What about?'

'This and that. I asked him how he was doing and so on. He kept fairly quiet about his own affairs – didn't seem comfortable talking to me. It was as if I reminded him of a past he didn't want to revisit. I had the feeling he was ashamed of being in a doorman's uniform. Maybe it was something else. I don't know. I asked him about his family and he said they'd lost touch. Then the conversation dried up and we said goodbye to each other.'

'Do you have any idea who could have wanted to kill Gudlaugur?' Erlendur asked.

'Not the faintest,' Gabríel said. 'How was he attacked? How was he killed?'

He asked cautiously, a mournful look in his eyes. There was no hint that he wished to gloat over it later; he simply wanted to know how the life of a promising boy he had once taught came to an end.

'I honestly can't go into that,' Erlendur said. 'It's information that we're trying to keep secret because of the investigation.'

'Yes, of course,' Gabríel said. 'I understand. A criminal investigation … are you making any headway? Of course, you can't talk about that either, listen to how I carry on. I can't imagine who would have wanted to kill him, but then I lost touch with him long ago. I just knew that he worked at this hotel.'

'He'd been working here for years as a doorman and sort of jack of all trades. Playing Santa Claus, for example.'

Gabríel sighed. 'What a fate.'

, 'The only thing we found in his room apart from these records was a film poster that he had on his wall. It's a Shirley Temple film from 1939 called *The Little Princess*. Do you have any idea why he would have kept it, or glorified it? There was almost nothing else in the room.'

'Shirley Temple?'

'The child star.'

'The connection's obvious,' Gabríel said. 'Gudlaugur saw himself as a child star and so did everyone around him. But I can't see any other significance as such.'

Gabríel stood up, put on his cap, buttoned his coat and wrapped his scarf around his neck. Neither of them said anything. Erlendur opened the door and walked out into the corridor with him.

'Thank you for coming to see me,' he said, offering his hand to shake.

'It was nothing,' Gabríel said. 'It was the least I could do for you. And for the dear boy.'

He dithered as if about to add something else, unsure exactly how to phrase it.

'He was terribly innocent,' he said eventually. 'A totally harmless boy. He'd been convinced that he was unique and he'd become famous, he could have had the world at his feet. The Vienna Boys' Choir. They make such an awful fuss about small things here in Iceland, even more now than they used to; it's a national trait in a country of under-achievers. He was bullied at school for being different; he suffered because of it. Then it turned out he was just an ordinary boy and his world fell apart in a single evening. He needed to be strong to put up with that.'

They exchanged farewells and Gabríel turned round and walked down the corridor. Erlendur watched him leaving with the feeling that telling the tale of Gudlaugur Egilsson had drained the old choirmaster's strength completely.

Erlendur shut the door. He sat down on the bed and thought about the choirboy and how he found him in a Santa suit with his trousers round his ankles. He wondered how his path had led to that little room and to death, at the end of a life paved with disappointment. He thought about Gudlaugur's father, paralysed in a wheelchair, with his thick horn-rimmed glasses, and about his sister with her hooked eagle's nose and her antipathy towards her brother. He thought about the fat hotel manager who had sacked him, and the man from reception who pretended not to know him. He thought about the hotel staff, who did not know who Gudlaugur was. He thought about Henry Wapshott who had travelled all that way to seek out the choirboy because the child Gudlaugur with his lovely voice still existed and always would.

Before he knew it he had started thinking about his brother.

Erlendur put the same record back on the turntable, stretched out, closed his eyes and let the song take him back home.

Maybe it was his song as well.

15

When Elínborg came back from Hafnarfjördur towards evening she went straight to the hotel to meet Erlendur.

She went up to his floor and knocked on the door, and again when she got no response, then a third time. She was turning away when the door opened at last and Erlendur let her in. He had been lying down thinking and had dozed off, and was rather vague when Elínborg began telling him what she had unearthed in Hafnarfjördur. She had spoken to the ex-headmaster of the primary school, an ancient man who remembered Gudlaugur well; his wife, who had died ten years before, had also been close to the boy. With the headmaster's help Elínborg tracked down three of Gudlaugur's classmates who were still living in Hafnarfjördur. One had been at the fateful concert. She talked to the family's old neighbours and people who were in touch with them in those days.

'No one is ever allowed to excel in this dwarf state,' Elínborg said, sitting down on the bed. 'No one's allowed to be different.'

Everyone knew that Gudlaugur's life was supposed to be something special. He never talked about it himself, never talked about himself at all really, but everyone knew. He was sent for piano lessons and learned to sing, first from his father and then with the choirmaster who was appointed to conduct the children's choir, and finally with a well-known singer who once lived in Germany but had come back to Iceland. People praised him to the skies, applauded him, and he would take a bow in his white shirt and black trousers, gentlemanly and sophisticated. Such a beautiful child, Gudlaugur, people said. And he made recordings of his singing. Soon he would be famous in other countries.

He was not from Hafnarfjördur. The family was from the north and had lived in Reykjavík for a while. His father was said to be the son of an organist who had studied singing abroad when he was younger. Rumour had it that he bought the house in Hafnarfjördur with what he inherited from his father, who had made money by trading with the American military after the war. It was said that he inherited enough to live comfortably afterwards. But he was never showy about his wealth. He kept a low profile in the community. Doffed his hat when he went out for walks with his wife and greeted people politely. She was said to be the daughter of a trawler owner. No one knew where. They made few friends in the town. Most of their friends were in Reykjavík, if they had any at all. They did not seem to have many visitors.

When the local boys and Gudlaugur's classmates called round for him the usual answer was that he had to stay in and do his homework, either for school or for singing and piano practice. Sometimes he was allowed to go out with them and they noticed that he was not as coarse as they were, and strangely sensitive. His clothes never got dirty, he never jumped in puddles, he was rather a wimp at football and spoke very properly. Sometimes he talked about people with foreign names. Some Schubert bloke. And when they told him about the latest action comics they were reading or what they had seen at the cinema, he told them he read poetry. Maybe not necessarily because he really wanted to, but because his father said it was good for him to read poetry. They had a hunch that his father set him lessons to learn and was very strict about it. One poem every evening.

His sister was different. Tougher. More like her father. The father did not seem to make such great demands on her as on the boy. She was learning the piano and like her brother, had joined the children's choir when it was set up. Her friends described how she was sometimes jealous of her brother when their father praised him; their mother appeared to favour the son as well. People thought Gudlaugur and his mother were close. She was like his guardian angel.

One of Gudlaugur's classmates was shown into the drawing room once while the family debated whether he could go out to play. The father stood on the stairs wearing his thick glasses, Gudlaugur on the landing and his mother by the door to the drawing room, and she said it did not matter if the boy went out to play. He did not have so many friends and they did not call for him very often. He could go on practising later.

'Get on with your exercises!' the father shouted. 'Do you think it's something you can pick up and put down as you please? You don't understand the dedication it involves, do you? You'll never understand that!'

'He's just a child,' his mother said. 'And he doesn't have many friends. You can't keep him shut up indoors all day. He must be allowed to be a child too.'

'It's all right,' Gudlaugur said, and walked over to the boy visiting him. 'I might come out later. Go home and I'll come afterwards.'

As the boy left, before the door closed behind him, he heard Gudlaugur's father shout down the stairs: 'You shall never do that again, argue with me in front of strangers.'

Over time Gudlaugur became isolated at school and the boys in the top form started to tease him. It was very innocent at first. They all teased each other and there were fights in the playground and pranks just as in all schools, but by the age of eleven Gudlaugur had clearly become the butt of the bullying and practical jokes. It was not a large school by modern standards and everyone knew that Gudlaugur was different. He was wan and sickly. A stay-at-home. The boys where he lived stopped calling for him and started teasing him at school. His satchel would go missing or be empty when he picked it up. Boys pushed him over. They ripped his clothes. He was beaten up. He was called names. No one invited him to birthday parties.

Gudlaugur did not know how to fight back. He did not understand what was going on. His father complained to the headmaster, who promised to put an end to it, but it proved to be beyond his control and Gudlaugur would go home from school as before covered in bruises and clutching his empty satchel. His father contemplated removing him from the school, even moving out of the town, but he was obstinate and refused to give in, having taken part in founding the children's choir. He was pleased with the young conductor, and, knowing that choir was a place for Gudlaugur to practise and draw attention to himself eventually, felt that the bullying – for which there was no word in the Icelandic language in those days, Elínborg interjected – was something Gudlaugur simply had to put up with.

The boy responded with total surrender and became a dreamy loner. He concentrated on singing and the piano and appeared to derive some peace of mind from them. In that field everything went in his favour. He could see what he was capable of. But most of the time he felt bad and when his mother died it was as if he turned to nothing.

He was always seen alone and tried to smile if he met children from the school. He made a record that was reported in the newspapers. It was as if his father had been right all the time. Gudlaugur would be something special in life.

And soon, because of a closely guarded secret, he earned a new name in the neighbourhood.

'What was he called?' Erlendur asked.

'The headmaster didn't know,' Elínborg said, 'and his classmates either pretended not to remember or refused to tell. But it had a profound effect on the boy. They all agreed on that.'

'What time is it anyway?' Erlendur suddenly asked, as if in panic.

'I suppose it must be past seven,' Elínborg said. 'Is something wrong?'

'Bugger it, I've slept all day,' Erlendur said, leaping to his feet. 'I have to find Henry Wapshott. They were supposed to take a sample from him at lunchtime and he wasn't here.'

Elínborg looked at the record player, loudspeakers and records.

'Is he any good?' she asked.

'He's brilliant,' Erlendur said. 'You ought to listen to him.'

'I'm going home,' Elínborg said, standing up now too. 'Are you going to stay at the hotel over Christmas? Aren't you going to get yourself home?'

'I don't know,' Erlendur said. 'I'll see.'

'You're welcome to join us. You know that. I'll be having cold leg of pork. And ox tongue.'

'Don't worry so much,' Erlendur said as he opened the door. 'You get off home, I'm going to check on Wapshott.'

'Where's Sigurdur Óli been all day?' Elínborg asked.

'He was going to see if he could find out anything about Wapshott from Scotland Yard. He's probably home by now.'

'Why's it so cold in your room?'

'The radiator's broken,' Erlendur said, closing the door behind them.

When they went down to the lobby he said goodbye to Elínborg and found the head of reception in his office. Henry Wapshott had not been seen at the hotel all day. His key card was not in the pigeon hole and he had not checked out. He still had to pay the bill. Erlendur knew that he was catching the evening flight to London and he had nothing concrete to prevent him from leaving the country. He had not heard from Sigurdur Óli. He dithered in the lobby.

'Could you let me into his room?' he asked the reception manager.

The manager shook his head.

'He could have fled,' Erlendur said. 'Do you know when the plane for London leaves tonight? What time?'

'The afternoon flight was badly delayed,' the man said. Knowing all about the flights was part of his job. 'It will take off around nine, they think.'

Erlendur made a couple of telephone calls. He found out that Henry Wapshott had a flight booked to London. He had not checked in yet. Erlendur took measures for passport control to apprehend him at the airport and have him sent back to Reykjavík. Needing to find a reason for the Keflavík police to detain him, he hesitated for a moment and wondered whether to invent something. He knew that the press would have a field day if he told the truth, but he couldn't think of a plausible lie on the spot, and in the end he said, which was true, that Wapshott was under suspicion in a murder inquiry.

'Can't you let me into his room?' Erlendur asked the manager again. 'I won't touch anything. I just need to know if he's done a runner. It would take me ages to get a warrant. I just need to put my head round the door.'

'He may yet check out,' the manager said stiffly. 'There's a good while before the flight yet and he has plenty of time to come back here, pack, pay his bill, check out and take the shuttle to Keflavík airport. Won't you hang on a while?'

Erlendur pondered.

'Can't you send someone up to tidy his room and I can walk past the door when it's open? Is that any problem?'

'You must understand the position I'm in,' the manager said. 'Above all we safeguard the interests of our guests. They're entitled to privacy, just like being at home. If I break that rule and word gets out or it's reported in the trial documents, our guests won't be able to trust us any longer. It couldn't be simpler. You must understand.'

'We're investigating a murder that was committed at this hotel,' Erlendur said. 'Isn't your reputation gone to buggery anyway?'

'Bring a warrant and there won't be any problem.'

Erlendur walked away from reception with a sigh. He took out his mobile and called Sigurdur Óli. The phone rang for a long while before he answered. Erlendur could hear voices in the background.

'Where on earth are you?' Erlendur asked.

'I'm doing the bread,' Sigurdur Óli said.

'Doing the bread?'

'Carving patterns in the wafer bread. For Christmas. With Bergthóra's family. It's a regular feature on our Christmas agenda. Have you gone home?'

'What did you find out from Scotland Yard about Henry Wapshott?'

'I'm waiting to hear. I'll find out tomorrow morning. Is anything happening with him?'

'I think he's trying to dodge the saliva sample,' Erlendur said, noticing the head of reception walking up with a sheet of paper in his hand. 'I think he's trying to leave the country without saying goodbye to us. I'll talk to you tomorrow. Don't cut your fingers.'

Erlendur put his mobile in his pocket. The manager was standing in front of him.

'I decided to check out about Henry Wapshott,' he said, handing Erlendur the piece of paper. 'To help you a bit. I shouldn't be doing this but ...'

'What is it?' Erlendur said as he looked at the paper. He saw Henry Wapshott's name and some dates.

'He's spent Christmas at this hotel for the past three years,' the manager said. 'If that helps at all.'

Erlendur stared at the dates.

'He said he's never been to Iceland before.'

'I don't know anything about that,' the man said. 'But he's been at this hotel before.'

'Do you remember him? Is he a regular?'

'I don't remember ever checking him in. There are more than two hundred rooms at this hotel and Christmas is always busy, so he can easily disappear into the crowd, besides which, he only makes short stops. Just a couple of days. I haven't noticed him this time around but the penny dropped when I looked at the printout. He's just like you in one respect. He has the same special needs.'

'What do you mean, like me? Special needs?' Erlendur could not imagine what he had in common with Henry Wapshott.

'He appears to be interested in music.'

'What are you talking about?'

'You can see here,' the manager said, pointing at the sheet of paper. 'We make a note of our guests' special requirements. In most cases.'

Erlendur read down the list.

'He wanted a player in his room,' the manager said. 'Not a smart CD player, but some old heap. Just like you.'

'Bloody liar,' Erlendur hissed, and took out his mobile again.

16

A warrant for Henry Wapshott's arrest was issued that evening. He was apprehended when he went to catch the plane for London. Wapshott was taken to the cells in the police station on Hverfisgata and Erlendur obtained a warrant to search his room. The forensics team arrived at the hotel around midnight. They combed the room in search of the murder weapon, but found nothing. All they found was a suitcase that Wapshott clearly intended to leave behind, his shaving kit in the bathroom, an old record player similar to the one Erlendur had borrowed from the hotel, a television and video player, and several British newspapers and magazines. Including *Record Collector*.

Fingerprint experts looked for clues that Gudlaugur had been in his room, scouring the edges of the table and the door frame. Erlendur stood out in the corridor watching the forensics team. He wanted a cigarette and even a glass of Chartreuse because Christmas was coming, wanted his armchair and books. He intended to go home. Did not really know why he stayed at that deathly hotel. Did not really know what to do with himself.

White dust from the fingerprinting sprinkled onto the floor.

Erlendur saw the hotel manager waddling along the corridor. He wielded his handkerchief and was puffing and blowing. After taking a look inside the room where the forensics team were at work, he smiled all over his face.

'I heard you've caught him,' he said, wiping his neck. 'And that it was a foreigner.'

'Where did you hear that?' Erlendur asked.

'On the radio,' the manager said, unable to conceal his glee at all this good news. The man had been found, it was not an Icelander who committed the deed and it was not one of the hotel staff either. The manager panted: 'They said on the news that he was arrested at Keflavík airport on his way to London. A Brit?'

Erlendur's mobile started ringing.

'We don't know whether he's the one we're looking for,' he said as he took out his phone.

'You don't need to come down to the station,' Sigurdur Óli said when Erlendur answered. 'Not for the time being.'

'Shouldn't you be doing the Christmas bread?' Erlendur asked, and turned away from the manager with his mobile in his hand.

'He's drunk,' Sigurdur Óli said. 'Henry Wapshott. It's pointless trying to talk to him. Shall we let him sleep it off tonight and talk to him in the morning?'

'Did he cause any trouble?'

'No, not at all. They told me he went along with them without saying a word. They stopped him immediately at passport control and kept him in the body search room, and when the police arrived they took him straight out to the van and drove to Reykjavík. No trouble. He was apparently very reticent and fell asleep in the van on his way into town. He's sleeping in his cell now.'

'It was on the news, so I'm told,' Erlendur said. 'About the arrest.' He looked at the manager. 'People are hoping we've got the right man.'

'He only had a case with him. A big briefcase.'

'Is there anything in it?'

'Records. Old ones. The same sort of vinyl crap we found in the room in the basement.'

'You mean Gudlaugur's records?'

'Looked like it. Not many. And he had some others. You can examine it all tomorrow.'

'He's hunting for Gudlaugur's records.'

'Maybe he managed to add to his collection,' Sigurdur Óli said. 'Should we meet down here at the station tomorrow morning?'

'We need a saliva sample from him,' Erlendur said.

'I'll see to that,' Sigurdur Óli said, and they rang off.

Erlendur put his mobile back in his pocket.

'Has he confessed?' the hotel manager asked. 'Did he confess?'

'Do you remember seeing him in the hotel before? Henry Wapshott. From Liverpool. Looks about sixty. He told me this was his first visit to Iceland, then it turns out that he's stayed here before.'

'I don't remember anyone by that name. Do you have a photograph of him?'

'I need to get one. Find out if any of the staff recognise him. It might ring a bell somewhere. Even the tiniest detail could be important.'

'Hopefully you'll get it all sorted,' the manager grunted. 'We've had cancellations because of the murder. Icelanders mostly. The tourists haven't heard so much about it. But the buffet's not so busy and our bookings are down. I should never have allowed him to live down there in the basement. Bloody kindness will be the death of me.'

'You positively ooze with it,' Erlendur said.

The manager looked at Erlendur, unsure whether he was mocking him. The head of forensics came out into the corridor to them, greeted the manager and drew Erlendur to one side.

'It all looks like a typical tourist in a double room in a Reykjavík hotel,' he said. 'The murder weapon isn't lying on his bedside table, if that's what you were hoping for, and there are no bloodstained clothes in his suitcase – nothing to connect him with the man in the basement really. The room's covered with fingerprints. But he's obviously done a runner. He left his room as if he was on his way down to the bar. His electric shaver is still plugged in. Spare pairs of shoes on the floor. And some slippers he'd brought with him. That's really all we can say at this stage. The man was in a hurry. He was fleeing.'

The head of forensics went back into the room and Erlendur walked over to the manager.

'Who does the cleaning on this corridor?' he asked. 'Who goes into the rooms? Don't the cleaners share the floors out between them?'

'I know which women do this floor,' the manager said. 'There are no men. For some reason.'

He said this sarcastically, as if cleaning was obviously not a man's job.

'And who are they then?' Erlendur asked.

'Well, the girl you talked to, for example.'

'Which girl I talked to?'

'The one in the basement,' the manager said. 'Who found the body. The girl who found the dead Santa. This is her floor.'

When Erlendur went back to his room two storeys above, Eva Lind was waiting for him in the corridor. She was sitting on the floor, leaning against the wall, with her knees up under her chin, and appeared to be asleep. When he walked over she looked up and smoothed out her clothes.

'It's fantastic coming to this hotel,' she said. 'When are you going to get your arse back home?'

'The plan was soon,' Erlendur said. 'I'm growing tired of this place too.'

He slid his card into the slot on the door. Eva Lind got to her feet and followed him inside. Erlendur closed the door and Eva threw herself flat out onto his bed. He sat down at the desk.

'Getting anywhere with the bizz?' Eva asked, lying on her stomach with her eyes closed as if trying to fall asleep.

'Very slowly,' Erlendur said. 'And stop calling it "bizz". What's wrong with "business", or even "case"?'

'Aw, shut your face,' Eva Lind said, her eyes still closed. Erlendur smiled. He looked at his daughter on the bed and wondered what kind of parent he would have been. Would he have made great demands on her? Signed her up for ballet classes? Hoped she was a little genius? Would he have hit her if she had knocked his chartreuse onto the floor?

'Are you there?' she asked, eyes still closed.

'Yes, I'm here,' Erlendur said wearily.

'Why don't you say anything?'

'What am I supposed to say? What are people ever supposed to say?'

'Well, what you're doing at this hotel, for instance. Seriously.'

'I don't know. I didn't want to go back to the flat. It's a bit of a change.'

'Change! What's the difference between hanging around by yourself in this room and hanging around by yourself at home?'

'Do you want to hear some music?' Erlendur asked, trying to steer the conversation away from himself. He began outlining the case to his daughter, point by point, to gain some kind of a picture of it himself. He told her about the girl who found a stabbed Santa, once an exceptionally gifted choirboy who had made two records that were sought-after by collectors. His voice was unique.

He reached for the record he had yet to listen to. It contained two hymns and was clearly designed for Christmas. On the sleeve was Gudlaugur wearing a Santa hat, with a wide smile showing his adult teeth, and Erlendur thought about the irony of fate. He put the record on and the choirboy's voice resounded around the room in beautiful, bitter-sweet song. Eva Lind opened her eyes and sat up on the bed.

'Are you joking?' she said.

'Don't you think it's magnificent?'

'I've never heard a kid sing like that,' Eva said. 'I don't think I've ever heard anyone sing so beautifully.' They sat in silence and listened to the end of the song. Erlendur reached over to the record player, turned the record over and played the hymn on the other side. They listened to it, and when it was over Eva Lind asked him to play it again.

Erlendur told her about Gudlaugur's family, the concert in Hafnarfjördur, his father and sister who had not been in touch with him for more than thirty years, and the British collector who tried to leave the country and was only interested in choirboys. Told her that Gudlaugur's records might be valuable today.

'Do you think that's why he got done?' Eva Lind asked. 'Because of the records? Because they're valuable now?'

'I don't know.'

'Are there any still around?'

'I don't think so,' Erlendur said, 'and that's probably what makes them collectors' items. Elínborg says collectors look for something that's unique. But that might not be important. Maybe someone at the hotel attacked him. Someone who didn't know about the choirboy at all.'

Erlendur decided not to tell his daughter about the way Gudlaugur was found. He knew that when she was taking drugs she had prostituted herself and knew how it operated in Reykjavík. Yet he flinched from broaching that subject with her. She lived her own life and had her own way without him ever having any say in the matter. But since he thought there was a possibility that Gudlaugur had paid for sex at the hotel, he asked her if she knew of any prostitution there.

Eva Lind looked at her father.

'Poor bloke,' she said without answering him. Her mind was still on the choirboy. 'There was a girl like that at my school. Primary school. She made a few records. Her name was Vala Dögg. You remember anything by her? She was really hyped. Sang Christmas carols. A pretty little blonde girl.'

Erlendur shook his head.

'She was a child star. Sang on children's hour and TV shows and sang really well, a little sweetie-pie sort of type. Her dad was some obscure pop singer but it was her mum who was a bit of a nutter and wanted to make a pop star out of her. She got teased big time. She was really nice, not a show-off or pretentious in the least, but people were always bugging her. Icelanders get jealous and annoyed so easily. She was bullied, so she left school and got a job. I met her a lot when I was doing dope and she'd turned into a total creep. Worse than me. Burned-out and forgotten. She told me it was the worst thing that ever happened to her.'

'Being a child star?'

'It ruined her. She never escaped from it. Was never allowed to be herself. Her mum was really bossy. Never asked her if it was what she wanted. She liked singing and being in the spotlight and all that, but she had no idea what was going on. She could never be anything more than the little cutie on children's hour. She was only allowed to have one dimension. She was pretty little Vala Dögg. And then she got teased about it, and couldn't understand why until she got older and realised that she'd never be anything but a pretty little dolly singing in her frock. That she'd never be a world-famous pop star like her mum always told her.'

Eva Lind stopped talking and looked at her father.

'She totally fell to bits. She said the bullying was the worst thing, it turns you into shit. You end up with exactly the same opinion of yourself as the people who persecute you.'

'Gudlaugur probably went through the same,' Erlendur said. 'He left home young. It must be a strain for kids having to go through all that.'

They fell silent.

'Of course there are tarts at this hotel,' Eva Lind suddenly said, throwing herself back on the bed. 'Obviously.'

'What do you know about it? Is there anything you could help me with?'

'There are tarts everywhere. You can dial a number and they wait for you at the hotel. Classy tarts. They don't call themselves tarts, they provide "escort services".'

'Do you know of any who work this hotel? Girls or women who do that?'

'They don't have to be Icelandic. They're imported too. They can come over as tourists for a couple of weeks, then they don't need any papers. Then come back a few months later.'

Eva Lind looked at her father.

'You could talk to Stína. She's my friend. She knows the game. Do you think it was a tart who killed him?'

'I have no idea.'

They fell silent. Outside in the darkness snowflakes glittered as they fell to the ground. Erlendur vaguely recalled a reference to snow in the Bible, sins and snow, and tried to remember it: though your sins be as scarlet, they shall be as white as snow.

'I'm freaking out,' Eva Lind said. There was no excitement in her voice. No eagerness.

'Maybe you can't handle it by yourself,' Erlendur said; he had urged his daughter to seek counselling. 'Maybe you need someone other than me to help you.'

'Don't give me that psychology bollocks,' Eva said.

'You haven't got over it and you don't look well, and soon you'll go and take the pain away the old way, then you're back in exactly the same mess as before.'

Erlendur was on the verge of saying the sentence he still had not dared to say out loud to his daughter.

'Preaching all the time,' Eva Lind said, instantly on edge, and she stood up.

He decided to fire away.

'You'd be failing the baby that died.'

Eva Lind stared at her father, her eyes black with rage.

'The other option you have is to come to terms with this fucking life, as you call it, and put up with the suffering it involves. Put up with the suffering we all have to endure, always, to get through that and find and enjoy the happiness and joy that it brings us as well, in spite of our being alive.'

'Speak for yourself! You can't even go home at Christmas because there's nothing there! Not a fucking thing and you can't go there because you know it's just a hole with nothing in it which you can't be bothered to crawl back into any more.'

'I'm always at home at Christmas,' Erlendur said.

Eva Lind looked confused.

'What are you talking about?'

'That's the worst thing about Christmas,' Erlendur said. 'I always go home.'

'I don't understand you,' Eva Lind said, opening the door. 'I'll never understand you.'

She slammed the door behind her. Erlendur stood up to run after her, but stopped. He knew that she would come back. He walked over to the window and watched his reflection in the glass until he could see through it into the darkness and the glittering snowflakes.

He had forgotten his decision to go home to the hole with nothing in it, as Eva Lind put it. He turned from the window and set Gudlaugur's hymns playing again, stretched out on his bed and listened to the boy who, much later, would be found murdered in a little room at a hotel, and thought about sins as white as snow.

FOURTH DAY

17

He woke up early in the morning, still in his clothes and lying on top of the quilt. It took him a long time to shake off the sleep. A dream about his father followed him into the dark morning and he struggled to remember it but caught only snatches: his father, younger in some way, fitter, smiled at him in a deserted forest.

His hotel room was dark and cold. The sun would not be up for a few hours yet. He lay thinking about the dream, his father and the loss of his brother. How the unbearable loss had made a hole in his world. And how the hole was continually growing and he stepped back from its edge to look down into the void that was ready to swallow him when finally he let go.

He shook off these waking fantasies and thought about his tasks for the day. What was Henry Wapshott hiding? Why did he tell lies and make a forlorn attempt to flee, drunk and without luggage? His behaviour puzzled Erlendur. And before long his thoughts stopped at the boy in the hospital bed and his father: Elínborg's case, which she had explained to him in detail.

Elínborg suspected that the boy had been maltreated before and there were strong indications that it happened at home. The father was under suspicion. She insisted on having him remanded in custody for the duration of the investigation. A week's custody was granted, against vociferous protests from both the father and his lawyer. When the warrant was issued Elínborg went to fetch him with four uniformed police officers and accompanied him down to Hverfisgata. She led him along the prison corridor and locked the door to his cell herself. She pulled back the hatch on the door and looked in at the man who was standing on the same spot with his back turned to her, hunched up and somehow helpless, like everyone who is removed from human society and kept like an animal in a cage.

He slowly turned round and looked her in the eye from the other side of the steel door, and she slid the hatch shut on him.

Early the next morning she began questioning him. Erlendur took part but Elínborg was in charge of the interrogation. The two of them sat facing him in the interrogation room. On the table between them was an ashtray screwed down to the table. The father was unshaven, wearing a crumpled suit and a scruffy white shirt buttoned at the neck with a tie knotted impeccably, as if it represented the last vestiges of his self-respect.

Elínborg switched on the tape recorder and recorded the interview, the names of those present and the number assigned to the case. She had prepared herself well. She had met the boy's supervisor from school who talked about dyslexia, attention deficit disorder and poor school performance; a psychologist, a friend of hers, who talked about disappointment, stress and denial; and talked to the boy's friends, neighbours, relatives, everyone whom it occurred to her to ask about the boy and his father.

The man would not yield. He accused them of persecution, announced that he would sue them, and refused to answer their questions. Elínborg looked at Erlendur. A warden appeared who pushed the man to his cell again.

Two days later he was brought back for questioning. His lawyer had brought him more comfortable clothes from home and he was now dressed in jeans and a T-shirt with a designer label on one of the breast pockets, which he wore like a medal rewarding him for absurdly expensive shopping. He was in a different frame of mind now. Three days in custody had dampened his arrogance, as it tends to do, and he saw that it depended on him alone whether he would stay confined in the cells or not.

Elínborg made sure that he came in for interrogation barefoot. His shoes and socks were taken away without explanation. When he sat down in front of them he tried to pull his feet under his chair.

Elínborg and Erlendur sat facing him, intractable. The tape recorder whirred softly.

'I talked to your son's teacher,' Elínborg said. 'And although what happens and passes between parent and teacher is confidential and she was very firm about that, she wanted to help the boy, help in the criminal case. She told me you assaulted him once in front of her.'

'Assaulted him! I gave him a little rap on the jaw. That's hardly what you call assault. He was being naughty, that's all. Fidgeting all over the place. He's difficult. You don't know about that sort of thing. The strain.'

'So it's right to punish him?'

'We're good friends, my boy and I,' the father said. 'I love him. I'm responsible for him all by myself. His mother …'

'I know about his mother,' Elínborg said. 'And of course it can be difficult bringing up a child by yourself. But what you did to him and do to him is … it's indescribable.'

The father sat and said nothing.

'I didn't do anything,' he said eventually.

Elínborg crossed her legs and caught her foot on the father's shin as she did so.

'Sorry,' Elínborg said.

He winced, unsure whether she had done it on purpose.

'The teacher said you make unrealistic demands on your son,' she said, unruffled. 'Is that true?'

'What's unrealistic? I want him to get an education and make something of himself.'

'Understandably,' Elínborg said. 'But he's eight years old, dyslexic and borderline hyperactive. You didn't finish school yourself.'

'I own and run my own business.'

'Which is bankrupt. You're losing your house, your fancy car, the wealth that's brought you a certain social status. People look up to you. When the old classmates have a reunion you're sure to be the big shot. Those golfing trips with your mates. You're losing everything. How infuriating, especially when you bear in mind that your wife is in a psychiatric ward and your son's behind at school. It all mounts up, and in the end you explode when Addi, who's surely spilled milk and dropped plates on the floor all his life, knocks a bottle of Drambuie onto the marble floor of your lounge.'

The father looked at her. His expression did not change.

Elínborg had visited his wife at Kleppur mental hospital. She suffered from schizophrenia and sometimes had to be admitted when she began hallucinating and the voices overwhelmed her. When Elínborg met her she was on such strong medication that she could hardly speak. Sat rocking backwards and forwards and asked Elínborg for a cigarette. Had no idea why she was visiting her.

'I'm trying to bring him up as best I can,' the father said in the interrogation room.

'By pricking the back of his hand with needles.'

'Shut your mouth.'

Elínborg had talked to the man's sister, who said she sometimes thought the boy's upbringing rather harsh. She cited one example from a visit to their home. The boy was four at the time and complained that he was not feeling well, he cried a little and she thought he might even have the flu. Her brother lost his patience when the boy had been moaning at him for some while, and he picked him up and held him.

'Is anything wrong?' he asked the child brashly.

'No,' Addi said, his voice low and nervous, as if giving in.

'You shouldn't be crying.'

'No,' the boy said.

'If there's nothing wrong, then stop crying.'

'Yes.'

'So is there anything wrong?'

'No.'

'So everything's OK.'

'Yes.'

'Good. You shouldn't blubber about nothing.'

Elínborg recounted this story to the father, but his expression remained unchanged.

'My sister and I don't get on,' he said. 'I don't remember that.'

'Did you assault your son with the result that he was admitted to hospital?' Elínborg asked.

The father looked at her.

Elínborg repeated the question.

'No,' he said. 'I didn't. Do you think any father would do that? He was beaten up at school.'

The boy was out of hospital. Child welfare had found a foster home for him and Elínborg went to see him when the interrogation was over. She sat down beside him and asked how he was doing. He hadn't said a word to her since the first time they met, but now he looked at her as if he wanted to say something.

He cleared his throat, faltering.

'I miss my dad,' he said, choking back the sobs.

Erlendur was sitting at the breakfast table when he saw Sigurdur Óli come in followed by Henry Wapshott. Two detectives sat down at another table behind them. The British record collector was scruffier than before, his ruffled hair standing out in all directions and a look of suffering on his face, which expressed total humiliation and a lost battle with a hangover and imprisonment.

'What's going on?' Erlendur asked Sigurdur Óli, and stood up. 'Why did you bring him here? And why isn't he done up?'

'Done up?'

'In handcuffs.'

'Does that look necessary to you?'

Erlendur looked at Wapshott.

'I couldn't be bothered to wait for you,' Sigurdur Óli said. 'We can only detain him until this evening, so you'll have to make a decision on charges as soon as possible. And he wanted to meet you here. Refused to talk to me. Just wanted to talk to you. Like you were old friends. He hasn't insisted on bail, hasn't asked for legal aid or help from his embassy. We've told him he can contact the embassy but he just shakes his head.'

'Have you found out anything about him from Scotland Yard?' Erlendur said with a glance at Wapshott, who was standing behind Sigurdur Óli, his head hung low.

'I'll explore that when you take him over,' said Sigurdur Óli, who had done nothing on the matter. 'I'll let you know what they've got on him, if anything.'

Sigurdur Óli said goodbye to Wapshott, stopped briefly with the two detectives, then left. Erlendur offered the British man a seat. Wapshott perched on a chair, looking down at the floor.

'I didn't kill him,' he said in a low voice. 'I could never have killed him. I've never been able to kill anything, not even flies. To say nothing of that wonderful choirboy.'

Erlendur looked at Wapshott.

'Are you talking about Gudlaugur?'

'Yes,' Wapshott said. 'Of course.'

'He was a long way from being a choirboy,' Erlendur said. 'Gudlaugur was almost fifty and played Santa Claus at Christmas parties.'

'You don't understand,' Wapshott said.

'No, I don't,' Erlendur said. 'Maybe you can explain it to me.'

'I wasn't at the hotel when he was attacked,' Wapshott said.

'Where were you?'

'I was looking for records.' Wapshott looked up and a pained smile passed across his face. 'I was looking at the stuff you Icelanders throw away. Seeing what comes out of that recycling plant. They told me a dead person's estate had come in. Including gramophone records for disposal.'

'Who?'

'Who what?'

'Told you about the dead person's things?'

'The staff. I give them a tip if they let me know. They have my card. I've told you that. I go to the collectors' shops, meet other collectors and go to the markets. Kolaportid, isn't that the name? I do what all collectors do, try to find something worth owning.'

'Was anyone with you at the time of the attack on Gudlaugur? Someone we can talk to?'

'No,' Wapshott said.

'But they must remember you at those places.'

'Of course.'

'And did you find anything worth having? Any choirboys?'

'Nothing. I haven't found anything on this trip.'

'Why were you running away from us?' Erlendur asked.

'I wanted to get home.'

'And you left all your stuff at the hotel?'

'Yes.'

'Apart from a few of Gudlaugur's records.'

'Yes.'

'Why did you tell me you'd never been to Iceland before?'

'I don't know. I didn't want to attract unnecessary attention. The murder has nothing to do with me.'

'It's very easy to prove the opposite. You must have known, when you were lying, that I'd find out. That I'd find out you'd been at this hotel before.'

'The murder is nothing to do with me.'

'But now you've convinced me it is something to do with you. You couldn't have drawn more attention to yourself.'

'I didn't kill him.'

'What was your relationship with Gudlaugur?'

'I've told you that story and I wasn't lying then. I became interested in his singing, in old records by him as a choirboy, and when I heard he was still alive I contacted him.'

'Why did you lie? You've been to Iceland before, you've stayed at this hotel before and you've definitely met Gudlaugur before.'

'It's nothing to do with me. The murder. When I heard about it I was afraid you'd find out that I knew him. I got more paranoid by the minute and I had to apply amazing self-discipline not to make a run for it at once, which would have pointed the finger at me. I had to let a few days go by, but then I couldn't stand it any longer and I had to get away. My nerves couldn't take it any more. But I didn't kill him.'

'How much did you know about Gudlaugur's background?'

'Not much.'

'Isn't the point about collecting records to dig up information about what you collect? Have you done that?'

'I don't know much,' Wapshott said. 'I know he lost his voice at a concert, only two recordings of his songs were released, he fell out with his father ...'

'Wait a minute, how did you hear about how he died?'

'What do you mean?'

'The hotel guests weren't told it was a murder, but an accident or heart attack. How did you find out he'd been murdered?'

'How did I find out? You told me.'

'Yes, I told you and you were very surprised, but now you say that when you heard about the murder you were afraid we would link you to him. In other words, it was before we met. Before we linked you to him.'

Wapshott stared at him. Erlendur could tell when people were stalling for time, and he let Wapshott have all the time he needed. The two detectives sat calmly at a suitable distance. Erlendur had been late for breakfast and there were few people in the dining hall. He caught a glimpse of the big chef who had gone berserk when the saliva sample was supposed to be taken. Erlendur's thoughts turned to Valgerdur. The biotechnician. What would she be doing? Sticking needles into children who were fighting back their tears or trying to kick her?

'I didn't want to get involved in this,' Wapshott said.

'What are you hiding? Why don't you want to talk to the British embassy? Why don't you want a lawyer?'

'I heard people talking about it down here. Hotel guests. They were saying someone had been murdered. Some Americans. That's how I heard. And I was worried that you would connect us and I'd end up in precisely the situation in which I now find myself. That's why I fled. It's as simple as that.'

Erlendur remembered the American Henry Bartlett and his wife. Cindy, she had told Sigurdur Óli with a smile.

'How much are Gudlaugur's records worth?'

'What do you mean?'

'They must be worth a lot to make you come all the way up to the cold north here in the middle of winter to get hold of them. How much are they worth? One record. What does it cost?'

'If you want to sell it you auction it, even on E-bay, and there's no telling how much it will fetch in the end.'

'But at a guess. What do you guess it would sell for?'

'I can't say.'

'Did you meet Gudlaugur before he died?'

Henry Wapshott hesitated.

'Yes,' he said at last.

'The note we found, 18.30, was that the time of your meeting?'

'That was the day before he was found dead. We sat down in his room and had a short meeting.'

'About what?'

'About his records.'

'What about his records?'

'I wanted to know, I've wanted to know for a long time, whether he had any more. Whether the handful I know about, in my own collection and others', are the only copies in the world. For some reason he wouldn't answer. I asked him first in a letter that I wrote him several years ago, and it was one of the first things I asked when I met him.'

'So, did he have any records for you?'

'He refused to say.'

'Did he know what his records were worth?'

'I gave him a fairly clear picture.'

'And how much are these records really worth?'

Wapshott did not reply immediately.

'When I met him the last time, he gave in,' he said. 'He wanted to talk about his records. I ...'

Wapshott hesitated again. He looked behind him and saw the two detectives who were guarding him.

'I gave him half a million.'

'Half a million?'

'Króna. As a down payment or—'

'You told me we weren't talking about huge sums.'

Wapshott shrugged and Erlendur thought he detected a smile.

'So that's another lie,' Erlendur said.

'Yes.'

'Down payment for what?'

'The records he owned. If he had any.'

'And did you let him have the money the last time you met him without knowing if he had any records?'

'Yes.'

'Then what?'

'Then he was killed.'

'We didn't find any money on him.'

'I don't know anything about that. I gave him half a million the day before he died.'

Erlendur recalled asking Sigurdur Óli to check Gudlaugur's bank account. He must remember to ask him what he had found out.

'Did you see the records in his room?'

'No.'

'Why should I believe that? You've lied about everything else. Why should I believe anything you say?'

Wapshott shrugged.

'So he had half a million on him when he was attacked?'

'I don't know. All I know is that I gave him the money and then later he was killed.'

'Why didn't you tell me about that money in the first place?'

'I wanted to be left alone,' Wapshott said. 'I didn't want you to think I'd killed him for the money.'

'Did you?'

'No.'

They paused.

'Are you going to charge me?' Wapshott asked.

'I think you're still hiding something,' Erlendur said. 'I can hold you until the evening. Then we'll see.'

'I could never have killed the choirboy. I worship him and still do. I've never heard such a beautiful voice from any boy.'

Erlendur looked at Henry Wapshott.

'Strange how alone you are in all this,' he said, before even realising it.

'What do you mean?'

'You're so alone in the world.'

'I didn't kill him,' Wapshott said. 'I didn't kill him.'

18

Wapshott left the hotel accompanied by the two policemen, while Erlendur found out that Ösp, the girl who had discovered the body, was currently working on the fourth floor. He took the lift and when he arrived there he saw her loading a trolley with dirty laundry outside one of the rooms. She did not notice him until he walked up to her and said her name. She looked up and recognised him at once.

'Oh, is it you again?' she said indifferently.

She looked even more tired and depressed than when he had met her in the staff coffee room, and Erlendur thought to himself that Christmas was probably no season of joy in her life either. Before he knew it he had asked her.

'Does Christmas get you down?'

Instead of answering him she pushed the trolley to the next door, knocked and waited a moment before taking out her master key and opening the door. She called into the room in case someone was inside but had not heard her knocking, then went in and began cleaning, made the bed, picked up the towels from the bathroom floor, squirted cleaner on the mirror. Erlendur wandered into the room after her and watched her at work, and after a while she seemed to notice that he was still there with her.

'You mustn't come into the room,' she said. 'It's private.'

'You do room 312 on the floor below,' Erlendur said. 'A weird Brit was there. Henry Wapshott. Did you notice anything unusual in his room?'

She gave him a look of not quite following what he meant.

'Like a bloodstained knife, for example?' Erlendur said and tried to smile.

'No,' Ösp said. She stopped to think. Then she asked: 'What knife? Did he kill Santa?'

'I don't quite remember how you put it the last time we spoke, but you said some of the guests grope you. I thought you were talking about sexual harassment. Was he one of them?'

'No, I only saw him once.'

'And was there nothing that—'

'He went ballistic,' she said. 'When I went into the room.'

'Ballistic?'

'I disturbed him and he threw me out. I went to check what was going on and it turned out he'd made a special request at reception not to have his room tidied. No one told me anything. None of this bloody crew ever says a word to us. So I walked in on him and when he saw me he totally lost it. Went for me, the old sod. As if I have any say at this hotel. He should have gone for the hotel manager.'

'He is a little mysterious.'

'He's a creep.'

'I mean that Wapshott.'

'Yes, both of them.'

'So you didn't notice anything unusual in his room?'

'It was a real mess, but that's nothing unusual.'

Ösp stopped working, stood still for a moment and looked pensively at Erlendur.

'Are you getting anywhere? With Santa?'

'A little,' Erlendur said. 'Why?'

'This is a weird hotel,' Ösp said, lowering her voice and looking out into the corridor.

'Weird?' Erlendur had a sudden feeling that she was not quite so self-confident. 'Are you afraid of something? Something here at the hotel?'

Ösp did not answer.

'Are you frightened of losing your job?'

She looked at Erlendur.

'Yeah right, this is the sort of job you don't want to lose.'

'So what is it?'

Ösp hesitated, then seemed to make a decision. As if what she wanted to say was not worth bothering about any longer.

'They steal from the kitchen,' she said. 'Everything they can. I don't think they've had to go shopping for years.'

'Steal?'

'Everything that's not bolted to the floor.'

'Who are they?'

'Don't say I told you. The head chef. Him for starters.'

'How do you know?'

'Gulli told me. He knew everything that went on at this hotel.'

Erlendur recalled when he stole the ox tongue from the buffet and the head chef saw him and chided him. Remembered his tone of indignation.

'When did he tell you this?'

'A couple of months ago.'

'So what? Did it worry him? Was he going to tell someone? Why did he tell you? I thought you didn't know him.'

'I didn't know him.' Ösp paused. 'They were having a go at me in the kitchen,' she continued. 'Talking dirty. "How you feeling down there?" and that sort of thing. All the pathetic crap morons like that come up with. Gulli heard it and talked to me. Told me not to worry. He said they were all thieves and he could get them caught if he wanted.'

'Did he threaten to get them caught?'

'He didn't threaten anything,' Ösp said. 'He just said it to cheer me up.'

'What do they steal?' Erlendur asked. 'Did he mention anything in particular?'

'He said the manager knew but didn't do anything, he's on the take too. He buys black market stuff. For the bars. Gulli told me that too. The head waiter's in on it with him.'

'Gudlaugur told you that?'

'Then they pocket the difference.'

'Why didn't you tell me this when I first talked to you?'

'Is it relevant?'

'It might be.'

Ösp shrugged.

'I didn't know and I wasn't quite myself after I found him. Gudlaugur. With the condom. And the knife wounds.'

'Did you see any money in his room?'

'Money?'

'He'd recently been paid some money but I don't know whether he had it on him when he was attacked.'

'I didn't see a penny.'

'No,' Erlendur said. 'You didn't take the money? When you found him?'

Ösp stopped working and threw her hands down by her sides.

'Do you mean, did I steal it?'

'These things happen.'

'You think I—'

'Did you take it?'

'No.'

'You had the chance.'

'So did the person who killed him.'

'That's true,' Erlendur said.

'I didn't see a penny.'

'No, all right.'

Ösp went back to her cleaning. Sprayed disinfectant into the toilet bowl and scrubbed it with the brush, acting as if Erlendur wasn't there. He watched her working for a little while, then thanked her.

'What do you mean, you disturbed him?' he said, stopping at the door. 'Henry Wapshott. You could hardly have got very far into his room if you called out first the way you did here.'

'He didn't hear me.'

'What was he doing?'

'I don't know if I can ...'

'It won't go any further.'

'He was watching TV,' Ösp said.

'He wouldn't want that to get around,' Erlendur whispered conspiratorially.

'Or, you know, a video,' Ösp said. 'It was porn. Disgusting.'

'Do they show porn films at the hotel?'

'Not that sort of film, they're banned everywhere.'

'What sort of film?'

'It was child pornography. I told the manager.'

'Child pornography? What sort of child pornography?'

'What sort? Do you want me to describe it?'

'What day was this?'

'Fucking pervert!'

'When was it?'

'The day I found Gulli.'

'What did the manager do?'

'Nothing,' Ösp said. 'Told me to keep my mouth shut about it.'

'Do you know who Gudlaugur was?'

'What do you mean, the doorman? He was the doorman. Was he something else?'

'Yes, when he was little. He was a choirboy and had a very good voice. I've heard his records.'

'A choirboy?'

'A child star, really. Then somehow everything went wrong in his life. He grew up and it was over.'

'I didn't know that.'

'No, no one knew about Gudlaugur any more,' Erlendur said.

They fell silent, deep in their own thoughts. Some minutes passed.

'Does Christmas get you down?' Erlendur asked again. It was as if he had found a soul mate.

She turned towards him.

'Christmas is for happy people.'

Erlendur looked at Ösp and a hint of a wry smile moved across his face.

'You'd get on with my daughter,' he said, and took out his mobile phone.

Sigurdur Óli was surprised when Erlendur told him about the money that had probably been in Gudlaugur's room. They discussed the need to verify Wapshott's claim that he had been roaming the record markets at the time the murder was committed. Sigurdur Óli was standing in front of Wapshott's cell when Erlendur phoned him, and he described the conditions under which his saliva sample had been taken.

The cell he was in had housed many poor unfortunates, the whole spectrum from wretched tramps to thugs and murderers, and they had covered the walls and scratched the paint with remarks about their miserable stay in custody.

In the cell was a toilet bowl and a bed, bolted to the floor. On top of it was a thin mattress and a hard pillow. There were no windows in the cell, but high above the prisoner was a strong fluorescent light that was never switched off, making it difficult for the occupants to tell whether it was day or night.

Henry Wapshott stood rigid against the wall, facing the heavy steel door. Two warders held him. Elínborg and Sigurdur Óli were also in the cell with a warrant ordering the test to be made, and Valgerdur was there too, cotton bud in hand, ready to take the sample.

Wapshott stared at her as if she were the devil incarnate, who had arrived to drag him down into eternal hell fire. His eyes were popping out of his head, he arched himself as far away from her as he could, and no matter how they tried, they could not make him open his mouth.

Eventually they laid him on the floor and held his nose until he had to give in and gasp for breath. Valgerdur seized the chance and rammed the cotton wool bud into his mouth, wiped it around until he retched, then whipped it back out of him and hurried from the cell.

19

When Erlendur went back down to the lobby on his way to the kitchen he saw Marion Briem standing at the reception desk in a shabby coat, wearing a hat and fidgeting. He noticed how badly his old boss had aged in the years since they had last met, but still had the same watchful and inquisitive eyes, and never wasted time on formalities.

'You look awful,' Marion said, sitting down. 'What's getting you down?' A cigarillo appeared from somewhere in the coat and a box of matches with it.

'This is a smoke-free zone, apparently,' Erlendur said.

'You can't smoke anywhere any more,' Marion said, lighting up. Marion wore a pained expression, the skin grey, slack and wrinkled. Pallid lips puckered around the cigarillo. Anaemic nails stood out from bony fingers that reached for the cigarillo again once the lungs had taken their fill.

For all the long and eventful history of their acquaintance, Marion and Erlendur had never got along particularly well. Marion had been Erlendur's boss for years and tried to teach him the profession. Erlendur was surly and did not accept guidance willingly; he couldn't stand his superiors in those days and nothing had changed. Marion would take umbrage at this and they often clashed, but Marion knew that a better detective was difficult to find, if only because Erlendur was not tied down by family and the time-consuming commitments that entailed. Erlendur did nothing but work. Marion was the same, a lifelong recluse.

'What's new with you?' Marion asked, puffing on the cigarillo.

'Nothing,' Erlendur said.

'Does Christmas annoy you?'

'I've never understood this Christmas business,' Erlendur said vaguely as he peered into the kitchen, on the lookout for the chef's hat.

'No,' Marion said. 'Too much cheer and joy, I would imagine. Why don't you get yourself a girlfriend? You're not that old. There are plenty of women who could take a fancy to an old fart like you.'

'I've tried that,' Erlendur said. 'What did you find out about—'

'Do you mean your wife?'

Erlendur didn't intend to spend the time discussing his private life.

'Stop it, will you?'

'I heard that—'

'I told you to stop it,' Erlendur said angrily.

'All right,' Marion said. 'It's none of my business how you live your life. All I know is that loneliness is a slow and painful death.' Marion paused. 'But of course you've got your children, haven't you?'

'Can't we just skip all this?' Erlendur said. 'You are—' He got no further.

'What am I?'

'What are you doing here? Couldn't you have phoned?'

Marion looked at Erlendur and the hint of a smile played across that old face.

'I'm told you've been sleeping at this hotel. That you won't go home for Christmas. What's happening to you? Why don't you go home?'

Erlendur didn't answer.

'Are you that fed up with yourself?'

'Can't we talk about something else?'

'I know the feeling. Being fed up with yourself. With the bastard that happens to be you and which you can't get out of your own head. You can get rid of it for a while but it always comes back and starts on the same old bollocks. You can try to drink it away. Have a change of scenery. Stay at hotels when it gets really bad.'

'Marion,' Erlendur pleaded, 'give me a break.'

'Anyone who owns Gudlaugur Egilsson's records,' Marion said, suddenly getting to the point, 'is sitting on a goldmine.'

'What makes you say that?'

'They're a treasure trove today. Admittedly not many people own them or know about them, but people in the know are prepared to pay incredible sums for them. Gudlaugur's records are a rarity in the collectors' world and very sought-after.'

'What kind of incredible sums? Tens of thousands?'

'Could be hundreds of thousands,' Marion said. 'For a single copy.'

'Hundreds of thousands? You're kidding.' Erlendur sat up in his seat. He thought about Henry Wapshott. Knew why he came to Iceland in search of Gudlaugur. In search of his records. It was not only admiration for choirboys that kindled his interest, as Wapshott would have him believe. Erlendur realised why he had given Gudlaugur half a million on the off-chance.

'As far as I've been able to find out, the boy made only two records,' Marion Briem said. 'And what makes them valuable, besides the boy's incredible singing, is that very few copies were cut and they hardly sold at all. There aren't many people who own those records today.'

'Does the actual singing matter?'

'It seems to, but the rule is still that the quality of the music, the quality of what is on the record, is less important than its condition. The music might be bad but if it's the right performer with the right song and the right label at the right time, it can be priceless. No one is interested solely in artistic value.'

'What happened to the copies? Do you know?'

'They've gone missing. They've been lost over the course of time or simply thrown away. That happens. Probably there weren't more than a couple of hundred to start with. The main reason that the records are so valuable is that there only seems to be a handful in the world. The short career helps too. I understand he lost his voice and never sang again.'

'It happened at a concert, the poor boy,' Erlendur said. 'A wolf in your voice, it's called. When your voice breaks.'

'Then decades later he's found murdered.'

'If those records are worth hundreds of thousands ...?'

'Well?'

'Isn't that ample motive for killing him? We found one copy of each record in his room. There was really nothing else in there.'

'Then the person who stabbed him can't have realised how much they are worth,' Marion Briem said.

'Because otherwise he would have stolen the records?'

'What were the copies like?'

'Pristine,' Erlendur said. 'Not a spot or crease on the sleeves and I can't see that they've ever been played ...'

He looked at Marion Briem.

'Could Gudlaugur possibly have acquired all the copies?' he said.

'Why not?' Marion said.

'We found some keys in his room that we can't figure out. Where might he have kept others?'

'It needn't be the whole lot,' Marion said. 'Maybe some of them. Who else would own them other than the choirboy himself?'

'I don't know,' Erlendur said. 'We've detained a collector who came over from the UK to meet Gudlaugur. A mysterious old sod who tried to run away from us and worships the ex-choirboy. He seems to be the only person around here who realises how much Gudlaugur's records are worth.'

'Is he a nutter?' Marion Briem asked.

'Sigurdur Óli's looking into that,' Erlendur said. 'Gudlaugur was the hotel Santa,' he added, as if Santa was an official appointment there.

A smile passed over Marion's grey old face.

'We found a note in Gudlaugur's room saying Henry and the time 18.30, as if he'd been to a meeting or was supposed to go at that time. Henry Wapshott says he met him at half past six on the day before the murder.'

Erlendur fell silent, deep in thought.

'What are you brooding over?' Marion asked.

'Wapshott told me he paid Gudlaugur half a million krónur to prove he meant business, or words to that effect. In buying the records. That money could have been in the room when he was attacked.'

'Do you mean someone knew about Wapshott and his dealings with Gudlaugur?'

'Possibly.'

'Another collector?'

'Maybe. I don't know. Wapshott's odd. I know he's hiding something from us. Whether it's about him or about Gudlaugur I don't know.'

'And of course the money was gone when you found him.'

'Yes.'

'I must be going,' Marion said, standing up. Erlendur got to his feet too. 'I can barely last half a day any more,' Marion said. 'I'm dying of exhaustion. How's your daughter doing?'

'Eva? I don't know. I don't think she feels too good.'

'Maybe you should spend Christmas with her.'

'Yes, maybe.'

'And your love life?'

'Stop going on about my love life,' Erlendur said, and his thoughts turned to Valgerdur. He wanted to phone her but lacked the nerve. What was he supposed to say? What business of hers was his past? What business of anyone's was his life? Ridiculous, asking her out like that. He didn't know what had come over him.

'I'm told you dined here with a woman,' Marion said. 'That hasn't happened for years to the best of our knowledge.'

'Who told you that?' Erlendur asked in astonishment.

'Who was the woman?' Marion asked back without answering him. 'I hear she's attractive.'

'There's no woman,' Erlendur snarled and strutted away. Marion Briem watched him and then walked slowly out of the hotel, chuckling.

On his way down to the lobby, Erlendur had wondered how he could politely accuse the head chef of theft, but Marion had wound him up. After taking the man aside in the kitchen he had not an iota of discretion left in him.

'Are you a thief?' he asked straight out. 'And all of you in the kitchen? Do you steal everything that isn't bolted to the floor?'

'What do you mean?'

'I mean that Santa might have been stabbed to death because he knew about a massive pilfering operation at this hotel. Maybe he was stabbed because he knew who ran the scam. Maybe you crept down to his hovel in the basement and stabbed him to death so he wouldn't go spilling the beans to everyone. What do you reckon to that theory? And you robbed him in the process.'

The chef stared at Erlendur. 'You're crazy!' he grunted.

'Do you steal from the kitchen?'

'Who have you been talking to?' the chef asked in a deadly serious tone. 'Who's been filling your head with lies? Was it someone from the hotel?'

'Have they taken your saliva sample?'

'Who told you?'

'Why didn't you want to give a sample?'

'It was done eventually. I think you're a retard. Taking samples from all the hotel staff! Why? To make us all look like a load of wankers!

And then you come calling me a thief. I've never stolen as much as a head of cabbage from this kitchen. Never! Who's been telling you these lies?'

'If Santa had some dirt on you, for thieving, could it just be that he blackmailed you into doing him favours? Like su—'

'Shut up!' the head chef shouted. 'Was it the pimp? Who told you these lies?'

Erlendur thought the chef was about to jump on him. He moved so close that their faces almost touched. His chef's hat bent forward.

'Was it the fucking pimp?' the chef hissed.

'Who's the pimp?'

'That fucking fat bastard of a manager,' the chef said through gritted teeth.

Erlendur's mobile started ringing in his pocket. They looked each other in the eye, neither of them prepared to back down. At last Erlendur took out his mobile. The chef walked off, seething.

The head of forensics was on the phone.

'It's about the saliva on the condom,' he told Erlendur.

'Yes,' Erlendur said, 'have you traced the owner?'

'No, we're still a long way from that,' the head of forensics said. 'But we've looked at it more closely, the composition I mean, and we found traces of tobacco.'

'Tobacco? You mean pipe tobacco?'

'Well, it's more like quid,' the voice said over the telephone.

'Quid? I'm not with you.'

'The chemical composition. You used to be able to buy quid in tobacco shops once but I'm not sure if it's still around. Maybe in sweetshops, I don't know if they're still allowed to sell it. We need to check that. You stick it under your lip, either in a lump or in a gauze, you must have heard of it.'

The chef kicked a cupboard door and spouted curses.

'You're talking about chewing tobacco,' Erlendur said. 'Are there traces of chewing tobacco in the sample from the condom?'

'Bingo,' the voice said.

'So what does that mean?'

'The person who was with Santa chews tobacco.'

'What do we gain by knowing that?'

'Nothing. Yet. I just thought you'd want to know. And there's another thing. You were asking about the cortisol in the saliva.'

'Yes.'

'There wasn't very much, in fact it was quite normal.'

'What does that tell us? It was all quiet on that front?'

'A high level of cortisol indicates a rise in blood pressure due to excitement or stress. The person who was with the doorman was as calm as a millpond all the time. No stress. No excitement. They didn't have anything to fear.'

'Until something happened,' Erlendur said.

'Yes,' the head of forensics said. 'Until something happened.'

They finished the conversation and Erlendur put his mobile back in his pocket. The head chef stood staring at him.

'Do you know anyone here who chews tobacco?' Erlendur asked.

'Fuck off!' the chef screamed.

Erlendur took a deep breath, clasped his hands over his face and rubbed it wearily, then suddenly saw an image of Henry Wapshott's tobacco-stained teeth.

20

Erlendur asked for the hotel manager at reception and was told he had popped out. The head chef refused to explain the pimp moniker when he mentioned the 'fucking fat bastard of a manager'. Erlendur had rarely met anyone with such a temper. The chef must have realised that in his agitation he had let slip something. Erlendur made no headway. All he could get out of him were snide remarks and abuse, since the man was on home ground in the kitchen. To level the playing field and irritate the chef even further Erlendur thought of arranging for four uniformed police officers to turn up at the hotel and take him off for questioning at the station on Hverfisgata.

After toying with the idea he decided to shelve it for the time being.

Instead, he went up to Henry Wapshott's room. He broke the police seal that had been put on the door. The forensics team had taken care not to move anything. Erlendur stood still for a long time, scanning all around. He was looking for some kind of wrapper from a packet of chewing tobacco.

It was a twin room with two single beds, both unmade as if Wapshott had either slept in both of them or had had a guest for the night. On one table was an old record player connected to an amplifier and two small speakers, and on the other was a 14-inch television set and a video player. Two tapes lay beside it. Erlendur put one in the player and turned on the television, but switched it off as soon as the picture came on. Ösp was right about the pornography.

He opened the drawer of the bedside table, took a good look inside Wapshott's suitcase, checked the cupboard and went into the bathroom, but did not find chewing tobacco anywhere. He looked in the wastepaper basket, but it was empty.

'Elínborg was right,' said Sigurdur Óli, who suddenly appeared in the room.

Erlendur turned round.

'What do you mean?' he said.

'Scotland Yard sent us some information about him at last,' Sigurdur Óli said, looking around the room.

'I'm looking for chewing tobacco,' Erlendur said. 'They found some on the condom.'

'I think I know why he doesn't want to contact his embassy or a lawyer and is just hoping all this will blow over,' Sigurdur Óli said before relaying Scotland Yard's information on the record collector.

Henry Wapshott, unmarried with no children, was born on the eve of the Second World War, in 1938, in Liverpool. His father's family owned several valuable properties in the city. Some were bombed during the war and rebuilt as quality residential and office premises, which ensured a certain degree of wealth. Wapshott had never needed to work. An only child, he had the best education, Eton and Oxford, but did not complete his degree. When his father died he took over the family business but, unlike the old man, he had little interest in property management and soon attended only the most important meetings, until he stopped that as well and handed over the operations entirely to his managers.

He always lived in his parents' house and his neighbours regarded him as an eccentric loner; kindly and polite but strange and withdrawn. His only interest was collecting records and he filled his house with albums that he bought from the estates of dead people or at markets. He did a great deal of travelling for his hobby and was said to own one of the largest private record collections in Britain.

He had twice been found guilty of a criminal offence and was on Scotland Yard's register of sex offenders. On the first occasion he was imprisoned for raping a twelve-year-old boy. The boy was a neighbour of Wapshott's and they got to know each other through a common interest in collecting records. The incident took place at Wapshott's parents' house, and when his mother heard of her son's behaviour she had a breakdown; it was blown up in the British media, especially the tabloids, which portrayed Wapshott, born into the privileged class, as a beast. Investigations revealed that he paid boys and young men handsomely to perform sexual acts.

By the time he finished his sentence his mother had died, and he sold his parents' house and moved to another district. Several years later he was back in the news when two boys in their early teens revealed how Wapshott had offered them money to undress at his home, and he was charged with rape again. When the matter came to light Wapshott was in Baden Baden in Germany and was arrested at Brenner's Hotel & Spa.

The second rape charge could not be proved and Wapshott moved abroad, to Thailand, but retained his British citizenship and kept his record collection in the UK, which he often visited on collecting missions. He used his mother's surname then, Wapshott; his real name was Henry Wilson. He had not fallen foul of the law since emigrating from Britain, but little was known about what he did in Thailand.

'So it's not surprising that he wanted to keep a low profile,' Erlendur said when Sigurdur Óli had finished his account.

'He sounds like a pervert big time,' Sigurdur Óli said. 'You can imagine why he chose Thailand.'

'Don't they have anything on him at the moment?' Erlendur asked. 'Scotland Yard.'

'No, but I'll bet they're relieved to be rid of him,' Sigurdur Óli said.

They had gone back to the ground floor and into the small bar there. The buffet table was packed. The tourists at the hotel were merry and noisy and gave the impression of being happy with everything they had seen and done, rosy-cheeked in their traditional Icelandic sweaters.

'Have you found any bank account in Gudlaugur's name?' Erlendur asked. He lit a cigarette, looked around him and noticed that he was the only smoker at the bar.

'I've still got to look into that,' Sigurdur Óli said, and sipped his beer.

Elínborg appeared in the doorway and Sigurdur Óli waved her over. She nodded and elbowed her way to the bar, bought a large beer and sat down with them. Sigurdur Óli gave Elínborg a résumé of Scotland Yard's dossier on Wapshott, and she took the liberty of smiling.

'I bloody knew it,' she said.

'What?'

'That his interest in choirboys was sexually motivated. His interest in Gudlaugur too for certain.'

'Do you mean that he was having a bit of fun with Gudlaugur downstairs?' Sigurdur Óli said.

'Maybe Gudlaugur was forced to take part,' Erlendur said. 'Someone was carrying a knife.'

'What a way to spend Christmas, having to puzzle all this out,' Elínborg sighed.

'Not exactly good for the appetite,' Erlendur said and finished his Chartreuse. He wanted another. Looked at his watch. If he had been at the office he would have finished work by now. The bar was a little less busy and he waved the waiter over.

'There must have been at least two people in there with him because you can't threaten anyone if you're down on your knees.' Sigurdur Óli cast a glance at Elínborg and thought he might have gone a little too far.

'It gets better all the time,' Elínborg said.

'Ruins the taste of the Christmas cookies,' Erlendur said.

'OK, but why did he stab Gudlaugur?' Sigurdur Óli said. 'Not just once, but repeatedly. As if he lost control of himself. If Wapshott attacked him first, something must have happened or been said in the basement room that made the pervert snap.'

Erlendur was going to order but the others declined and looked at their watches – Christmas was drawing quickly closer.

'I reckon he had a woman in there,' Sigurdur Óli said.

'They measured the level of cortisol in the saliva on the condom,' Erlendur said. 'It was normal. Any woman who was with Gudlaugur could have been gone by the time he was murdered.'

'I don't think that's likely, judging from how we found him,' Elínborg said.

'Whoever was with him wasn't forced into anything,' Erlendur said. 'I think that's established. If any level of cortisol had been found it would have been a sign of excitement or tension in the body.'

'So it was a whore then,' Sigurdur Óli said, 'going about her job.'

'Can't we talk about something nicer?' Elínborg asked.

'It could be that they were fleecing the hotel and Santa knew about it,' Erlendur said.

'And that's why he was killed?' Sigurdur Óli said.

'I don't know. There might also be some low-key prostitution going on with the manager's complicity. I haven't quite worked out all this but we may need to look into these things.'

'Was Gudlaugur tied up in it in any way?' Elínborg asked.

'Judging from the state he was in when he was found, we can't rule it out,' Sigurdur Óli said.

'How's it going with your man?' Erlendur asked.

'He was poker-faced in the district court,' Elínborg said, sipping her beer.

'The boy still hasn't testified against his father, has he?' asked Sigurdur Óli, who was also familiar with the case.

'Silent as the grave, poor kid,' Erlendur said. 'And that bastard sticks to his statement. Flatly denies hitting the boy. And he's got good lawyers too.'

'So he'll get the boy back?'

'It could well be.'

'And the boy?' Erlendur asked. 'Does he want to go back?'

'That's the weirdest part of all,' Elínborg said. 'He's still attached to his father. It's as if he feels he deserved it.'

They fell silent.

'Are you going to spend Christmas at this hotel, Erlendur?' Elínborg asked. There was a tone of accusation in her voice.

'No, I suppose I'll get myself home,' Erlendur said. 'Spend some time with Eva. Boil some smoked lamb.'

'How's she doing?' Elínborg asked.

'So-so,' Erlendur said. 'Fine, I suppose.' He thought they could tell that he was lying. They were well aware of the problems his daughter had run into but rarely mentioned them. They knew he wanted to discuss them as little as possible and never asked in detail.

'St Thorlac's Day tomorrow,' Sigurdur Óli said. 'Got everything done, Elínborg?'

'Nothing.' She sighed.

'I'm wondering about that record collecting,' Erlendur said.

'What about it?' Elínborg said.

'Isn't it something that starts in childhood?' Erlendur said. 'Not that I know anything about it. I've never collected anything. But isn't it an interest that develops when you're a kid, when you collect cards and model planes, stamps of course, theatre programmes, records? Most people grow out of it but some go on collecting books and records until their dying day.'

'What are you trying to tell us?'

'I'm wondering about record collectors like Wapshott, although of course they're not all perverts like him, whether the collecting fad is connected with some kind of yearning for lost youth. Connected with a need to keep hold of something that otherwise would disappear from their lives but which they want to retain for as long as they can. Isn't collecting an attempt to preserve something from your childhood? Something to do with your memories, something you don't want to let go but keep on cultivating and nourishing with this obsession?'

'So Wapshott's record collecting, the choirboys, is some kind of nostalgia for youth?' Elínborg asked.

'And then when the nostalgia for youth appears before him in the flesh at this hotel, something snaps inside him?' said Sigurdur Óli. 'The boy turned into a middle-aged man. Do you mean something like that?'

'I don't know.'

Erlendur vacantly watched the tourists at the bar and noticed one who was middle-aged, Asian in appearance and American-sounding. He had a new video camera and was filming his friends. Suddenly it occurred to Erlendur that there might be security cameras at the hotel. The hotel manager had not mentioned it, nor the reception manager. He looked at Sigurdur Óli and Elínborg.

'Did you ask if there were security cameras at this hotel?' he asked.

They looked at each other.

'Weren't you going to?' Sigurdur Óli said.

'I just forgot,' Elínborg said. 'Christmas and all that. It completely slipped my mind.'

The reception manager looked at Erlendur and shook his head. He said the hotel had a very firm policy on this issue. There were no security cameras on the hotel premises, neither in the lobby nor lifts, corridors nor rooms. Especially not in the rooms, of course.

'Then we wouldn't have any guests,' the manager said seriously.

'Yes, that had occurred to me,' Erlendur said, disappointed. For a moment he had entertained the vague hope that something had been caught on camera, something that did not tally with the stories and statements, something at odds with what the police had discovered.

He turned away from the reception to head back to the bar when the manager called out to him.

'There's a bank in the south wing, on the other side of the building. There are souvenir shops and a bank, and you can enter the hotel from there. Fewer people use it as an entrance. The bank's bound to have security cameras. But they'll hardly show anyone besides their customers.'

Erlendur had noticed the bank and souvenir shops, and he went straight there but saw that the bank was closed. Looking up, he saw the almost invisible eye of a camera above the door. No one was working in the bank. He knocked on the glass door so hard that it rattled, but nothing happened. Eventually he took out his mobile and insisted on having the bank manager fetched.

While he was waiting Erlendur looked at the souvenirs in the shop, sold at inflated prices: plates with pictures of Gullfoss and Geysir painted on them, a carved figurine of Thor with his hammer, key rings with fox fur, posters showing whale species off the Icelandic coast, a sealskin jacket that would set him back a month's salary. He thought about buying a memento of this peculiar Tourist-Iceland that exists only in the minds of rich foreigners, but he couldn't see anything cheap enough.

The bank manager, a woman of about forty, had been on her way to a Christmas party and was far from amused about being interrupted; at first she thought there had been a robbery at the bank. She had not been told what was going on when two uniformed police officers knocked on the door of her house and asked her to accompany them. She glared at Erlendur in front of the bank when he explained to her that he needed access to her security cameras. She lit a fresh cigarette with the butt of the old one and Erlendur thought to himself that he had not encounted a proper smoker like her for years.

'Couldn't this wait until the morning?' she asked coldly, so coldly that he could almost hear the icicles dropping from her words, and thought that he would not like to owe this woman any money.

'Those things will kill you,' Erlendur said, pointing to the cigarette.

'They haven't yet,' she said. 'Why did you drag me out here?'

'Because of the murder,' Erlendur said. 'At the hotel.'

'And?' she said, unimpressed by murder.

'We're trying to speed up the investigation.' He smiled, but it was pointless.

'Bloody farce this is,' she said, and ordered Erlendur to follow her inside. The two police officers had left, clearly relieved at being rid of the woman, who had hurled abuse at them on the way. She took him to the staff entrance to the bank, keyed in her PIN, opened the door and commanded him to hurry.

It was a small branch and inside her office the manager had four monitors connected to the security cameras: one behind each of the two cashiers, in the waiting area and above the entrance. She switched on the monitors and explained to Erlendur that the cameras rolled all day and night, and that tapes were kept for three weeks and then rewritten. The recorders were in a small basement below the bank.

Already on her third cigarette, she led him downstairs and pointed to the tapes, which were clearly labelled with the dates and locations of the cameras. The tapes were kept in a locked safe.

'A security guard comes here from the bank every day,' she said, 'and takes care of it all. I don't know how to use it and would ask you not to go fiddling with anything that's none of your business.'

'Thank you,' Erlendur said humbly. 'I want to start on the day the murder was committed.'

'Be my guest,' she said, dropping her smoked cigarette on the floor where she diligently stamped it out.

He found the date he wanted on a tape labelled 'Entrance' and put it in a video player that was connected to a small television. He didn't think he needed to look at the tapes from the cashiers' cameras.

The bank manager looked at her gold watch.

'There's a full twenty-four-hour period on each tape,' she groaned.

'How do you manage?' Erlendur asked. 'At work?'

'What do you mean, how do I manage?'

'Smoking? What do you do?'

'What business is that of yours?'

'None at all,' Erlendur hastened to say.

'Can't you just take the tapes?' she said. 'I don't have time for this. I was supposed to be somewhere else ages ago and I don't plan to hang around here while you go through all of these.'

'No, you're right,' Erlendur said. He looked at the tapes in the cupboard. 'I'll take the fortnight before the murder. That's fourteen tapes.'

'Do you know who killed the man?'

'Not yet,' Erlendur said.

'I remember him well,' she said. 'The doorman. I've been manager here for seven years,' she added as if by way of explanation. 'He struck me as a nice enough chap.'

'Did he talk to you at all recently?'

'I never talked to him. Not a word.'

'Was this his bank?' Erlendur asked.

'No, he didn't have an account here. Not as far as I know. I never saw him in this branch. Did he have any money?'

Erlendur took the fourteen tapes up to his room and had a television and video player installed. He had started watching the first tape towards evening when his mobile rang. It was Sigurdur Óli.

'We've got to charge him or let him go,' he said. 'Really we don't have anything on him.'

'Is he complaining?'

'He hasn't said a word.'

'Has he asked for a lawyer?'

'No.'

'Make a charge for child pornography.'

'Child pornography?'

'He had tapes in his room containing child pornography. Possession of them is illegal. We have a witness who saw him watching that filth. We'll take him for the porn and then we'll see. I don't want to let him go back to Thailand just yet. We need to find out if his story of going into town the day that Gudlaugur was murdered holds good. Let him sweat in his cell a bit and we'll see what happens.'

21

Erlendur watched the tapes for almost the whole night.

He soon got the hang of using fast forward when no one walked past the camera. As expected, the heaviest footfall in front of the bank was over the period from nine in the morning to four in the afternoon, after which it slowed down sharply, and even further when the souvenir shops closed at six. The entrance to the hotel was open round the clock and there was an ATM but little traffic around it in the dead of night.

He saw nothing noteworthy the day Gudlaugur was murdered. The faces of the people going through the lobby were quite clearly visible but Erlendur didn't recognise any of them. When he fast-forwarded through the night recordings, figures would dart in through the door and stop at the cash machine before rushing out again. An occasional person went into the hotel itself. He scrutinised them but couldn't link any with Gudlaugur.

He saw that the hotel staff used the bank entrance. The head of reception, the fat hotel manager and Ösp could be seen rushing past, and he thought to himself how relieved she probably felt to get away after her day at work. In one place he saw Gudlaugur cross the lobby, and he stopped the tape. This was three days before the murder. Gudlaugur, alone, paced slowly in front of the camera, looked inside the bank, turned his head, looked over at the souvenir shops and then went back to the hotel. Erlendur rewound and watched Gudlaugur again, then again and a fourth time. He found it odd to see him alive. He stopped the tape when Gudlaugur looked inside the bank and watched his frozen face on the screen. It was the choirboy in the flesh. The man who once had that lovely voice, that tear-jerking boy soprano. The boy who forced Erlendur to probe into his own most painful memories when he heard him.

There was a knock on the door, and he turned off the video and opened for Eva Lind.

'Were you asleep?' she asked, squeezing past him. 'What are these tapes?'

'They're to do with the case,' Erlendur said.

'Getting anywhere?'

'No. Nowhere.'

'Did you talk to Stína?'

'Stína?'

'The one I told you about. Stína! You were asking about tarts and the hotels.'

'No, I haven't spoken to her. Tell me something else, do you know a girl of your age called Ösp who works at this hotel? You have a similar attitude to life.'

'Meaning?' Eva Lind offered her father a cigarette, gave him a light and flopped down onto the bed. Erlendur sat at the desk and looked out through the window into the pitch-black night. Two days to Christmas, he thought. Then we'll be back to normal.

'Pretty negative,' he said.

'Do you reckon I'm really negative?' Eva Lind said.

Erlendur said nothing, and Eva snorted, sending billows of smoke out through her nose.

'And what, you're the picture of happiness?'

Erlendur smiled.

'I don't know any Ösp,' Eva said. 'What's she got to do with it?'

'She has nothing to do with it,' Erlendur said. 'At least I don't think so. She found the body and seems to know a few things about what goes on in this place. Quite a smart girl. A survivor, with a mouth on her. Reminds me a bit of you.'

'I don't know her,' Eva said. Then she fell silent and stared at nothing, and he looked at her and said nothing either, and time went by. Sometimes they had nothing to say to each other. Sometimes they argued furiously. They never made small talk. Never talked about the weather or prices in the shops, politics, sport or clothes, or whatever it was that people spent their time discussing, which they both regarded as idle chatter. Only the two of them, their past and present, the family that was never a family because Erlendur walked out on it, the tragic circumstances of Eva and her brother Sindri, their mother's malice towards Erlendur – that was all that mattered, their topic of conversation that coloured all contact between them.

'What do you want for Christmas?' Erlendur suddenly broke the silence.

'For Christmas?' Eva said.

'Yes.'

'I don't want anything.'

'You must want something.'

'What did you get for Christmas? When you were a boy?'

Erlendur thought. He remembered some mittens.

'Little things,' he said.

'I always thought Mum gave Sindri better presents than me,' Eva Lind said. 'Then she stopped giving me presents. Said I sold them to buy dope. She gave me a ring once and I sold it. Did your brother get better presents than you?'

Erlendur felt the way she cautiously probed him. Usually she went straight to the point and shocked him with her candour. At other times, much less frequently, she seemed to want to be delicate.

When Eva was in intensive care after her miscarriage, in a coma, the doctor told Erlendur to try to be with her as much as possible and talk to her all the same. One topic that Erlendur talked about to Eva was his brother's disappearance and how he himself was rescued from the moor. When Eva regained consciousness and moved in with him he asked her whether she remembered what he had said to her, but she did not recall a word. Her curiosity was aroused and she pressed him until he repeated what he had told her, what he had never told anyone about before and no one knew about. He had never talked to her about his past and Eva, who never tired of calling him to account, felt that she moved a little closer to him, felt she knew her father a fraction better, although she also knew that she was a long way from understanding him fully. One question that haunted Eva made her angry and spiteful towards him, and shaped their relationship more than anything else. Divorces were common, she realised that. Couples were always getting divorced and some divorces were worse than others, when the partners never spoke again. Aware of this, she did not question it. But she was totally incapable of fathoming why Erlendur divorced his children too. Why he took no interest in them after he left. Why he continually neglected them until Eva herself sought him out and found him alone in a dark block of flats. She had discussed all this with her father, who so far could provide no answers to her questions.

'Better presents?' he said. 'It was all the same. Really just like in the old Christmas rhyme: a candle and a pack of cards. Sometimes we would have liked something more exciting, but our family was poor. Everyone was poor in those days.'

'What about after he died? Your brother.'

Erlendur said nothing.

'Erlendur?' Eva said.

'Christmas disappeared with him,' Erlendur said.

*

The birth of the Saviour was not celebrated after his brother died. More than a month had elapsed since his disappearance and there was no joy in the home, no presents and no visitors. It was a custom for Erlendur's mother's family to visit them on Christmas Eve when they would all sing Christmas carols. It was a small house and everyone sat close together, emanating warmth and light. His mother refused all visitors that Christmas. His father had sunk into a deep depression and spent most days in bed. He took no part in the search for his son, as if he knew it was futile, as if he knew he had failed; his son was dead and he could do nothing about it, nor anyone ever, and that it was his fault and no one else's.

His mother was indefatigable. She made sure that Erlendur was nursed properly. She urged on the search party and took part herself. She was the last to come down from the moors when darkness fell and searching became futile, exhausted, and was the first to set off back into the highlands when it grew light again. After it became obvious that her son must be dead she kept on searching just as energetically. It was not until winter had set in completely, the snows were so deep and the weather so treacherous that she was forced to give up. Forced to face up to the fact that the boy had died in the wilds and she would have to wait until spring to look for his earthly remains. She turned towards the mountains every day, sometimes cursing. 'May the trolls eat you who took my boy!'

The thought of his dead body lying up there was unbearable to Erlendur, who began seeing him in nightmares from which he awoke screaming and crying, fighting the blizzard, submerged in the snow, his little back turned against the howling wind and death by his side.

Erlendur did not understand how his father could sit motionless at home while all the others were hard at work. The incident seemed to break him completely, turn him into a zombie, and Erlendur thought about the power of grief, because his father was a strong, vigorous man. The loss of his son gradually drained him of the will to live and he never recovered.

Later, when it was all over, his parents argued for the first and only time about what happened, and Erlendur found out that their mother had not wanted their father to go up onto the moors that day, but he did not listen to her. 'Well,' she said, 'since you're going anyway, leave the boys at home.' He paid no heed.

And Christmas was never the same again. His parents reached some kind of accord as time went by. She never mentioned that he had ignored her wishes. He never mentioned that he had been seized by stubbornness at hearing her tell him not to go and not to take the boys. There was nothing wrong with the weather and he felt she was meddling. They chose never to talk about what happened between them, as if breaking the silence would leave nothing to keep them together. It was in this silence that Erlendur tackled the guilt that swamped him at being the one who survived.

'Why's it so cold in here?' Eva Lind asked, wrapping her coat tighter.

'It's the radiator,' Erlendur said. 'It doesn't get warm. Any news about you?'

'Nothing. Mum got off with some bloke. She met him at the old-time dancing at Ölver. You can't imagine how gross that freak is. I think he still uses Brylcreem, he combs his hair into a quiff and wears shirts with sort of huge collars and he clicks his fingers when he hears some old crap on the radio. "My bonnie lies over the ocean ..."'

Erlendur smiled. Eva was never as bitchy about anything as when she described her mother's 'blokes', who seemed to become more pathetic with every year that went by.

Then they fell silent again.

'I'm trying to remember what I was like when I was eight,' Eva suddenly said. 'I don't really remember anything except my birthday. I can't remember the party, just the day it was my birthday. I was standing in the car park outside the block and I knew it was my birthday that day and I was eight, and somehow this memory that is totally irrelevant has stuck with me ever since. Just that, I knew it was my birthday and I was eight.'

She looked at Erlendur.

'You said he was eight. When he died.'

'It was his birthday that summer.'

'Why was he never found?'

'I don't know.'

'But he's up there on the moor?'

'Yes.'

'His skeleton.'

'Yes.'

'Eight years old.'

'Yes.'

'Was it your fault? That he died?'

'I was ten.'

'Yes, but ...'

'It was no one's fault.'

'But you must have thought ...'

'What are you driving at, Eva? What do you want to know?'

'Why you never contacted me and Sindri after you left us,' Eva Lind said. 'Why didn't you try to be with us?'

'Eva ...'

'We weren't worth it, were we?'

Erlendur looked out of the window in silence. It had started snowing again.

'Are you drawing a parallel?' he said eventually.

'I've never been given an explanation. It crossed my mind ...'

'That it was something to do with my brother. The way he died. You want to associate the two?'

'I don't know,' Eva said. 'I don't know you in the slightest. It's a couple of years since I first met you and I was the one who located you. That business with your brother is all I know about you apart from the fact you're a cop. I've never been able to understand how you could leave Sindri and me. Your children.'

'I left it to your mother to decide. Maybe I should have been firmer about gaining access but ...'

'You weren't interested,' Eva finished the sentence for him.

'That's not true.'

'Sure it is. Why didn't you take care of your children like you were supposed to?'

Erlendur said nothing and stared down at the floor. Eva stubbed out her third cigarette. Then she stood up, went to the door and opened it.

'Stína's going to meet you here at the hotel tomorrow,' she said. 'At lunchtime. You can't miss her with those new tits of hers.'

'Thanks for talking to her.'

'It was nothing,' Eva said.

She hesitated in the doorway.

'What do you want?' Erlendur asked.

'I don't know.'

'No, I mean for Christmas.'

Eva looked at her father.

'I wish I could have my baby back,' she said, and quietly closed the door behind her.

Erlendur heaved a deep sigh and sat on the edge of his bed for a long while before he resumed watching the tapes. People going about their Christmas errands rushed across the screen, many of them carrying bags and parcels of Christmas shopping.

He had reached the fifth day before Gudlaugur was murdered when he saw her. Initially he overlooked it but a flash went off somewhere in his mind and he stopped the recorder, rewound the tape and went back over the scene. It was not her face that caught Erlendur's attention, but her bearing; her walk and haughtiness. He pressed 'Play' again and saw her clearly, walking into the hotel. He fast-forwarded again. About half an hour later she reappeared on the screen when she left the hotel and strode past the bank and souvenir shops looking neither left nor right.

He stood up from the bed and stared at the screen.

It was Gudlaugur's sister.

Who had not set eyes on her brother for decades.

FIFTH DAY

22

It was late when the noise woke Erlendur up the following morning. It took him a long time to stir after a dreamless night, and at first he did not realise what the awful din was that resounded in his little room. He had stayed up all night watching a succession of tapes, but only saw Gudlaugur's sister that one day. Erlendur couldn't believe it was purely coincidence that she went to the hotel – that she had business there other than to meet her brother, with whom she claimed to have had no contact for decades.

Erlendur had unearthed a lie and he knew there was nothing more valuable for a criminal investigation.

The noise refused to stop, and gradually Erlendur realised that it was his telephone. He answered and heard the hotel manager's voice.

'You must come down to the kitchen,' the manager said. 'There's someone here you should talk to.'

'Who is it?' Erlendur asked.

'A lad who went home sick the day we found Gudlaugur,' the manager said. 'You ought to come.'

Erlendur got out of bed. He was still in his clothes. He went into the bathroom, looked in the mirror and perused the several days' stubble, which made a noise like sandpaper being rubbed over rough timber when he stroked it. His beard was dense and coarse like his father's.

Before going downstairs he telephoned Sigurdur Óli and told him to go to with Elínborg to Hafnarfjördur to take Gudlaugur's sister in for questioning. He would meet them later that day. He did not explain why he wanted to talk to her. He did not want them to blurt it out. Wanted to see her expression when she realised that he knew she had been lying.

When Erlendur went into the kitchen he saw the hotel manager standing with an exceptionally skinny man in his twenties. Erlendur wondered whether the contrast with the manager was playing tricks on his vision; beside him, everyone looked skinny.

'There you are,' the manager said. 'Anyone would think I'm taking over this investigation of yours, locating witnesses and whatever.'

He looked at his employee.

'Tell him what you know.'

The young man began his account. He was fairly precise about details and explained that he had started to feel ill around noon on the day Gudlaugur was found in his room. In the end he vomited and just managed to grab a rubbish sack in the kitchen.

The man gave the manager a sheepish look.

He was allowed to go home and went to bed with a bad fever, a temperature and aches. Since he lived alone and did not watch the news he hadn't mentioned to anyone what he knew until this morning when he came back to work and heard about Gudlaugur's death. And he was certainly surprised to hear what had happened, and even though he didn't know the man well – he had only been working in the hotel for just over a year – he did sometimes talk to him and even went down to his room and—

'Yes, yes, yes,' the manager said impatiently. 'We're not interested in that, Denni. Just get on with it.'

'Before I went home that morning Gulli came into the kitchen and asked if I could get him a knife.'

'He asked to borrow a knife from the kitchen?' Erlendur said.

'Yes. At first he wanted scissors, but I couldn't find any so then he asked for a knife.'

'Why did he need scissors or a knife, did he tell you?'

'It was something to do with the Santa suit.'

'The Santa suit?'

'He didn't go into detail, just some stitches he needed to unpick.'

'Did he return the knife?'

'No, not while I was here, then I left at noon and that's all I know.'

'What sort of a knife was it?'

'He said it had to be a sharp one,' Denni said.

'It was the same kind as this,' the manager said, reaching into a drawer to take out a small steak knife with a wooden handle and fine-serated blade. 'We lay these for people who order our T-bone steak. Have you tried one? Delicious. The knives go through them like butter.'

Erlendur took the knife, examined it and thought to himself that Gudlaugur may have provided his murderer with the weapon that was used to kill him. Wondered whether that business about the stitching of his Santa suit was just a ploy. Whether Gudlaugur had expected someone in his room and wanted to have the knife at hand; or had the knife been lying on his desk because he needed to mend his Santa suit and the attack was sudden, unpremeditated and sparked by something that happened in the little room? In that case, the attacker had not gone to Gudlaugur's room armed, not gone there with the purpose of killing him.

'I need to take that knife,' he said. 'We need to know if the size and type of blade match the wounds. Is that all right?'

The hotel manager nodded.

'Isn't it that British chap?' he said. 'Have you got anyone else?'

'I'd like to have a quick word with Denni here,' Erlendur said without answering him.

The manager nodded again and stayed where he was, until the

penny dropped and he gave Erlendur an offended look. He was accustomed to being the centre of attention. When he did get the message he noisily invented some business to attend to in his office and disappeared. Denni's relief when his boss was no longer present proved short-lived.

'Did you go down to the basement and stab him?' Erlendur asked.

Denni looked at him like a doomed man.

'No,' he said hesitantly, as if not quite sure himself. The next question left him even more in doubt.

'Do you chew tobacco?' Erlendur asked.

'No,' he said. 'Chew tobacco? What …?'

'Have you had a sample taken?'

'Eh?'

'Do you use condoms?'

'Condoms?' said Denni, still at a total loss.

'No girlfriend?'

'Girlfriend?'

'That you have to make sure you don't get pregnant?'

Denni said nothing.

'I don't have a girlfriend,' he said in the end; Erlendur sensed a note of regret. 'What are you asking me all this for?'

'Don't worry about it,' Erlendur said. 'You knew Gudlaugur. What kind of a man was he?'

'He was cool.'

Denni told Erlendur that Gudlaugur had felt comfortable at the hotel, did not want to leave and in fact feared moving out after he was sacked. He used all the hotel services and was the only member of staff who got away with that for years. He ate cheaply at the hotel, put his clothes in with the hotel laundry and didn't pay a penny for his little room in the basement. Redundancy came as a shock to him, but he said he could manage if he lived frugally and might not even have to earn himself a living any more.

'What did he mean by that?' Erlendur asked.

Denni shrugged.

'I don't know. He was quite mysterious sometimes. Said lots of things I couldn't suss out.'

'Like what?'

'I don't know, something about music. Sometimes. When he drank. Most of the time he was just normal.'

'Did he drink a lot?'

'No, not at all. Sometimes at weekends. He never missed a day's work. Never. He was proud of that although it's not such a remarkable job. Being a doorman and stuff.'

'What did he say to you about music?'

'He liked beautiful music. I don't remember exactly what he said.'

'Why do you think he said he didn't need to earn himself a living any more?'

'He seemed to have money. And he never paid for anything so he could save up for ever. I guess that's what he meant. That he'd saved enough.'

Erlendur remembered asking Sigurdur Óli to check Gudlaugur's bank accounts and resolved to remind him. He left Denni in the kitchen in a state of confusion, wondering about chewing tobacco and condoms and girlfriends. As he walked past the lobby he caught sight of a young woman arguing noisily with the head of reception. He seemed to want her out of the hotel, but she refused to leave. It crossed Erlendur's mind that the woman who wanted to invoice this man for his night of fun had shown up, and he was about to go away when the young woman noticed him and stared.

'Are you the cop?' she called out.

'Get out of here!' the head of reception said in an unusually harsh tone.

'You look exactly like Eva Lind described you,' she said, sizing up Erlendur. 'I'm Stína. She told me to talk to you.'

They sat down in the bar. Erlendur bought them coffee. He tried to ignore her breasts but had his work cut out doing so. Never in his life had he seen such a huge bosom on such a slim and delicate body. She was wearing an ankle-length beige coat with a fur collar, and she draped it over the chair at their table to reveal a skin-tight red top that hardly covered her stomach and black flared trousers that barely stretched above the crease between her buttocks. She was heavily painted, wore thick, dark lipstick and smiled to reveal a beautiful set of teeth.

'Three hundred thousand,' she said, carefully rubbing under her right breast as if it itched. 'Were you wondering about the tits?'

'Are you all right?'

'It's the stitches.' She winced. 'I mustn't scratch them too much. Have to be careful.'

'What—?'

'New silicon,' Stína interrupted him. 'I had a boob job the other day.'

Erlendur took care not to stare at her new breasts.

'How do you know Eva Lind?' he asked.

'She said you'd ask that and told me to tell you that you don't want to know. She's right. Trust me. And she also told me you'd help me with a little business and then I could help you, know what I mean?'

'No,' Erlendur said. 'I don't know what you mean.'

'Eva said you would.'

'Eva was lying. What are you talking about? A little business, what does that involve?'

Stína sighed.

'My friend was busted with some hash at Keflavík airport. Not much, but enough for them to put him away for maybe three years. They sentence them like murderers, those fuckers. A bit of hash. And a few tabs, right! He says he'll get three years. Three! Paedophiles get three months, suspended. Fucking wankers!'

Erlendur didn't see how he could help her. She was like a child, unaware of how big and complicated and difficult it is to deal with the world.

'Was he caught at the terminal?'

'Yeah.'

'I can't do anything,' Erlendur said. 'And I don't feel inclined to. You don't keep particularly good company. Dope smuggling and prostitution. What about a straightforward office job?'

'Won't you just try?' Stína said. 'Talk to someone. He mustn't get three years!'

'To get this perfectly straight,' Erlendur said with a nod, 'you're a prostitute?'

'Prostitute, prostitute,' Stína said, producing a cigarette from a little black handbag over her shoulder. 'I dance at The Marquis. She leaned forwards and whispered conspiratorially to Erlendur: 'But there's more money in the other business.'

'And you've had customers at this hotel?'

'A few,' Stína said.

'And you've been working at this hotel?'

'I've never worked here.'

'I mean do you pick up the customers here or bring them over from town?'

'Whatever I please. They used to let me be here until Fatso threw me out.'

'Why?'

Stína started itching under her breasts again and gave the spot a cautious rub. She winced and forced a smile at Erlendur, but clearly didn't feel particularly well.

'A girl I know went for a boob job that went wrong,' she said. 'Her tits are like empty bin liners.'

'Do you really need all that breast?' Erlendur couldn't refrain from asking.

'Don't you like them?' she said, thrusting them forward but grimacing as she did. 'These stitches are killing me,' she groaned.

'Well, they are ... big,' Erlendur admitted.

'And straight off the shelf,' Stína boasted.

Erlendur saw the hotel manager enter the bar with the head of reception and stride over to them in all his majesty. Looking around to make sure no one else was in the bar, he hissed at Stína when he was still a few metres away from her.

'Out! Get out, girl! This minute! Out of here!'

Stína looked over her shoulder at the hotel manager, then back at Erlendur and rolled her eyes.

'Christ,' she said.

'We don't want whores like you at this hotel!' the manager shouted.

He grabbed her as if to throw her out.

'Leave me alone,' Stína said. 'I'm talking to this man here.'

'Watch her tits!' Erlendur shouted, not knowing what else to say. The hotel manager looked at him, dumbfounded. 'They're new,' Erlendur added by way of explanation.

He stood up, blocked the hotel manager's path and tried to push him away, but with little success. Stína did her utmost to protect her breasts, while the head of reception stood at a distance, watching the goings-on. Eventually he came to Erlendur's aid and they managed to shuffle the furious hotel manager out of reach of Stína.

'Everything ... she ... says about ... me is ... fucking lies!' he wheezed. The effort was almost too much for him; his face poured with sweat and he was panting for breath after the struggle.

'She hasn't said anything about you,' Erlendur said to calm him down.

'I want ... her ... to ... get out ... of here.' The hotel manager slumped down in a chair, took out his handkerchief and started mopping his face.

'Cool it, Fatso,' Stína said. 'He's a meat merchant, you know that?'

'A meat merchant?' Erlendur didn't immediately grasp the meaning.

'He takes a slice from all of us who work at this hotel,' Stína said.

'A slice?' Erlendur said.

'A slice. His commission! He takes a cut from us.'

'It's a lie!' the hotel manager shouted. 'Get out, you fucking whore!'

'He wanted more than half a share for himself and the head waiter,' Stína said as she carefully rearranged her breasts, 'and when I refused he told me to fuck off and never come back.'

'She's lying,' the hotel manager said, slightly calmer. 'I've always thrown those girls out, and her too. We don't want whores at this hotel.'

'The head waiter?' Erlendur said, visualising the thin moustache. Rósant, he thought the name was.

'Always thrown them out,' Stína snorted as she turned to Erlendur. 'He's the one who phones us. If he knows one of the guests is up for it or has money he phones to let us know and plants us in the bar. Says it makes the hotel more popular. They're conference guests and the like. Foreigners. Lonely old men. If there's a big conference on, he phones.'

'Are there many of you?' Erlendur asked.

'A few of us run an escort service,' Stína said. 'Really high class.'

Stína gave the impression that she was not as proud of anything as being a prostitute, apart perhaps from her new breasts.

'They don't run a bloody escort service,' the manager said, breathing normally again. 'They hang around the hotel and try to hook guests and take them up to the rooms, and she's lying about me phoning them. You fucking bitch of a whore!'

Thinking it inadvisable to continue the conversation with Stína at the bar, Erlendur said he needed to borrow the head of reception's office for a moment – otherwise they could all go down to the police station and resume there. The hotel manager let out a groan and gave Stína the evil eye. Erlendur followed her out of the bar and into the office. The hotel manager stayed behind. All the wind seemed to have been knocked out of him, and he shooed the head of reception away when he went over to attend to him.

'She's lying, Erlendur,' he shouted after them. 'It's all a pack of lies!'

Erlendur sat down at the manager's desk while Stína stood and lit a cigarette, as if immune to the fact that smoking was prohibited throughout the hotel except conceivably at the bar.

'Did you know the doorman at this hotel?' Erlendur asked. 'Gudlaugur?'

'He was really nice. He collected Fatso's cut from us. And then he got killed.'

'He was—'

'Do you reckon Fatso killed him?' Stína interrupted. 'He's the biggest creep I know. Do you know why I'm not allowed at this shitty hotel of his any more?'

'No.'

'He didn't only want a cut from us girls, but, you know …'

'What?'

'Wanted us to do stuff for him too. Personal. You know …'

'And?'

'I refused. Put my foot down. Those rolls of fat on the bastard. He's gross. He could have killed Gudlaugur. I could see him doing that. I bet he sat on him.'

'But what was your relationship with Gudlaugur? Did you do things for him?'

'Never. He wasn't interested.'

'He certainly was,' Erlendur said, imagining Gudlaugur's corpse in his little room with his trousers round his ankles. 'I'm afraid he wasn't entirely uninterested.'

'He never took an interest in me anyway,' Stína said, carefully hitching up her breasts. 'And none of us girls.'

'Is the head waiter in on this with the manager?'

'Rósant? Yeah.'

'What about the man from reception?'

'He doesn't want us. He doesn't want any tarts but the other two decide. The man from reception wants to get rid of Rósant, but Fatso makes too much money out of him.'

'Tell me something else. Do you ever chew tobacco? In a kind of gauze, like miniature teabags. People keep it under their lip. Pressed against the gums.'

'Yuk, no,' Stína said. 'Are you crazy? I take really good care of my teeth.'

'Does anyone you know chew tobacco?'

'No.'

They said nothing more until Erlendur felt compelled to do a spot of moralising. He had Eva Lind in mind. How she had been caught up in drugs and surely went in for prostitution to pay for her habit, although it probably didn't take place at any of the finer hotels in the city. He thought what a terrible lot it was for a woman to sell her favours to any dirty old man whatever, wherever and whenever.

'Why are you doing this?' he asked, trying to conceal the tone of accusation in his voice. 'The silicon implants in your breasts. Sleeping with conference guests in hotel rooms. Why?'

'Eva Lind said you'd ask that too. Don't try to understand it,' Stína said, and stubbed her cigarette out on the floor. 'Don't even try.'

She happened to glance through the open door to the office and into the lobby, and saw Ösp walking by.

'Is Ösp still working here?' she said.

'Ösp? Do you know her?' Erlendur's mobile began ringing in his pocket.

'I thought she'd quit. I used to talk to her sometimes when I was here.'

'How did you know her?'

'We were just together in—'

'She wasn't whoring with you, was she?' Erlendur took out his mobile and was about to answer.

'No,' Stína said. 'She's not like her little brother.'

'Her brother?' Erlendur said. 'Has she got a brother?'

'He's a bigger tart than I am.'

23

Erlendur stared at Stína while he tried to puzzle out her comment about Ösp's brother. Stína dithered in front of him.

'What?' she said. 'What's wrong? Aren't you going to answer the phone?'

'Why did you think Ösp had quit?'

'It's just a shitty job.'

Erlendur answered his phone almost absent-mindedly.

'About time too,' Elínborg said down the line.

She and Sigurdur Óli had gone to Hafnarfjördur to bring Gudlaugur's sister in for questioning at the police station in Reykjavík, but she refused to go with them. When she asked for an explanation they refused to give one, and then she said she could not abandon her father in his wheelchair. They offered to provide a carer for him and also invited her to talk to a lawyer, who could be present, but she didn't seem to realise the seriousness of the matter. She would not entertain the notion of going to the police station, so Elínborg suggested a compromise, flatly against Sigurdur Óli's wishes. They would take her to Erlendur at the hotel and after he had talked to her they would decide the next move. She thought about it. On the verge of losing his patience, Sigurdur Óli was about to drag her off forcibly when she agreed. She phoned a neighbour who came round immediately, clearly accustomed to looking after the old man when needed. Then she began resisting again, which infuriated Sigurdur Óli.

'He's on his way to you with her,' Elínborg said over the telephone. 'He would have much preferred to have had her locked up. She kept asking us why we wanted to talk to her and wouldn't believe us when we said we didn't know. Why do you want to talk to her anyway?'

'She came to the hotel a few days before her brother was murdered but told us she hadn't seen him for decades. I want to know why she didn't tell us that, why she's lying. See the look on her face.'

'She might be rather peeved,' Elínborg said. 'Sigurdur Óli wasn't exactly pleased at the way she behaved.'

'What happened?'

'He'll tell you.'

Erlendur rang off.

'What do you mean, he's a bigger tart than you?' he said to Stína, who was peering into her bag and wondering whether she could be bothered to light another cigarette. 'Ösp's brother. What are you talking about?'

'Eh?'

'Ösp's brother. You said he was a bigger tart than you.'

'Ask her,' Stína said.

'I will, but I mean, what … he's her little brother, didn't you say?'

'Yes, and he's a ... bye-bye, baby.'

'A bye-bye baby. You mean a …?'

'Bisexual.'

'And, does he prostitute himself?' Erlendur asked. 'Like you?'

'You bet. A junkie. There's always someone wanting to beat him up because he owes them money.'

'And what about Ösp? How do you know her?'

'We were at school together. So was he. He's only a year younger than her. We're the same age. We were in the same class. She isn't that bright.' Stína pointed at her head. 'Not up there,' she said. 'Left school at fifteen. Failed the lot. I passed them all. Finished secondary school.'

Stína gave a broad smile.

Erlendur sized her up.

'I know you're my daughter's friend and you've been helpful,' he said, 'but you shouldn't go comparing yourself with Ösp. For a start, she doesn't have itchy stitches.'

Stína looked at him, still smiling out of one corner of her mouth, then walked out of the office without a word and through the lobby. On the way she swung her fur-collared coat over her, but now her motions lacked all dignity. She came face to face with Sigurdur Óli and Gudlaugur's sister as they entered the lobby, and Erlendur saw Sigurdur Óli goggle at Stína's breasts. He thought to himself that she must have got her money's worth after all.

The hotel manager stood nearby as if he had been waiting for Erlendur's meeting to finish. Ösp was standing by the lift and watched Stína leave the hotel. It was obvious that Ösp recognised her. When Stína walked past the head of reception who was sitting at his desk, he looked up and watched her go out through the door. He glanced over at the hotel manager who waddled off in the direction of the kitchen, and Ösp entered the lift, which closed behind her.

'What's behind all this tomfoolery, may I ask?' Erlendur heard Gudlaugur's sister say as she approached him. 'What's the meaning of such effrontery and rudeness?'

'Effrontery and rudeness?' Erlendur said in a quizzical voice. 'That doesn't sound familiar.'

'This man here,' the sister said, clearly unaware of Sigurdur Óli's name, 'this man has been rude to me and I demand an apology.'

'Out of the question,' Sigurdur Óli said.

'He pushed me and led me out of my home like a common criminal.'

'I handcuffed her,' Sigurdur Óli said. 'And I won't apologise. She can forget that. She called me plenty of names and Elínborg too, and she resisted. I want to lock her up. She was impeding a police officer in the execution of his duty.'

Stefanía Egilsdóttir looked at Erlendur and said nothing.

'I'm not accustomed to such treatment,' she said at last.

'Take her down the station,' Erlendur said to Sigurdur Óli. 'Put her in the cell next to Henry Wapshott. We'll talk to her tomorrow.' He looked at the woman. 'Or the day after.'

'You can't do this,' Stefanía said, and Erlendur could tell that she was severely taken aback. 'You have no reason to treat me like this. Why do you think you can throw me in prison? What have I done?'

'You've been lying,' Erlendur said. 'Goodbye.' And then to Sigurdur Óli, 'We'll be in touch.'

He turned away from them and set off in the direction the hotel manager had gone. Sigurdur Óli took Stefanía by the arm and was about to lead her away, but she stood rooted to the spot and stared at Erlendur's retreating back.

'All right,' she called after him. She tried to shake off Sigurdur Óli. 'This is not necessary,' she said. 'We can sit down and talk this over like human beings.'

Erlendur stopped and turned around.

'My brother,' she said. 'Let's talk about my brother if you want. But I don't know what you'll gain by it.'

They sat down in Gudlaugur's little room. She said she wanted to go there. Erlendur asked whether she had been there before and she denied it. When he asked whether she had not met her brother in all those years, she repeated what she had said before, that she had not been in contact with her brother. Erlendur was convinced that she was lying. That her business at the hotel five days before Gudlaugur's murder was in some way connected with him, not mere coincidence.

She looked at the poster of Shirley Temple in the role of the Little Princess without the slightest change of expression or word of comment. Opening the wardrobe, she saw his doorman's uniform. Finally she sat down on the only chair in the room, while Erlendur propped himself up against the wardrobe. Sigurdur Óli had meetings scheduled in Hafnarfjördur with more of Gudlaugur's old classmates and left when they went down to the basement.

'He died here,' the sister said without a hint of regret in her voice, and Erlendur wondered, just as he had at their first meeting, why this woman apparently lacked all feeling towards her brother.

'Stabbed through the heart,' Erlendur said. 'Probably with a knife from the kitchen,' he added. 'There is blood on the bed.'

'How sparse,' she said, looking around the room. 'That he should have lived here all those years. What was the man thinking of?'

'I was hoping you could help me with that one.'

She looked at him and said nothing.

'I don't know,' Erlendur went on. 'He regarded it as ample. Some people can only live in a villa five hundred metres square. I understand that he benefited from living and working at the hotel. There were plenty of perks.'

'Have you found the murder weapon?' she asked.

'No, but perhaps something resembling it,' Erlendur said. Then he stopped and waited for her to speak, but she did not utter a word and a good while elapsed until she broke the silence.

'Why do you claim I'm lying to you?'

'I don't know how much of it is a lie but I do know that you're not telling me everything. You're not telling me the truth. But of course above all you're not telling me anything and I'm astonished at your and your father's reaction to Gudlaugur's death. It's as if he was nothing to do with you.'

She took a good long look at Erlendur, then seemed to make a decision.

'There were three years between us,' she said suddenly, 'and, young as I was, I still remember the first time they brought him home. One of my first memories in life, I expect. He was the apple of his father's eye from day one. Dad was always devoted to him and I think he had great things in mind for him from the very start. It didn't come of its own accord, as it should have done perhaps – our father always had something big planned for when Gudlaugur grew up.'

'What about you?' Erlendur asked. 'Didn't he see you as a genius?'

'He was always kind to me,' she said, 'but he worshipped Gudlaugur.'

'And drove him on until he broke down.'

'You want to have things simple,' she said. 'Things rarely are. I would have thought that a man like you, a policeman, realised that.'

'I don't think this revolves around me,' Erlendur said.

'No,' she said. 'Of course not.'

'How did Gudlaugur end up alone and abandoned in this little room? Why did you hate him so much? I could conceivably under-stand your father's attitude if Gudlaugur cost him his health but I don't understand why you take such a harsh stand against him.'

'Cost him his health?' she said, looking at Erlendur in surprise.

'When he pushed him down the stairs,' Erlendur said. 'I've heard that story.'

'From whom?'

'That's not important. Is it true? Did he cripple your father?'

'I don't think that's any of your business.'

'Definitely not,' Erlendur said. 'Unless it concerns the investigation. Then I'm afraid it's more people's business than just you two.'

Saying nothing, Stefanía looked at the blood on the bed, while Erlendur pondered why she wanted to talk to him in the room where her brother had been murdered. He thought of asking her, but could not bring himself to.

'It can't always have been that way,' he said instead. 'The choirmaster told me you came to your brother's rescue when he lost his voice on stage. At some point you were friends. At some point he was your brother.'

'How do you know what happened? How did you dig that up? Who have you been talking to?'

'We're gathering information. People from Hafnarfjördur remember it well. You weren't totally indifferent to him then. When you were children.'

Stefanía remained silent.

'The whole thing was a nightmare,' she said at last. 'A terrible nightmare.'

*

In their house in Hafnarfjördur they spent the whole day excitedly looking forward to when he would sing at the cinema. She woke up early, made breakfast and thought about her mother, feeling that she had assumed that role in the household and was proud of it. Her father mentioned how helpful she was at looking after the two of them after her mother died. How grown-up and responsible she was in everything she did. Normally he never said anything about her. Ignored her. Always had.

She missed her mother. One of the last things her mother said to her in hospital was that now she would need to look after her father and brother. She must not let them down. 'Promise me that,' her mother said. 'It won't always be easy. It hasn't always been easy. Your father can be so stubborn and strict and I don't know whether Gudlaugur can take it. But if it ever comes to that you must stand with him, Gudlaugur, promise me that too,' her mother said, and she nodded and promised that too. And they held hands until her mother fell asleep, and then she stroked her hair and kissed her on the forehead.

Two days later she was dead.

'We'll let Gudlaugur sleep a little bit longer,' her father said when he came down into the kitchen. 'It's an important day for him.'

An important day for him.

She did not recall any day being important for her. Everything revolved around him. His singing. The recording sessions. The two records that had been released. The invitation to tour Scandinavia. The concerts in Hafnarfjörður. The concert tonight. His voice. His singing practice when she had to sneak around the house so as not to disturb them as he stood by the piano and his father played the accompaniment, instructing and encouraging him and showing him love and understanding if he felt he did well, but being strict and firm if he did not think he concentrated enough. Sometimes he lost his temper and scolded him. Sometimes he hugged him and said he was wonderful.

If only she had received a fraction of the attention lavished on him and the encouragement that he was given every day for having that beautiful voice. She felt unimportant, devoid of any talent that could attract her father's attention. He sometimes said it was a shame that she did not have a voice. He regarded teaching her to sing as a hopeless task, but she knew that wasn't the case. She knew that he could not be bothered to expend his energy on her, because she did not have a special voice. She lacked her brother's gift. She could sing in a choir and hammer out a tune on the piano, but both her father, and the piano teacher he sent her to because he did not have the time to attend to her himself, talked about her lack of musical talent.

Her brother, on the other hand, had a wonderful voice and a profound feeling for music, but was still just a normal boy like she was a normal girl. She did not know what it was that distinguished them from each other. He was no different from her. To some extent she was in charge of his upbringing, especially after their mother fell ill. He obeyed her, did what she told him and respected her. Similarly, she loved him, but also felt jealous of the praise he earned. She was afraid of that feeling and mentioned it to no one.

She heard Gudlaugur coming down the stairs, and then he appeared in the kitchen and sat down beside their father.

'Just like Mum,' he said as he watched his sister pour coffee into their father's cup.

He often talked about their mother and she knew he missed her terribly. He had turned to her when something went wrong, when the boys bullied him or their father lost his temper, or simply when he needed someone to hold him without it being a special reward for a good performance.

Expectation and excitement reigned in the house all day and had reached an almost unbearable pitch when towards evening they put on their best clothes and set off for the cinema. The two of them accompanied Gudlaugur backstage, their father greeted the choirmaster, and then they crept out into the auditorium as it began to fill up. The lights in the auditorium dimmed. The curtain rose. Quite big for his age, handsome and peculiarly determined as he stood on stage, Gudlaugur finally began to sing in his melancholy boy soprano.

She held her breath and closed her eyes.

The next thing she knew was her father grabbing her by the arm so tightly that it hurt, and hearing him moan: 'Oh my God!'

She opened her eyes and saw her father's face, pale as death, and when she looked up at the stage she saw Gudlaugur trying to sing, but something had happened to his voice. It was like yodelling. She rose to her feet, looked all around the auditorium behind her and saw that people had started to smile and some were laughing. She ran up onto the stage to her brother and tried to lead him away. The choirmaster came to her assistance and eventually they managed to take him backstage. She saw her father standing rigid in the front row, staring up at her like the god of thunder.

When she lay in bed that evening and thought back to that terrible moment her heart missed a beat, not from fear or horror at what had happened or how her brother must have felt, but from a mysterious glee for which she had no explanation and which she repressed like an evil crime.

*

'Did you have a guilty conscience about those thoughts?' Erlendur asked.

'They were completely alien to me,' Stefanía said. 'I'd never thought anything like that before.'

'I don't suppose there's anything abnormal about gloating over other people's misfortunes,' Erlendur said. 'Even people close to us. It may be an instinct, a kind of defence mechanism for dealing with shock.'

'I shouldn't be telling you this in such detail,' Stefanía said. 'It doesn't paint a very appealing picture of me. And you may be right. We all suffered shock. An enormous shock, as you can imagine.'

'What was their relationship like after this happened?' Erlendur asked. 'Gudlaugur and his father.'

Stefanía ignored his question.

'Do you know what it's like not to be the favourite?' she asked instead. 'What it's like just being ordinary and never earning any particular attention. It's like you don't exist. You're taken for granted, not favoured or shown any special care. And all the time someone you consider your equal is championed like the chosen one, born to bring infinite joy to his parents and the whole world. You watch it day after day, week after week and year after year and it never ceases, if anything it increases over the years, almost … almost worship.'

She looked up at Erlendur.

'It can only spawn jealousy,' she said. 'Anything else would not be human. And instead of suppressing it the next thing you know is that you're nourished by it, because in some odd way it makes you feel better.'

'Is that the explanation for gloating over your brother's misfortune?'

'I don't know,' Stefanía said. 'I couldn't control that feeling. It hit me like a slap in the face and I trembled and shivered and tried to get rid of it, but it wouldn't go. I didn't think that could happen.'

They fell silent.

'You envied your brother,' Erlendur said then.

'Maybe I did, for a while. Later I began to pity him.'

'And eventually hate him.'

She looked at Erlendur.

'What do you know about hate?' she said.

'Not much,' Erlendur said. 'But I do know that it can be dangerous. Why did you tell us that you hadn't been in contact with your brother for almost three decades?'

'Because it's true,' Stefanía said.

'It's not true,' Erlendur said. 'You're lying. Why are you lying about that?'

'Are you going to send me to prison for lying?'

'If I need to I will,' Erlendur said. 'We know that you came to this hotel five days before he was murdered. You told us you hadn't seen or been in contact with your brother for decades. Then we discover that you came to the hotel a few days before his death. On what business? And why did you lie to us?'

'I could have come to the hotel without meeting him. It's a big hotel. Did that ever occur to you?'

'I doubt that. I don't think it's a coincidence that you came to the hotel just before he died.'

He saw that she was prevaricating. Saw that she was mulling over whether to take the next step. She had patently prepared herself to give a more detailed account than at their first meeting, and now was the moment to decide whether to take the plunge.

'He had a key,' she said in such a low voice that Erlendur could barely hear it. 'The one you showed to me and my father.'

Erlendur remembered the key ring that was found in Gudlaugur's room and the little pink penknife with a picture of a pirate on it. There were two keys on the ring, one that he thought was a door key and the other that could well fit a chest, cupboard or box.

'What about that key?' Erlendur asked. 'Did you recognise it? Do you know what it fits?'

Stefanía smiled.

'I have an identical key,' she said.

'What key is it?'

'It's the key to our house in Hafnarfjördur.'

'You mean your home?'

'Yes,' Stefanía said. 'Where my father and I live. The key fits the basement door at the back of the house. Some narrow steps lead up from the basement to the hall and from there you can get into the living room and kitchen.'

'Do you mean …?' Erlendur tried to work out the implications of what she was saying. 'Do you mean he went in the house?'

'Yes.'

'But I thought you weren't in contact. You said you and your father hadn't had anything to do with him for decades. That you didn't want to have any contact with him. Why were you lying?'

'Because Dad didn't know.'

'Didn't know what?'

'That he came. Gudlaugur must have missed us. I didn't ask him, but he must have done. For him to do that.'

'What was it precisely that your father didn't know?'

'That Gudlaugur sometimes came to our house at night without us being aware, sat in the living room without making a sound and left before we woke up. He did it for years and we never knew.'

She looked at the bloodstains on the bed.

'Until I woke up in the middle of the night once and saw him.'

24

Erlendur watched Stefanía, her words racing through his mind. She was not as haughty as at their first meeting when Erlendur had been outraged at her lack of feeling for her brother, and he thought he may have judged her too quickly. He knew neither her nor her story well enough to be able to sit on his high horse, and suddenly he regretted his remark on her lack of conscience. It was not up to him to judge others, though he was always falling into that trap. To all intents and purposes he knew nothing about this woman who had suddenly turned so pitiful and terribly lonely in front of him. He realised that her life had been no bed of roses, first as a child living in her brother's shadow, then a motherless teenager and finally a woman who never left her father's side and probably sacrificed her life for him.

A good while passed in this way, each of them engrossed in their respective thoughts. The door to the little room was open and Erlendur went out into the corridor. All of a sudden he wanted to reassure himself that no one was outside, no one was eavesdropping. He looked along the poorly lit corridor but saw nobody. Turning round, he looked down to the end, but it was pitch dark. He thought to himself that anyone who went down there would have had to walk past the door and that he would have noticed. The corridor was empty. All the same, he had a strong feeling that they were not alone in the basement when he went back into the room. The smell in the corridor was the same as the first time he went there: something burning that he could not place. He did not feel comfortable. His first sight of the body was etched in his mind and the more he found out about the man in the Santa suit, the more wretched was the mental image he preserved and knew he could never shake off.

'Is everything all right?' Stefanía asked, still sitting on the chair.

'Yes, fine,' Erlendur said. 'A silly idea of mine. I had a feeling someone was in the corridor. Shouldn't we go somewhere else? For coffee maybe?'

She looked across the room, nodded and stood up. They walked along the corridor in silence, up the stairs and across the lobby to the dining room where Erlendur ordered two coffees. They sat down to one side and tried not to let all the tourists disturb them.

'My father wouldn't be pleased with me now,' Stefanía said. 'He's always forbidden me to talk about the family. He can't stand any invasion of his privacy.'

'Is he in good health?'

'He's in quite good health for his age. But I don't know ...' Her words trailed off.

'There's no such thing as privacy when the police are involved,' Erlendur said. 'Not to mention when murder has been committed.'

'I'm starting to realise that. We were going to shake this off like it was none of our business, but I don't expect anyone can claim immunity in these dreadful circumstances. I don't suppose that's part of the deal.'

'If I understand you correctly,' Erlendur said, 'you and your father had broken off all contact with Gudlaugur but he sneaked into the house at night without being noticed. What was his motive? What did he do? Why did he do this?'

'I never got a satisfactory answer out of him. He just sat still in the living room for an hour or two. Otherwise I'd have noticed him much earlier. He'd been doing it several times a year for years on end. Then one night about two years ago I couldn't sleep and was lying in bed in a drowsy state at about four in the morning, when I heard a creaking noise in the sitting room downstairs, which of course startled me. My father's room is downstairs and his door is always open at night, and I thought he was trying to get my attention. I heard another creak and wondered if it was a burglar, so I crept downstairs. I saw that the door to my father's room was just as I'd left it, but when I entered the hall I saw someone dart down the stairs, and I called out to him. To my horror he stopped on the stairs, turned round and came back up.'

Stefanía paused and stared ahead as if transported away from time and place.

'I thought he would attack me,' she began again. 'I stood in the kitchen doorway and turned on the light, and there he was in front of me. I hadn't seen him face to face for years, ever since he was a young man, and it took me a little while to realise that it was my brother.'

'How did you react to it?' Erlendur asked.

'It threw me completely. I was terrified too, because if it had been a burglar I should have rung the police instead of making all that fuss. I was trembling with fright and let out a scream when I switched on the light and saw his face. It must have been funny to see me so scared and nervous, because he started laughing.'

*

'Don't wake Dad,' he said, putting a finger to his lips to hush her.

She couldn't believe her eyes.

'Is that you?' she gasped.

He wasn't like the image she retained of him from his youth, and she saw how badly he had aged. He had bags under his eyes and his thin lips were pale; wisps of hair stood out in all directions and he regarded her with infinitely sad eyes. She automatically began working out how old he really was. He looked so much older.

'What are you doing here?' she whispered.

'Nothing,' he said. 'I'm not doing anything. Sometimes I just want to come home.'

*

'That was the only explanation he gave for why he sometimes sneaked into the living room at night without letting anyone know,' Stefanía said. 'Sometimes he wanted to go home. I don't know what he meant by that. Whether he associated it with childhood, when Mum was still alive, or whether he meant the years before he pushed Dad down the stairs. I don't know. Maybe the house itself held some meaning for him, because he never had another home. Just a dirty little room in the basement of this hotel.'

*

'You ought to leave,' she said. 'He might wake up.'

'Yes, I know,' he said. 'How is he? Is he all right?'

'He's doing fine. But he needs constant care. He has to be fed and washed and dressed and taken out and put down in front of the television. He likes films.'

'You don't know how bad I've felt about this,' he said. 'All these years. I didn't want it to turn out like this. It was all a huge mistake.'

'Yes, it was,' she said.

'I never wanted to be famous. That was his dream. My part was just to make it come true.'

They fell silent.

'Does he ever ask about me?'

'No,' she said. 'Never. I've tried to get him to talk about you but he won't even hear your name mentioned.'

'He still hates me.'

'I don't think he'll ever get that out of his system.'

'Because of the way I am. He can't stand me because I'm …'

'That's something between the two of you that …'

'I would have done anything for him, you know that.'

'Yes.'

'Always.'

'Yes.'

'All those demands he made on me. Endless practising. Concerts. Recordings. It was all his dream, not mine. He was happy and then everything was fine.'

'I know.'

'So why can't he forgive me? Why can't he make up with me? I miss him. Will you tell him that? I miss when we were together. When I used to sing for him. You are my family.'

'I'll try to talk to him.'

'Will you? Will you tell him I miss him?'

'I'll do that.'

'He can't stand me because of the way I am.'

Stefanía said nothing.

'Maybe it was a rebellion against him. I don't know. I tried to hide it but I can't be anything else than what I am.'

'You ought to go now,' she said.

'Yes.'

He hesitated.

'What about you?'

'What about me?'

'Do you hate me too?'

'You ought to go. He might wake up.'

'Because it's all my fault. The situation you're in, having to look after him all the time. You must …'

'Go,' she said.

'Sorry.'

*

'After he left home, after the accident, what happened then?' Erlendur asked. 'Was he just erased as if he'd never existed?'

'More or less. I know Dad listened to his records now and again. He didn't want me to know, but I saw it sometimes when I got home from work. He'd forget to put the sleeve away or take the record off. Occasionally we heard something about him and years ago we read an interview with him in a magazine. It was an article about former child stars. "Where are they now?" was the headline or something equally appalling. The magazine had dug him up and he seemed willing to talk about his old fame. I don't know why he opened up like that. He didn't say anything in the interview except that it was fun being the main attraction.'

'So someone remembered him. He wasn't completely forgotten.'

'There's always someone who remembers.'

'In the magazine he didn't mention being bullied at school or your father's demands, losing his mother and how his hopes, which I expect your father kindled, were dashed and he was forced to leave home?'

'What do you know about the bullying at school?'

'We know that he was bullied for being different. Isn't that right?'

'I don't think my father kindled any expectations. He's a very down-to-earth and realistic man. I don't know why you talk like that. For a while it looked as if my brother would go a long way as a singer, performing abroad and commanding attention on a scale unknown in our little community. My father explained that to him but I also think he told him that even though it would take a lot of work, dedication and talent, he still shouldn't set his hopes too high. My father isn't stupid. Don't you go thinking that.'

'I don't think anything of the sort.'

'Good.'

'Did Gudlaugur never try to contact you two? Or you him? All that time?'

'No. I think I've already answered your question. Apart from sneaking in sometimes without us noticing. He told me he'd been doing it for years.'

'You didn't try to track him down?'

'No, we didn't.'

'Were he and his mother close?' Erlendur asked.

'She meant the world to him,' Stefanía said.

'So her death was a tragedy to him.'

'Her death was a tragedy to us all.'

Stefanía heaved a deep sigh.

'I suppose something died inside us when she passed away. Something that made us a family. I don't think I realised until long afterwards that it was her who tied us together, created a balance. She and Dad never agreed about Gudlaugur, and they quarrelled about his upbringing, if you could call it quarrelling. She wanted to let him be the way he was, and even if he did sing beautifully not to make too much of it.'

She looked at Erlendur.

'I don't think our father ever regarded him as a child, more of a task. Something for him alone to shape and create.'

'And you? What was your standpoint?'

'Me? I was never asked.'

They stopped talking, listened to the murmuring in the dining room and watched the tourists chatting together and laughing. Erlendur looked at Stefanía, who seemed to have withdrawn inside her shell and the memories of her fragile family life.

'Did you have any part in your brother's murder?' Erlendur asked cautiously.

It was as if she did not hear what he said, so he repeated the question. She looked up.

'Not in the slightest,' she said. 'I wish he was still alive so that I could ...'

Stefanía did not finish.

'So you could what?' Erlendur asked.

'I don't know, maybe make up for ...'

She stopped again.

'It was all so terrible. All of it. It started with trivial things and then escalated beyond control. I'm not making light of him pushing our father down the stairs. But you take sides and don't do much to change it. Because you don't want to, I suppose. And time goes by and the years pass until you've really forgotten the feeling, the reason that set it all in motion, and you've forgotten, on purpose or accidentally, the opportunities you had to make up for what went wrong, and then suddenly it's too late to set things straight. All those years have gone by and ...' She groaned.

'What did you do after you caught him in the kitchen?'

'I talked to Dad. He didn't want to know about Gulli, and that was that. I didn't tell him about the night-time visits. A few times I tried to talk to him about a reconciliation. Said I'd bumped into Gulli in the street and he wanted to see his father, but Dad was absolutely immovable.'

'Did your brother never go back to the house after that?'

'Not as far as I know.'

She looked at Erlendur.

'That was two years ago and that was the last I saw of him.'

25

Stefanía stood up, about to leave. It was as if she'd said all she had to say. Erlendur still had an inkling that she had been selective about what she wanted to go on record, and was keeping the rest to herself. He stood up as well, wondering whether to let that suffice for the time being or press her further. He decided to leave the choice to her. She was much more cooperative than before and that suited him for now. But he could not refrain from asking her about an enigma that she had left unexplained.

'I could understand your father's lifelong anger at him because of the accident,' Erlendur said. 'If he blamed him for the paralysis that has confined him to a wheelchair ever since. But you I can't quite figure out. Why you reacted the same way. Why you took your father's side. Why you turned against your brother and had no contact with him for all those years.'

'I think I've helped you enough,' Stefanía said. 'His death is nothing to do with my father and me. It's connected with some other life that my brother led and neither I nor my father know. I hope you appreciate the fact that I've tried to be honest and helpful, and you won't disturb us any more. You won't handcuff me in my own home.'

She held out her hand as if wanting to seal some kind of pact that she and her father would be left undisturbed in future. Erlendur shook her hand and tried to smile. He knew the pact would be broken sooner or later. Too many questions, he thought to himself. Too few real answers. He wasn't ready to let her off the hook just yet and thought he could tell that she was still lying to him, or at least circumventing the truth.

'You didn't come to the hotel to meet your brother a few days before his death?' he said.

'No, I met a friend in this dining room. We had coffee together. You ask her if you think it's not true. I'd forgotten that he worked here and I didn't see him while I was here.'

'I might check that,' Erlendur said, and wrote down the woman's name. 'Then there's something else: do you know a man called Henry Wapshott? He's British and he was in contact with your brother.'

'Wapshott?'

'He's a record collector. Interested in your brother's recordings. It just so happens that he collects records of choral music and specialises in choirboys.'

'I've never heard of him,' Stefanía said. 'Specialises in choirboys?'

'Actually there are stranger collectors than him,' Erlendur said, but did not venture into an account of airline sick bags. 'He says your brother's records are very valuable today, do you know anything about that?'

'No, not a thing,' Stefanía said. 'What was he suggesting? What does it mean?'

'I don't know for sure,' Erlendur said. 'But they're valuable enough for Wapshott to want to come up here to Iceland to meet him. Did Gudlaugur have any of his own records?'

'Not that I know of.'

'Do you know what happened to the copies that were released?'

'I think they just sold out,' Stefanía said. 'Would they be worth anything if they were still around?'

Erlendur sensed a note of eagerness in her voice and wondered whether she was masquerading, whether she was much better informed about all this than he was and was trying to establish just what he knew.

'Could well be,' Erlendur said.

'Is this British man still in the country?' she asked.

'He's in police custody,' Erlendur said. 'He may know more about your brother and his death than he wants to tell us.'

'Do you think he killed him?'

'You haven't heard the news?'

'No.'

'He's a candidate, no more than that.'

'Who is this man?'

Erlendur was about to tell her about the information from Scotland Yard and the child pornography that was found in Wapshott's room. Instead, he repeated that Wapshott was a record collector who was interested in choirboys and had stayed at the hotel and been in contact with Gudlaugur, and was suspicious enough to be remanded in custody.

They exchanged cordial farewells and Erlendur watched her leave the dining room for the lobby. His mobile rang in his pocket. He fumbled for it and answered. To his surprise, Valgerdur was on the other end.

'Could I meet you tonight?' she asked without preamble. 'Will you be at the hotel?'

'I can be,' Erlendur said, not bothering to conceal the surprise in his voice. 'I thought ...'

'Shall we say eight? In the bar?'

'All right,' Erlendur said. 'Let's say that. What—?'

He was going to ask Valgerdur what was bothering her when she rang off and all he could hear was silence. Putting away his mobile, he wondered what she wanted. He had written off any chance of getting to know her and concluded he was probably a total loser as far as women were concerned. Then this telephone call came out of the blue and he didn't know what to read into it.

It was well past noon and Erlendur was starving, but instead of eating in the dining room he went upstairs and had room service send up some lunch. He still had several tapes to go through, so he put one in the player and let it roll while he waited for his food.

He soon lost his concentration, his mind wandered from the screen and he started mulling over Stefanía's words. Why had Gudlaugur crept into their house at night? He had told his sister that he wanted to go home. *Sometimes I just want to come home.* What did those words imply? Did his sister know? What was *home* in Gudlaugur's mind? What did he miss? He was no longer part of the family and the person who had been closest to him, his mother, had died long before. He did not disturb his father and sister when he visited them. He did not come by day as normal people would do – if there was such a thing as normal people – to settle scores, to tackle differences and the anger and even hatred that had formed between him and his family. He came by cover of night, taking care not to disturb anyone, and sneaked back out unnoticed. Instead of reconciliation or forgiveness, he seemed to be looking for something perhaps more important to him, something that only he could understand and which was beyond explanation, enshrined in that single word.

Home.

What was that?

Perhaps a feeling for the childhood he spent in his parents' house before life's incomprehensible complexities and destinies descended upon him. When he had run around that house in the knowledge that his father, mother and sister were his companions and loved ones. He must have gone to the house to gather memories that he did not want to lose and from which he drew nourishment when life weighed him down.

Perhaps he went to the house to come to terms with what fate had meted out to him. The unyielding demands that his father made, the bullying that went with being considered different, the motherly love that was more precious to him than all other things, and the big sister who protected him too; the shock when he returned home after the concert at Hafnarfjördur cinema, his world in ruins and his father's hopes dashed. What could be worse for a boy like him than to fail to live up to his father's expectations? After all the effort he had expended, all the effort his father had made, all the effort his family had made. He had sacrificed his childhood for something too large for him then to comprehend or control – and which then failed to materialise. His father had played a game with his childhood, and in effect deprived him of it.

Erlendur sighed.

Who doesn't want to come home sometimes?

He was flat out on his bed when suddenly he heard a noise in the room. At first he couldn't tell where it was coming from. He thought the turntable had started up and the needle had missed the record.

Sitting up, he looked at the record player and saw that it was switched off. He heard the same noise again and looked all around. It was dark and he couldn't see very clearly. A vague light emanated from the lamp post on the other side of the road. He was about to switch on the bedside lamp when he heard the noise again, louder than before. He didn't dare move. Then he remembered where he had heard the noise before.

He sat up in bed and looked towards the door. In the weak glow he saw a small figure, blue with cold, huddled up in the alcove by the door, staring at him, shaking and shivering so that its head bobbed, sniffling.

The sniffling was the noise that Erlendur recognised.

He stared at the figure and it stared back at him, trying to smile but unable to do so for the cold.

'Is that you?' Erlendur gasped.

In that instant the figure disappeared from the alcove and Erlendur started from his sleep, half out of bed, and stared at the door.

'Was that you?' he groaned, seeing snatches of the dream, the woollen mittens, the cap, the winter jacket and scarf. The clothing they were wearing when they left their house.

The clothing of his brother.

Who sat shivering in the cold room.

26

For a long time he stood in silence at the window, watching the snow fall.

Eventually he sat down to continue watching the tapes. Gudlaugur's sister didn't reappear, nor anyone he knew apart from some employees he recognised from the hotel, hurrying to or from work.

The hotel telephone rang and Erlendur answered.

'I reckon Wapshott's telling the truth,' Elínborg said. 'They know him well at the collectors' shops and the flea market.'

'Was he down there at the time he claimed?'

'I showed them photos of him and asked about the times, and they were pretty close. Close enough to stop us putting him at the hotel when Gudlaugur was attacked.'

'He doesn't give the impression of being a murderer either.'

'He's a paedophile, but maybe not a murderer. What are you going to do with him?'

'I suppose we'll send him to the UK.'

The conversation ended and Erlendur sat pondering Gudlaugur's murder, without reaching any conclusion. He thought about Elínborg and his mind soon returned to the case of the boy whose father abused him and whom Elínborg hated for it.

'You're not the only one,' Elínborg had said to the father. She wasn't trying to console him. Her tone was accusatory, as if she wanted him to know he was only one of many sadists who maltreated their children. She wanted to let him hear what he was a part of. The statistics that applied to him.

She had studied the statistics. Well over three hundred children had been examined at the Children's Hospital in connection with suspected maltreatment over the period 1980–99. Of these, 232 cases involved suspected sexual abuse and 43 suspected physical abuse or violence. Including toxic poisoning. Elínborg repeated the words for emphasis. Including toxic poisoning and wilful neglect. She read from a sheet of paper, calm and collected: head injuries, broken bones, burns, cuts, bites. She reread the list and stared into the father's eyes.

'It is suspected that two children died from physical violence over that twenty-year period,' she said. 'Neither case went to court.'

The experts, she told him, considered that this was an underlying problem, which in plain language meant there were probably many more cases.

'In the UK,' she said, 'four children die every week from maltreatment. Four children,' she reiterated. 'Every week.

'Do you want to know what reasons are given?' she continued. Erlendur sat in the interrogation room but kept a low profile. He was only there to help Elínborg if necessary, but she did not appear to need any assistance.

The father stared into his lap. He looked at the tape recorder. It wasn't switched on. It wasn't a proper interrogation. His lawyer had not been notified but the father had not objected nor complained, yet.

'I shall name some,' Elínborg said, and began listing the reasons that parents are violent to their children: 'Stress,' she said. 'Financial problems, sickness, unemployment, isolation, poor partner support and momentary insanity.'

Elínborg looked at the father.

'Do you think any of this applies to you? Momentary insanity?'

He didn't answer.

'Some people lose control of themselves, and there are documented cases of parents who are so disturbed by a guilty conscience that they want to be caught. Does that sound familiar?'

He said nothing.

'They take the child to the doctor, maybe their GP, because it has, let's say, a persistent cold. But it's not the cold that motivates them; they want the doctor to notice the wounds on the child, the bruises. They want to get caught. You know why?'

He still sat in silence.

'Because they want to put an end to it. Want someone to intervene. Intervene in a process they have no control over. They are incapable of doing so themselves and hope the doctor will see that something's wrong.'

She looked at the father. Erlendur watched in silence. He was worried that Elínborg was going too far. She seemed to draw on every ounce of strength to act professionally, to show that she was not upset by the case. It seemed to be a hopeless struggle and he thought she realised. She was too emotional.

'I spoke to your GP,' Elínborg said. 'He said he had twice reported the boy's injuries to the child welfare agency. The agency investigated both times but found no conclusive evidence. It didn't help that the boy said nothing and you admitted nothing. It's two different things, wanting to be found out for the violence and confessing to it. I read the reports. In the second one, your son is asked about his relationship with you, but he does not seem to understand the question. They repeat the question: "Who do you trust most of all?" And he replies: "My Dad. I trust my Dad most of all."'

Elínborg paused.

'Don't you think that's appalling?' she said.

She looked over towards Erlendur and back to the father.

'Don't you think that's just appalling?'

Erlendur thought to himself that there was a time when he would have given the same answer. He would have named his father.

When spring came and the snow thawed his father went up to the mountains to look for his lost son, trying to calculate his route in the storm from where Erlendur had been found. He seemed to have made a partial recovery, but was nevertheless tormented by guilt.

He roamed the moors and the mountains, beyond where there was any chance of his son reaching, but never found anything. He stayed in a tent up there, Erlendur went with him and his mother took part in the search, and sometimes local folk came to help them, but the boy was never discovered. It was crucial to find the body. Until then, he was not dead in the proper sense, only lost to them. The wound remained open and immeasurable sorrow seeped from it.

Erlendur fought that sorrow alone. He felt bad, and not only about losing his brother. His own rescue he attributed to luck, but a strange sense of guilt preyed on him because it was him and not his younger brother who was saved. Not only had he lost his grip on his brother in the storm, he was also haunted by the thought that he should rather have died himself. He was older and was responsible for his sibling. It had always been that way. He had taken care of him. In all their games. When they were home alone. When they were sent off on errands. He had lived up to those expectations. On this occasion he had failed, and perhaps he did not deserve to be saved since his brother had died. He didn't know why he survived. But he sometimes thought it would have been better if he were the one lying lost on the moor.

He never mentioned these thoughts to his parents and in his lone-liness he sometimes felt that they must think the same about him. His father had sunk down into his own guilt and wanted to be left alone. His mother was overwhelmed with grief. They both blamed

themselves in part for what happened. Between them reigned a curi-
ous silence that drowned out the loudest of shouts, while Erlendur
fought his own battle in solitude, reflecting on responsibility, blame
and luck.

If they had not found him, would they have found his brother
instead?

Standing by the hotel window, he wondered what mark his brother's death had left on his life, and whether it was more than he
realised. He had pondered those events when Eva Lind began asking
him questions. Although he had no simple answers, he knew deep
down where they were to be found. He had often asked himself the
same questions as Eva Lind did when she quizzed him about his
past.

Erlendur heard a knock on his door and turned away from the
window.

'Come in!' he called out. 'It's not locked.'

Sigurdur Óli opened the door and entered.

He had spent the whole day in Hafnarfjördur, talking to people
who knew Gudlaugur.

'Anything new?' Erlendur asked.

'I found out the name he was called. You remember, the one after
everything had collapsed around him.'

'Yes, who told you?'

Sigurdur Óli sighed and sat down on the bed. His wife Bergthóra
had been complaining how much he had been away from home
recently when Christmas was drawing near; she had to handle all
the preparations by herself. He intended to go home and take her to
buy a Christmas tree, but first he needed to see Erlendur. Over the
telephone on his way to the hotel, he explained this to her and said he
would hurry, but she had heard that story too often to believe it and
was in a huff by the time they finished speaking.

'Are you going to spend the whole of Christmas in this room?' Sigurdur Óli asked.

'No,' Erlendur said. 'What did you find out in Hafnarfjördur.'

'Why's it so cold in here?'

'The radiator,' Erlendur said. 'It won't heat up. Won't you get to the point?'

Sigurdur Óli smiled.

'Do you buy a Christmas tree? For Christmas?'

'If I did buy a Christmas tree, I'd do it at Christmas.'

'I located a man who, after waffling a bit, told me he knew Gudlaugur in the old days,' Sigurdur Óli said. He knew he had information that could change the course of the investigation and enjoyed keeping Erlendur in suspense.

Sigurdur Óli and Elínborg had set themselves the goal of talking to everyone who had been at school with Gudlaugur or knew him as a boy. Most of them remembered him and vaguely recalled his promising career as a singer and the bullying that accompanied his celebrity. The occasional person remembered him well and knew what happened when he left his father paralysed. One had a closer relationship with him than Sigurdur Óli could ever have imagined.

An old female schoolmate of Gudlaugur's pointed him out to Sigurdur Óli. She lived in a big house in the newest quarter of Hafnarfjördur. He had telephoned her that morning, so she was expecting him when he arrived. They shook hands and she invited him inside. A pilot's wife, she worked part time in a book shop; her children were grown up and had left home.

She told him all the details of her acquaintance with Gudlaugur, even though it was only slight, and also had a dim recollection of his sister, who she knew was older. She thought she remembered him losing his voice, but didn't know what had happened to him after they left school, and was shocked to see the reports that he was the man who was found murdered in the little basement room at the hotel.

Sigurdur Óli listened to all this distractedly. He had heard most of it from Gudlaugur's other classmates. When she finished, he asked whether she knew any name that Gudlaugur was called as a child and teased with. She didn't remember any, but added, when she saw Sigurdur Óli was about to leave, that she had heard something about him a long time ago that the police might be interested in, if they didn't know it already.

'What's that?' Sigurdur Óli asked, standing up to leave.

She told him, and was pleased to see that she had managed to arouse the detective's interest.

'And is this man still alive?' Sigurdur Óli asked the woman, who said that for all she knew he was, and gave his name. She stood up to fetch the telephone directory and Sigurdur Óli found the man's name and address. He lived in Reykjavík. His name was Baldur.

'Are you sure this is the guy?' Sigurdur Óli asked.

'As far as I know,' the woman said, smiling in the hope that she had provided some assistance. 'It was the talk of the town,' she added.

Sigurdur Óli decided to go there immediately on the off-chance that the man would be at home. It was late in the day. The traffic to Reykjavík was heavy and on the way Sigurdur Óli called Bergthóra who—

'Please stop beating about the bush,' Erlendur impatiently interrupted Sigurdur Óli's account.

'No, this part involves you,' Sigurdur Óli said with a teasing grin. 'Bergthóra wanted to know if I'd invited you round for Christmas Eve. I told her I had, but you hadn't given an answer.'

'I'm spending Christmas Eve with Eva Lind,' Erlendur said. 'That's the answer. Will you please get to the point.'

'Right on,' Sigurdur Óli said.

'And stop staying "right on".'

'Right on.'

*

Baldur lived in a neat wooden house in the Thingholt district near the city centre and had just got home; he was an architect. Sigurdur Óli rang his doorbell and introduced himself as a detective investigating the murder of Gudlaugur Egilsson. The man showed no surprise. He looked Sigurdur Óli up and down and invited him inside.

'To tell the truth I've been expecting you,' he said. 'Or one of you. I was wondering about getting in touch, but I've been putting it off. It's never nice talking to the police.' Smiling again, he offered to hang up Sigurdur Óli's coat.

Everything in the house was spick and span. There were lit candles in the sitting room and a decorated Christmas tree. The man offered Sigurdur Óli a glass of liqueur, which he declined. He was of average height, slim, jolly and balding, but what hair was left had clearly been tinted to enhance its ginger colour. Sigurdur Óli thought he recognised Frank Sinatra crooning from speakers.

'Why were you expecting me, or us?' Sigurdur Óli asked as he sat down on a large red sofa.

'Because of Gulli,' the man said, sitting opposite him. 'I knew you'd dig this up.'

'This what?' Sigurdur Óli asked.

'That I was with Gulli in the old days,' the man said.

'What do you mean, he was with Gudlaugur in the old days?' Erlendur butted in again. 'What could he mean by that?'

'That's the way he phrased it,' Sigurdur Óli said.

'That he was with Gudlaugur?'

'Yes.'

'What does that mean?'

'That they were together.'

'You mean Gudlaugur was …?' Countless thoughts rushed through Erlendur's mind, all screeching to a halt at the stern expressions on the faces of Gudlaugur's sister and his father in the wheelchair.

'That's what this Baldur guy says,' Sigurdur Óli said. 'But Gudlaugur didn't want anyone to know.'

'Didn't want anyone to know about their relationship?'

'He wanted to hide the fact that he was gay.'

27

The man from Thingholt told Sigurdur Óli that his relationship with Gudlaugur began when they were about twenty-five. It was during the disco era when Baldur rented a basement flat in the Vogar district. Neither of them had come out of the closet. 'Attitudes to being gay were different then,' he said with a smile. 'But it was starting to change.'

'And we didn't really live together,' Baldur added. 'Men didn't live together then like they do today, without anyone giving it a second thought. Gays could hardly survive in Iceland in those days. Most of us felt compelled to go abroad, as you may know. He often used to visit me, shall we say. Stayed the night with me. He had a room of his own in the west of town and I went there a couple of times, but he was maybe not quite houseproud enough for my taste so I stopped going there. We were mainly at my place.'

'How did you meet?' Sigurdur Óli asked.

'There were places where gays used to meet then. One was just off the city centre, in fact not far from here in Thingholt. Not a club, but a sort of meeting place we had in someone's house. You never knew what to expect at the clubs and you sometimes got thrown out for dancing with other men. This home was a hotchpotch of everything, a coffee bar, guesthouse, night club, advice centre and shelter. He came there one evening with some friends. That was the first time I saw him. Sorry, silly me, can I offer you coffee?'

Sigurdur Óli looked at his watch.

'Maybe you're in a terrible hurry,' the man said, carefully smoothing down his thin, dyed hair.

'No, it's not that, I wouldn't mind a cup of tea if you have any,' Sigurdur Óli said, his thoughts on Bergthóra. She sometimes got angry when his time-keeping failed. She was very petty about punctuality and would nag him long afterwards if he turned up late.

The man went into the kitchen to make the tea.

'He was awfully repressed,' he said from the kitchen, raising his voice so that Sigurdur Óli could hear him better. 'I sometimes thought he hated his own sexuality. As if he still hadn't fully admitted it. I think he was partly using his relationship with me to help find his way along. He was still searching even at that age. But of course that's nothing new. People come out in their forties, maybe having been married with four kids.'

'Yes, there are all sorts of permutations,' said Sigurdur Óli, who had no idea what he was talking about.

'Oh yes there are, my dear. Do you like it well brewed?'

'Were you together for long?' Sigurdur Óli asked, adding that he did like his tea strong.

'Three years or so, but it was very on and off towards the end.'

'And you haven't been in touch with him since?'

'No. I knew about him, sort of,' the man said, returning to the sitting room. 'The gay community isn't that big.'

'In what way was he repressed?' Sigurdur Óli asked while the man put two cups on the table. He had brought in a bowl of cookies, which he recognised as the sort Bergthóra baked every Christmas. He tried in vain to remember what they were called.

'He was very mysterious and rarely opened up, or only if we got drunk. It was something to do with his father though, I think. He had no contact with him or with his older sister, who had turned against him, but he missed them terribly. His mother had been dead for years when I met him, but he talked more about her than the rest of his family. He could go on for ever about his mother and it could be very tiring, to tell the truth.'

'How did she turn against him? His sister?'

'This was a long time ago and he never described it exactly. All I know is that he fought what he was. You know what I mean? As if he should have been something else.'

Sigurdur Óli shook his head.

'He thought it was dirty. Something unnatural about it. Being gay.'

'And fought it?'

'Yes and no. He wavered about it. I don't think he knew which foot to stand on. Poor thing. He didn't have much self-confidence. Sometimes I think he hated himself.'

'Did you know about his past? As a child star?'

'Yes,' the man said, then he stood up to go to the kitchen and returned with a pot of piping-hot tea which he poured into the cups. He took the pot back to the kitchen and they sipped their tea.

'Can't you speed this up a bit?' Erlendur said to Sigurdur Óli, making no attempt to conceal his impatience as he sat at his hotel room desk listening to the account.

'I'm trying to make it as detailed as possible,' Sigurdur Óli said with a glance at his watch. He was already three-quarters of an hour late for Bergthóra.

'Yes, yes, get on with it ...'

'Did he ever talk about it?' Sigurdur Óli asked, putting down his teacup and helping himself to a cookie. 'His childhood brush with fame?'

'He said he lost his voice,' Baldur said.

'And was he bitter about that?'

'Terribly. It happened at an awful time for him. But he would never tell me about it. He said he was bullied at school for being famous, and that got him down. But he didn't call it being famous. He didn't regard himself as ever having been famous. His father wanted him to be, and apparently he came very close to it. But he felt unhappy, and on top of that these feelings started to come out, his gay side. He was reluctant to talk about it. Preferred to say as little as possible about his family. Do have another cookie.'

'No, thanks,' Sigurdur Óli said. 'Do you know of anyone who may have wanted to kill him? Someone who wanted to hurt him?'

'Good Lord, no! He was such a pussy cat, he would never have harmed a fly. I don't know who could have done it. The poor man, going like that. Are you getting anywhere in your enquiries?'

'No,' Sigurdur Óli said. 'Did you ever listen to his records, or do you have them?'

'You bet,' the man said. 'He was absolutely brilliant. It's wonderful the way he sang. I don't think I've ever heard a child sing so well.'

'Was he proud of his singing when he was older? When you knew him?'

'He never listened to himself. Didn't want to hear his records. Never. No matter how I tried.'

'Why not?'

'It was just impossible to get him to. He never gave any explanation, he just didn't listen to his own records.'

Baldur stood up, went to a cupboard in the sitting room, fetched Gudlaugur's two records and put them on the table in front of Sigurdur Óli.

'He gave them to me after I helped him move.'

'Move?'

'He lost his room on the west side of town and asked me to help him move. He got himself another room and put all his stuff in there. He never really owned anything apart from records.'

'Did he have a lot?'

'Tons of them.'

'Was there anything special that he listened to?'

'No, you see,' Baldur said, 'they were all the same records. These ones here,' he said, pointing to Gudlaugur's two records. 'He had loads of these. He said he'd acquired all the copies.'

'So, he had boxes full of these?' Sigurdur Óli said, unable to conceal his eagerness.

'Yes, at least two.'

'Do you know where they might be?'

'Me? No, I haven't the foggiest. Are they a hot number these days?'

'I know of someone who might be prepared to kill for them,' Sigurdur Óli said.

Baldur's face was now a huge question mark.

'What do you mean?'

'Nothing,' Sigurdur Óli said, looking at his watch. 'I must be going. I might need to contact you again to fill in a few details. It would also be helpful if you phoned me if you remember anything, no matter how trivial it may seem.'

'To tell the truth we didn't have much choice in those days,' the man said. 'Not like today when half the population is gay and the other half pretends it is.'

He smiled at Sigurdur Óli, who choked on his tea.

'Excuse me,' Sigurdur Óli said.

'It is a little strong.'

Sigurdur Óli stood up and so did Baldur, who followed him to the door.

'We know that Gudlaugur was bullied at school,' Sigurdur Óli said when he was about to leave, 'and they called him names. Do you remember if he ever mentioned that to you?'

'It was quite obvious that he'd been bullied for being in a choir and having a beautiful voice and not playing football, and being a bit girlish. He gave the impression of being a little unsure of himself with other people. He talked to me as if he understood why they teased him. But I don't remember him mentioning any names ...'

Baldur hesitated.

'Yes,' Sigurdur Óli said.

'When we were together, you know ...'

Sigurdur Óli shook his head vacantly.

'In bed ...'

'Yes?'

'Sometimes he wanted me to call him "my Little Princess",' Baldur said, a smile playing across his lips.

Erlendur stared at Sigurdur Óli.

'My Little Princess?'

'That's what he said.' Sigurdur Óli stood up from Erlendur's bed. 'And now I really must be going. Bergthóra will be going bananas. So you'll be home for Christmas?'

'And what about the boxes of records?' Erlendur said. 'Where could they be?'

'The guy didn't have any idea.'

'The Little Princess? As in the Shirley Temple film? How does that all fit together? Did that man explain it?'

'No, he didn't know what it meant.'

'It doesn't have to mean anything in particular,' Erlendur said, as if thinking out loud. 'Some gay patois no one else understands. Maybe no stranger than a lot of other things. So, he hated himself then?'

'Not much self-confidence, his friend said. He was indecisive.'

'About his homosexual feelings or something else?'

'I don't know.'

'You didn't ask?'

'We can always talk to him again, but he didn't really seem to know that much about Gudlaugur.'

'And nor do we,' Erlendur said languidly. 'If he wanted to hide the fact that he was gay twenty or thirty years ago, do we assume he went on hiding it?'

'That's the question.'

'I haven't met anyone else who mentioned that he was gay.'

'Yes, well, I'm off anyway,' Sigurdur Óli said, moving to the door. 'Was there anything else for today?'

'No,' Erlendur said. 'That's fine. Thanks for the invitation. Give my regards to Bergthóra, and try to treat her decently.'

'I always do,' Sigurdur Óli said and hurried out. Erlendur looked at his watch and saw that it was time to meet Valgerdur. He took the last tape from the bank out of the video player and put it on the top of the stack. Immediately his mobile began to ring.

It was Elínborg. She told him she had spoken to the State Prosecutor's office about the father who assaulted his son.

'What do they reckon he'll get?' Erlendur asked.

'They think he might even get off,' Elínborg said. 'He won't be convicted if he stands firm. If he just denies it. Won't spend a minute inside.'

'What about the evidence? The footprints on the stairs? The bottle of Drambuie? Everything suggests that—'

'I don't know why we bother. A case of assault came up for sentence yesterday. A man was repeatedly stabbed with a knife. The attacker got eight months in prison, four of them suspended, which means that he goes to jail for two months. Where's the justice in that?'

'Will he get the boy back?'

'He's bound to. The only positive thing, if it can be called positive, is that the boy seriously seems to miss his father. That's what I don't understand. How can he feel attached to his father if the man beats the shit out of him? I just can't figure this case out. Something must be missing. Something we've overlooked. It just doesn't add up.'

'I'll talk to you later,' Erlendur said and looked at his watch. He was late for his meeting with Valgerdur. 'Can you do one thing for me? Stefanía Egilsdóttir said she was with a friend at the hotel the other day. Would you talk to the woman and confirm it?' Erlendur gave her the woman's name.

'Aren't you going to get yourself back home from that hotel?' Elínborg asked.

'Stop nagging me,' Erlendur said and rang off.

28

When Erlendur went down to the lobby he saw Rósant, the head waiter. He hesitated, uncertain whether to make a move. Valgerdur was bound to be waiting for him. Erlendur looked at his watch, pulled a face and went up to the head waiter. This shouldn't take long.

'Tell me about the whores,' he said without preamble. Rósant was talking courteously to two hotel guests. They were clearly Icelandic, because they looked at him in astonishment.

Rósant smiled, raising his little moustache. He apologised politely to the guests, bowed and took Erlendur aside.

'A hotel is just people and our job is to make them feel good, wasn't it some kind of crap like that?' Erlendur said.

'It's not crap. They taught us that at catering college.'

'Did they also teach head waiters to be pimps?'

'I don't know what you're talking about.'

'I'll tell you then. You run a little knocking shop at this hotel.'

Rósant smiled.

'A knocking shop?'

'Has it got anything to do with Gudlaugur, your pimping?'

Rósant shook his head.

'Who was with Gudlaugur when he was murdered?'

They fixed each other's gaze until Rósant backed off and stared down at the floor.

'There was no one I know of,' he finally said.

'Not you?'

'One of your people took a statement from me. I have an alibi.'

'Was Gudlaugur involved with the whores?'

'No. And there are no whores under my charge. I don't know where you get these stories from about pilfering from the kitchen and whores. They're nonsense. I'm not a pimp.'

'But—'

'We have certain information for people, for visitors. Foreigners at conferences. Icelanders too. They ask for company and we try to assist. If they meet pretty women at the bars here and feel good about it—'

'Then everyone's happy. Aren't they grateful customers?'

'Extremely.'

'So you're an escort provider, so to speak,' Erlendur said.

'I ...'

'And how romantic you make it all sound. The hotel manager's in it with you. What about the head of reception?'

Rósant hesitated.

'What about the head of reception?' Erlendur repeated.

'He doesn't share our desire to fulfil the customers' diverse needs.'

'The customers' diverse needs,' Erlendur mimicked. 'Where did you learn to talk like that?'

'At catering college.'

'And how do the head of reception's views fit in with yours?'

'There are occasional conflicts.'

Erlendur remembered the man from reception denying that there were prostitutes at the hotel, and thought to himself that he was probably the only member of the management who tried to safeguard the hotel's reputation.

'But you're trying to eliminate these conflicts, aren't you?'

'I don't know what you're talking about.'

'Does he get in your way?'

Rósant did not answer.

'It was you who set that whore on him, wasn't it? A little warning in case he was planning to say anything. You were out on the town, saw him and set one of your whores on him.'

Rósant stalled.

'I don't know what you're talking about,' he repeated.

'No, I bet you don't.'

'He's just so awfully honest,' Rósant said, his moustache lifting alarmingly. 'He refuses to understand that it's better for us to run this ourselves.'

Valgerdur was waiting for Erlendur at the bar. As at their previous meeting, she was wearing light make-up that accentuated her features, with a white silk blouse under a leather coat. They shook hands and she gave a faltering smile. He wondered whether this meeting would be like a fresh start to their acquaintance. He couldn't work out what she wanted from him, after apparently saying the final word about their friendship the time they met in the lobby. With a smile, she asked him if she could buy him a drink from the bar, or was he perhaps on duty?

'In films, cops aren't supposed to drink if they're on duty,' she said.

'I don't watch films.' Erlendur smiled.

'No,' she said. 'You read books about pain and death.'

They took a seat in one corner of the bar and sat in silence, watching the people milling around. As Christmas drew closer, Erlendur felt that the guests were growing noisier, there were endless carols playing over the sound system, the tourists brought in gaudy parcels and drank beer as if unaware that it was the most expensive in Europe, if not the world.

'You managed to get a sample from Wapshott,' he said.

'What kind of guy is he anyway? They had to knock him to the floor and force his mouth open. It was awesome to see the way he acted, the way he fought them off inside his cell.'

'I can't work him out really,' Erlendur said. 'I don't know exactly what he's doing here and I don't know exactly what he's hiding.'

He didn't want to go into details about Wapshott, nor talk about the child pornography and the sentences he had received in the UK for sex crimes. He didn't feel that was an appropriate topic of conversation with Valgerdur, besides which Wapshott had the right, in spite of everything, that Erlendur did not go blathering about his private life to everyone he met.

'I expect you're much more accustomed to this than I am,' Valgerdur said.

'I've never taken a saliva sample from a man who has been knocked to the floor and lies there screaming and shouting.'

Valgerdur laughed.

'I didn't mean that,' she said. 'I mean, I haven't sat down by myself with a man other than my husband for – I guess it must be thirty years. So you have to excuse me if I act … sheepish.'

'I'm just as clumsy,' Erlendur said. 'I don't have much experience either. It's almost a quarter of a century since I divorced my wife. You can count the women in my life on three fingers.'

'I think I'm divorcing him,' Valgerdur said gloomily, looking at Erlendur.

'What do you mean? Divorcing your husband?'

'I think it's over between us and I wanted to apologise to you.'

'To me?'

'Yes, you,' Valgerdur said. 'I'm such an idiot,' she groaned. 'I was going to use you to take revenge.'

'I don't follow,' Erlendur said.

'I hardly know myself. It's been awful ever since I found out.'

'What?'

'He's having an affair.'

She said this just like any other fact she had to live with and Erlendur couldn't discern how she felt, sensed only the emptiness behind her words.

'I don't know when it started or why,' she went on.

Then she stopped talking and Erlendur, at a loss for something to say, kept silent as well.

'Did you cheat on your wife?' she suddenly asked.

'No,' Erlendur said. 'It wasn't like that. We were young and we weren't compatible.'

'Compatible,' Valgerdur repeated after him, vacantly. 'What's that?'

'And you're going to divorce him?'

'I'm trying to get my bearings,' she said. 'It may depend on what he does.'

'What kind of an affair is it?'

'What kind? Is there any difference between affairs?'

'Has it been going on for years or has he just started? Has he had more than one maybe?'

'He says he's been with the same woman for two years. I haven't had the guts to ask him about the past, whether there were any others. That I never knew about. You never know anything. You trust your people, your husband, and the next thing you know is one day he starts talking about the marriage, then that he knows this woman and he's known her for two years, and you're like a total idiot. Don't realise what he's talking about. Then it turns out they've been meeting at hotels like this one ...'

Valgerdur stopped.

'Is she married, this woman?'

'Divorced. She's five years younger than him.'

'Has he given any explanation for the affair? Why he—?'

'Do you mean whether it's my fault?' Valgerdur interjected.

'No, I didn't mean ...'

'Maybe it is my fault,' she said. 'I don't know. There have been no explanations. Just anger and incomprehension, I think.'

'And your two sons?'

'We haven't told them. They've both left home. Not enough time for ourselves while they were there, too much time when they'd moved out. Maybe we didn't know each other any longer. Two strangers after all those years.'

They fell silent.

'You don't have to apologise to me for anything,' Erlendur said eventually, looking at her. 'Far from it. I'm the one who should apologise for not being straight with you. For lying to you.'

'Lying to me?'

'You asked why I was interested in deaths in the mountains, in storms and up on the moors, and I didn't tell you the truth. It's because I've hardly ever talked about it and find it difficult, I suppose. I don't think it's anyone else's business. Not my children's business either. My daughter had a near-fatal experience and I thought she was going to die – it was only then that I felt the need to talk about it to her. To tell her about it.'

'Talk about what?' Valgerdur asked. 'Was it something that happened?'

'My brother froze to death,' Erlendur said. 'When he was eight. He was never found and still hasn't been found.'

He had told a complete stranger, a woman at a hotel bar, what had been weighing down his heart for almost as long as he could remember. Maybe it was a long-awaited dream. Maybe he did not want to wage that war any longer.

'There's a story about us in one of those books on tragedies that I'm always reading,' he said. 'The story of what happened when my brother died, the search and the gloom and grief that engulfed our home. A remarkably accurate account actually, related by one of the leaders of the search party, which a friend of my father's wrote down.

All our names are given, it describes our household and my father's reaction, which was considered strange because he was overwhelmed by total hopelessness and self-recrimination, and sat in his room rigid and staring into space while everyone else was searching for all they were worth. We weren't asked permission when the account was published and my parents were extremely upset by it. I can show it to you some time if you want.'

Valgerdur nodded.

Erlendur began to tell her, she sat and listened, and when he had finished she leaned back in her seat and sighed.

'So you never found him?' she said.

Erlendur shook his head.

'Long after this happened, even sometimes today, I imagine he's not dead. That he got down from the moor, weatherbeaten and having lost his memory, and that I'll meet him some time later. I look for him in crowds and try to imagine what he looks like. Apparently this is not an uncommon reaction when no bodily remains are found. I know that from being in the police. Hope lives on when nothing else is left.'

'You must have been close,' Valgerdur said. 'You and your brother.'

'We were good friends,' Erlendur said.

They sat in deep silence, watching the hustle and bustle at the hotel from their respective worlds. Their glasses were empty and neither thought of ordering more. A good while passed until Erlendur cleared his throat, leaned over to her and asked her in a hesitant voice a question that had been preying on his mind ever since she started talking about her husband's infidelities.

'Do you still want to take revenge on him?'

Valgerdur looked at him and nodded.

'But not yet,' she said. 'I can't ...'

'No,' Erlendur said. 'You're right. Of course.'

'Why don't you tell me about one of those missing persons you're so interested in? That you're always reading about.'

Erlendur smiled, thought for a moment and then started telling her about a man who disappeared right in front of everyone's eyes: Jón Bergthórsson, a thief from Skagafjördur.

He went out onto the sea ice off the Skagi coast to fetch a shark that had been hauled up through a hole in the ice the previous day. Suddenly a southerly wind set in, it began to rain and the ice split and drifted out to sea with Jón on it. Rescuing him by boat was ruled out because of the storm, and the ice drifted northwards out of the fjord, driven by the southerly wind.

The last time Jón was seen was through a pair of binoculars as he scurried back and forth across the iceberg on the distant northern horizon.

29

The soft bar music had a soporific effect and they sat in silence until Valgerdur reached over and took hold of his hand.

'I'd better be going now,' she said.

Erlendur nodded and they both stood up. She kissed him on the cheek and stood pressed up against him for a moment.

Neither of them noticed when Eva Lind walked into the bar and saw them from a distance. Saw them stand up, saw her kiss him and apparently snuggle up against him. Eva Lind shuddered and marched over.

'Who's this old cow?' Eva said, staring at them.

'Eva,' Erlendur reproached her, startled at suddenly seeing his daughter in the bar. 'Be polite.'

Valgerdur held out her hand and Eva Lind looked at it, looked Valgerdur in the face and then back at the outstretched hand. Erlendur watched them both in turn and ended up glaring at Eva.

'Her name's Valgerdur and she's a good friend of mine,' he said.

Eva Lind looked at her father and at Valgerdur again but did not shake her hand. With an embarrassed smile, Valgerdur turned round. Erlendur followed her out of the bar and watched her cross the lobby. Eva Lind went over to him.

'What was that?' she said. 'Have you started buying the tarts at the bar here?'

'How could you be so rude?' Erlendur said. 'How could you think of behaving like that? It's none of your business. Leave me in bloody peace!'

'Right! You can go poking your nose into my business 24-fucking-7 but I'm not allowed to know who you're shagging at this hotel!'

'Stop talking such filth! What makes you think you can talk to me like that?'

Eva Lind stopped but glared angrily at her father. He stared at her, furious.

'What the hell do you want from me, child?' he shouted in her face, then ran after Valgerdur. She had left the hotel and through the revolving doors he saw her stepping into a taxi. When he came out onto the pavement in front of the hotel he saw the taxi's red rear lights fading in the distance and finally vanish around the corner.

Erlendur cursed as he watched the tail lights disappear. Not in any mood to go back to the bar where Eva Lind was waiting for him, he went back inside absent-mindedly and down the stairs to the basement, and before he realised he was in the corridor where Gudlaugur's room was. He found a switch and turned it on, and the few remaining working bulbs cast a gloomy light onto the corridor. He fumbled his way along until he reached the little room, opened the door and turned on the light. The Shirley Temple poster greeted his eyes.

The Little Princess.

He heard light footsteps along the corridor and Eva Lind appeared in the doorway.

'The girl upstairs said she saw you go down to the basement,' Eva said, looking into the room. Her gaze stopped at the bloodstains on the bed. 'Was it here that it happened?' she asked.

'Yes,' Erlendur said.

'What's that poster?'

'I don't know,' Erlendur said. 'I don't understand the way you act sometimes. You shouldn't go calling her an old cow and refuse to shake her hand. She hasn't done you any harm.'

Eva Lind said nothing.

'You ought to be ashamed of yourself,' Erlendur said.

'Sorry,' Eva said.

Erlendur didn't reply. He stood staring at the poster. Shirley Temple in a pretty summer frock with a ribbon in her hair, smiling in Technicolor. *The Little Princess*. Made in 1939, based on the story by Frances Hodgson Burnett. Temple played a lively girl who was sent to a London boarding school when her father went abroad: he left her in the care of a harsh headmistress.

Sigurdur Óli had found an entry about the film on the Internet. It left them none the wiser about why Gudlaugur had hung up the poster in his room.

The Little Princess, Erlendur thought to himself.

'I couldn't help thinking about Mum,' Eva Lind said behind him. 'When I saw her with you at the bar. And about me and Sindri, who you've never shown any interest in. Started thinking about all of us. Us as a family, because however you look at it we are still a family. In my mind anyway.'

She stopped.

Erlendur turned to face her.

'I don't understand that neglectfulness,' she went on. 'Especially towards me and Sindri. I don't get it. And you're not exactly helpful. Never want to talk about anything that involves you. Never talk about anything. Never say anything. It's like talking to a brick wall.'

'Why do you need explanations for everything?' Erlendur said. 'Some things can't be explained. And some things don't need to be explained.'

'Says the cop!'

'People talk too much,' Erlendur said. 'People should shut up more often. Then they wouldn't give themselves away so much.'

'You're talking about criminals. You're always thinking about criminals. We're your family!'

They fell silent.

'I've probably made mistakes,' Erlendur said at last. 'Not with your mother, I think. Though I might have. I don't know. People get divorced all the time and I found living with her unbearable. But I definitely did wrong by you and Sindri. And perhaps I didn't even appreciate it until you found me and started visiting me, and sometimes dragged your brother along with you. Didn't realise that I had two children I hadn't been in touch with for the whole of their childhood, who'd gone astray so early in life, and I started wondering whether my lack of action played any part in it. I've thought a lot about why that was. Just like you. Why I didn't go to court and secure my parental rights, fight tooth and nail to have you with me. Or try harder to persuade your mother and reach an agreement. Or just hang around outside your school to kidnap you.'

'You just weren't interested in us,' Eva Lind said. 'Isn't that the point?'

Erlendur said nothing.

'Isn't that the point?' Eva repeated.

Erlendur shook his head.

'No,' he said. 'I wish it were that simple.'

'Simple? What do you mean?'

'I think ...'

'What?'

'I don't know how to put this. I think ...'

'Yes.'

'I think I lost my life up on the moors too.'

'When your brother died?'

'It's hard to explain and maybe I can't. Maybe you can't explain everything and some things may be better left unexplained.'

'What do you mean, lost your life?'

'I'm not ... a part of me died.'

'Please ...'

'I was found and rescued, but I died too. Something inside me. Something I had before. I don't know exactly what it was. My brother died and I think something inside me died too. I always felt he was my responsibility, and I failed him. That's the way I've felt ever since. I've been guilty that it was me and not him who survived. I've avoided looking anything in the face ever since. And even if I wasn't directly neglected, the way I neglected you and Sindri, it was as if I no longer mattered. I don't know if I'm right and I never will know, but I felt it as soon as I came down from the moor and I've felt it ever since.'

'All these years?'

'You can't measure time in feelings.'

'Because it was you and not him who survived.'

'Instead of trying to rebuild something from the ruins, which I think I was trying to do when I met your mother, I dug myself down deeper into it because it's comfortable there and it looks like sanctuary. Like when you take drugs. It's more comfortable that way. That's your sanctuary. And as you know, even if you are aware that you're doing other people wrong, your own self matters most. That's why you go on taking drugs. That's why I dig myself down over and again into the snowdrift.'

Eva Lind stared at her father, and although she did not fully comprehend him, she realised that he was making an absolutely candid attempt to explain what had puzzled her all the time and had prompted her to track him down when she did. She understood that she had penetrated a place within him that no one else had ever been to, not even him, except to make sure that everything there remained undisturbed.

'And that woman? Where does she come into the picture?'

Erlendur shrugged, and started to close the door that had come ajar.

'I don't know,' he said.

They stayed silent for a while until Eva Lind made her excuses and left. Unsure which direction to take, she peered into the darkness at the end of the corridor, and Erlendur suddenly noticed she was sniffing at the air like a dog.

'Can you smell that?' she said, sticking her nose up into the air.

'Smell what?' Erlendur said. 'What are you talking about?'

'Hash,' Eva Lind said. 'Dope. Do you mean to tell me you've never smelled hash?'

'Hash?'

'Can't you smell it?'

Erlendur went out into the corridor and started sniffing into the air as well.

'Is that what it is?' he said.

'You're asking the expert,' she said.

She was still sniffing at the air.

'Someone's been smoking hash down here, and not very long ago,' she said.

Erlendur knew that forensics had lit up the end of the corridor when the body was taken away, but was uncertain whether it had been fine-combed.

He looked at Eva Lind.

'Hash?'

'You're on the scent,' she said.

He went back into the room, took a chair and placed it in the corridor underneath one of the functional light bulbs, which he unscrewed. The bulb was scorching and he had to use the sleeve of his jacket to grip it. He found a blown bulb at the dark end of the corridor and swapped them. Suddenly it was illuminated and Erlendur jumped down from the chair.

At first they could see nothing of note, until Eva Lind pointed out to her father how spotlessly clean the alcove at the end seemed to be compared with the rest of the corridor. Erlendur nodded. It was as if every single spot on the floor had been cleaned and the walls wiped down.

Erlendur got down on all fours and scanned the floor. Heating pipes ran along all the walls at floor level and he looked under the pipes and crawled alongside them.

Eva Lind saw him stop and fish under the pipe to fetch something that had caught his attention. He got to his feet, walked over to her and showed her what he had found.

'At first I thought it was rat droppings,' he said, holding up a little brown lump between his fingers.

'What is it?' Eva Lind asked.

'It's a gauze,' Erlendur said.

'A gauze?'

'Yes, containing chewing tobacco that you put under your lip. Someone has thrown away or spat out his chewing tobacco here in this corridor.'

'But who? Who could have been in this corridor?'

Erlendur looked at Eva Lind.

'Someone who's a bigger tart than I am,' he said.

CHRISTMAS EVE

30

He found out that Ösp was working on the floor above his room, and he went up the stairs after having coffee and toast from the breakfast buffet.

He contacted Sigurdur Óli about some information he needed him to gather and phoned Elínborg to find out whether she had remembered to question the woman Stefanía claimed to have met at the hotel when she was captured on the security camera. Elínborg had gone out and did not answer her mobile.

Erlendur had lain awake in bed until almost morning, in pitch darkness. When he finally got up he looked out of the hotel window. It would be a white Christmas this year. The snow was setting in seriously. He could see it in the light from the lamp posts. Thick snow fell into the light they shed and formed a kind of backdrop for Christmas Eve.

Eva Lind had said goodbye to him in the basement corridor. She was going to meet him at home that evening. They were going to boil some smoked lamb and when he woke up he started wondering what to give her for Christmas. He had given her small presents after she began spending Christmas with him and she had given him socks, which she admitted she had stolen, and once a pair of gloves, which she said she had bought and he soon lost. She never asked about them. Perhaps the aspect of his daughter's character that he liked most was that she never asked about anything unless it mattered.

Sigurdur Óli called him with the information. It wasn't much, but enough to go on. Erlendur didn't know exactly what he was looking for, but thought his hypothesis was worth putting to the test.

He watched her working on her hotel floor as before, until she noticed him. She did not show any particular surprise at seeing him.

'Are you up?' she said, as if he was the laziest guest at the hotel.

'It took me ages to get to sleep,' he said. 'Actually I was thinking about you all night.'

'Me?' Ösp said, putting a heap of towels into a laundry basket. 'Nothing dirty, I hope. I've had enough of dirty old men at this hotel.'

'No,' Erlendur said. 'Nothing dirty.'

'Fatso asked me if I'd been grassing to you, telling you shit. And the chef shouted at me like I was stealing from his buffet. They knew we'd been talking.'

'Everyone knows more or less everything about everyone else at this hotel,' Erlendur said. 'But they never *really* say anything about anyone. Such people are very difficult to deal with. Like you, for example.'

'Me?' Ösp went into the room she was cleaning and Erlendur followed her inside as he had done before.

'You tell me everything and I believe every word because you create an honest and truthful impression, but actually you're only telling a fraction of what you know, which is also a lie of sorts. No less serious for us, the police. That sort of lie. Do you know what I'm talking about?'

Ösp did not reply. She was busy changing the beds. Erlendur watched her. He couldn't read what she was thinking. She acted as if he wasn't in the room. As if she could shake him off if she just pretended he was not there.

'For example, you didn't tell me that you have a brother,' Erlendur said.

'Why should I tell you that?'

'Because he's in trouble.'

'He's not in any trouble.'

'Not with me, he's not,' Erlendur said. 'I haven't got him into trouble. But he is in trouble and he sometimes goes to his sister for help when he needs it.'

'I don't get you,' Ösp said.

'I'll tell you. He's been in prison twice, not long stretches, for burglary and theft. Some of it has been found out, other things doubtless haven't, that's the way it goes. These are typical petty offences by a small-time criminal. Typical crimes by a junkie who's in debt. He's on the most expensive stuff now and never has enough money. But dealers don't do things by halves. They've caught him more than once and beaten him up. Once they threatened to kneecap him. So he needs to do odd jobs besides stealing to buy his drugs. To cover his debts.'

Ösp put down the linen.

'He has various recourses for financing his habit,' Erlendur said. 'You probably know that. Like all those kids do. Kids who are hopeless junkies.'

Ösp remained silent.

'Do you understand what I'm saying?'

'Did Stína tell you this?' Ösp said. 'I saw her here yesterday. I've often seen her here and if anyone's a tart it's her.'

'She didn't tell me any of this,' Erlendur said, not allowing Ösp to change the subject. 'It wasn't long ago your brother was in the corridor where Gudlaugur was living. He could even have been there since the murder. He may have been there very recently. His smell's still there, for those who recognise it. For people who smoke hash and use speed and cook heroin.'

Ösp stared at him. Erlendur didn't have much to work on when he went to see her. Only the fact that the alcove was spotlessly clean, but he could tell from her reaction that what he was saying was not so wide of the mark. He wondered whether to take an even greater gamble. After deliberating for a while, he decided to give it a shot.

'We found his chewing tobacco too,' Erlendur said. 'Has he been using that for long?'

Ösp was still staring at him without saying a word. Finally she looked down at the bed. Took a long look, until she seemed to resign herself.

'Since he was fifteen,' she said, almost inaudibly.

He waited for her to go on, but she added nothing and they stood facing each other in the hotel room, and Erlendur allowed the silence to reign for a while. In the end Ösp sighed and sat down on the bed.

'He's always broke,' she said softly. 'Owes everyone money. All the time. And then they threaten him and beat him up, but he still keeps on and his debts mount up. Sometimes he gets money and can pay part of it off. Mum and Dad gave up on him ages ago. Threw him out when he was seventeen. They sent him to rehab and he ran away. He didn't come home for a week or so and they put a missing persons announcement in the papers. He didn't give a shit. He's been dossing around ever since. I'm the only one in the family who keeps in touch with him. Sometimes I let him into the basement in the winter. He's slept in the alcove when he needs to hide. I've banned him from having drugs down there but I can't control him either. No one has any control over him.'

'Have you given him money? To pay off those debts?'

'Sometimes, but it's never enough. They've been round to Mum and Dad threatening blue murder and they smashed Dad's car in, so now they're paying to try to get the thugs off their backs, but it's just so much. They charge ridiculous interest on those debts and when they talk to the police, guys like you, the cops say they can't do anything because it's only threats, and apparently it's OK to threaten people.'

She looked at Erlendur.

'If they kill Dad, maybe you'll look into the matter.'

'Did your brother know Gudlaugur? They must have known about each other. From the basement.'

'They knew each other,' Ösp said gloomily.

'How?'

'Gulli paid him for …' Ösp stopped.

'For what?'

'Favours he did.'

'Sexual favours?'

'Yes, sexual favours.'

'How do you know that?'

'My brother told me.'

'Was he with Gudlaugur that afternoon?'

'I don't know. I haven't seen him for days, not since …' She stopped. 'I haven't seen him since Gudlaugur was stabbed,' she then said. 'He hasn't been in touch.'

'I think he may have been in the corridor not so long ago. Since Gudlaugur's murder.'

'I haven't seen him.'

'Do you think he attacked Gudlaugur?'

'I don't know,' Ösp said. 'All I know is that he's never attacked anyone. And he's constantly on the run and he must be on the run now because of this, even though he didn't do anything. He could never hurt anyone.'

'And you don't know where he is now?'

'No, I haven't heard from him.'

'Do you know whether he knew that British man I mentioned to you. Henry Wapshott? The one with the child pornography.'

'No, he didn't know him. I don't think so anyway. What are you asking that for?'

'Is he gay? Your brother?'

Ösp looked at him.

'I know he does anything for money,' she said. 'But I don't think he's gay.'

'Will you tell him I want to talk to him. If he noticed anything in the basement I need to speak to him about it. I also need to ask him about his relationship with Gudlaugur. I need to know whether he saw him the day he was murdered. Will you do that for me? Tell him I need to talk to him?'

'Do you think he did it? Killed Gudlaugur?'

'I don't know,' Erlendur said. 'If I don't hear from him very soon I'll have to declare him wanted for questioning.'

Ösp showed no reaction.

'Did you know that Gudlaugur was gay?' he asked.

Ösp looked up.

'Judging from what my brother said he seems to have been. And judging from what he paid my brother for being with him ...'

Ösp stopped.

'Did you know that Gudlaugur was dead when you were asked to go and fetch him?' Erlendur asked.

She looked at him.

'No, I didn't know. Don't try to pin this on me. Is that what you're trying to do? Do you reckon I killed him?'

'You didn't tell me about your brother in the basement.'

'He's always in trouble but I know he didn't do that. I know he could never do anything like that. Never.'

'You two must be close, the way you take care of him.'

'We've always been good friends,' Ösp said as she stood up. 'I'll talk to him if he gets in touch. Tell him you need to meet him in case he knows anything about what happened.'

With a nod, Erlendur said he would be at the hotel for most of the day and she could always find him there.

'It has to happen right away, Ösp,' he said.

31

When Erlendur went back down to the lobby he noticed Elínborg at the reception desk. The head of reception pointed towards him and Elínborg turned round. She was looking for him and walked over briskly wearing a concerned expression that Erlendur seldom saw.

'Is something the matter?' he asked as she approached.

'Can we sit down somewhere?' she said. 'Is the bar open yet? God, what a pathetic job this is! I don't know why I bother.'

'What's up?' Erlendur asked, taking her by the arm and leading her to the bar. The door was closed but not locked, and they went inside. Although the room was open, the bar itself seemed to be closed. Erlendur saw a sign saying it would not open for another hour. They sat down in one of the booths.

'And my Christmas is being ruined,' Elínborg said. 'I've never done so little baking. And all the in-laws are coming tonight and—'

'Tell me what happened,' Erlendur said.

'What a cock-up,' Elínborg said. 'I don't understand him. I simply don't understand him.'

'Who?'

'The boy!' Elínborg said. 'I don't understand what he means.'

She told Erlendur that, instead of going home and baking cookies the previous evening, she had dropped in at Kleppur mental hospital. Exactly why she did not know, but she couldn't get the case of the boy and his father out of her mind. When Erlendur chipped in that she may just have had enough of baking for her in-laws, she didn't even smile.

She had been to the mental hospital once before to try to talk to the boy's mother, but the woman was so ill then that she hardly uttered a word of sense. The same happened again on this second visit. His mother sat rocking back and forth, in a world of her own. Elínborg wasn't quite sure what she wanted to hear her say, but thought she might know something about the relationship between the father and the son that had not yet come to light.

She knew that his mother would only be in hospital temporarily. She was admitted intermittently, when she went through a phase of flushing her psychiatric medication down the toilet. When she took her pills she was generally in reasonable condition. She took good care of their home. When Elínborg mentioned the boy's mother to his teachers, they also said she seemed to look after him well.

Elínborg sat in the hospital lounge where the nurse had brought the boy's mother, and watched her twiddling her hair around her index finger, muttering something Elínborg could not make out. She tried to talk to her but the mother seemed to be miles away. Offered no response to her questions. It was as though she was sleepwalking.

After sitting with her for a while, Elínborg started thinking about all the assortments of cookies that she still had to bake. She stood up to fetch someone to take the woman back to the ward and found a warder in the corridor. He was about thirty and looked like a body-builder. He was wearing white trousers and a white T-shirt, and his strong biceps rippled with every movement of his body. His hair was crewcut and he had a round, chubby face with little eyes sunk deep into his head. Elínborg didn't ask his name.

He followed her into the lounge.

'Oh, it's old Dóra,' the warder said, walking over and taking the woman by the arm. 'You're pretty quiet tonight.'

The woman stood up, just as confused as ever.

'Stoned out of your tree again, are you, old girl,' the warder said in a tone that Elínborg disliked. It was like he was talking to a five-year-old. And what did he mean by saying she was pretty quiet tonight? Elínborg couldn't hold herself back.

'Will you stop talking to her like a little kid,' she said, more brashly than she had intended.

The warder looked at her.

'Is that any of your business?' he said.

'She's entitled to be treated with respect just like everyone else,' Elínborg said, but desisted from saying she was from the police.

'Maybe she is,' the warder said. 'And I don't think I'm treating her disrespectfully. Come on, Dóra,' he went on, leading her out into the corridor.

Elínborg followed close behind.

'What did you mean when you said she's pretty quiet tonight?'

'Quiet tonight?' the warder repeated, turning his head towards Elínborg.

'You said she was pretty quiet tonight,' Elínborg said. 'Wasn't she supposed to be?'

'I sometimes call her the Fugitive,' the warder said. 'She's always on the run.'

Elínborg didn't follow.

'What are you talking about?'

'Haven't you seen the movie?' the warder asked.

'Does she escape?' Elínborg said. 'From this hospital?'

'Or when we take them on trips into town,' the warder said. 'She ran away the last time we went. We were shitting bricks when you found her at the bus station and brought her back here to the ward. You didn't treat her with much respect then.'

'I found her?'

'I know you're from the cops. The cops literally threw her at us.'

'What day was this?'

He thought about it. He had been accompanying her and two other patients when she slipped away. They were on Laekjartorg square at the time. He remembered the date well, it was the same day that he set his personal best on the bench press.

The date matched that of the attack on the boy.

'Wasn't her husband informed when she ran away from you?' Elínborg asked.

'We were about to phone him when you found her. We always give them a few hours to come back. Otherwise we'd spend all our time on the phone.'

'Does her husband know that you call her that? The Fugitive.'

'We don't call her that. It's only me. He doesn't know.'

'Does he know that she runs away?'

'I haven't told him. She always comes back.'

'I don't believe this,' Elínborg said.

'When she comes in here she has to be drugged right up to stop her running off,' the warder said.

'This changes everything!'

'Come on, Dóra old girl,' the warder said, and the door to the ward closed behind him.

Elínborg stared at Erlendur.

'I was positive it was him. The father. Now she could have run away, gone home, assaulted the boy and hopped back out. If only the boy would open his mouth!'

'Why should she assault her son?'

'I've no idea,' Elínborg said. 'Maybe she hears voices.'

'And the broken fingers and bruises? All that over the years? Is it always her then?'

'I don't know.'

'Have you spoken to the father?'

'I've just come from seeing him.'

'And?'

'Naturally, we're not the best of friends. He hasn't been allowed to see the boy since we burst into their home and turned everything upside-down. He showered me with abuse and—'

'Did he say anything about his wife, the boy's mother?' Erlendur butted in impatiently. 'He must have suspected her.'

'And the boy hasn't said a thing,' Elínborg continued.

'Except that he misses his father,' Erlendur said.

'Yes, apart from that. So his father finds him in his room upstairs and thinks he's crawled home from school in that state.'

'You visited the boy in hospital and asked if it was his father who assaulted him, and he made some reaction that convinced you it was.'

'I must have misunderstood him,' Elínborg said, her head bowed. 'I read something into his manner ...'

'But we have nothing to prove it was the mother. We have nothing to prove it wasn't the father.'

'I told him, the boy's father, that I'd been to the hospital to talk to his wife and that we know nothing about her whereabouts on the day of the assault. He was surprised. As if it never occurred to him that she could escape from the hospital. He's still convinced it was the boys in the school playground. He said the boy would tell us if his mother had assaulted him. He's convinced of that.'

'So why doesn't the boy name her?'

'He's in a state of shock, poor thing. I don't know.'

'Love?' Erlendur said. 'In spite of everything she's done to him.'

'Or fear,' Elínborg said. 'Maybe a huge fear that she'll do it again. Either way he might be keeping quiet to protect his mother. It's impossible to say.'

'What do you want us to do? Should we drop the charges against the father?'

'I'm going to talk to the State Prosecutor's office and find out what they say.'

'Start with that. Tell me another thing, did you phone the woman who was with Stefanía Egilsdóttir at this hotel a few days before Gudlaugur was stabbed?'

'Yes,' Elínborg said vacantly. 'She asked her friend to vouch for her but when it came to the crunch she couldn't go through with the lie.'

'You mean lie for Stefanía?'

'She began by saying that they'd been sitting here, but she was very hesitant about it, and she was such a bad liar that when I said I had to bring her down to the station to make a statement she started crying over the phone. She told me how Stefanía phoned her, they're old friends from a music society, and asked her to say they were together at this hotel if she was asked. She said she refused, but Stefanía appears to have some hold over her and she won't tell me what it is.'

'It was a poor lie from the start,' Erlendur said. 'We both knew she let it slip out. I don't know why she's holding up the investigation like this unless she knows it's her fault.'

'You mean that she killed her brother?'

'Or she knows who did.'

They lingered at their table for a while and talked about the boy, his father and mother and the difficult family circumstances, which prompted Elínborg to ask Erlendur once again what he was going to do for Christmas. He said he was going to be with Eva Lind.

He told Elínborg about his discovery in the basement corridor and his suspicions that Ösp's brother was somehow involved, a delinquent with endless money problems. He thanked Elínborg for the invitation and told her to take off the rest of the time until Christmas.

'There isn't any time until Christmas.' Elínborg smiled, and shrugged as if Christmas no longer mattered, what with all the cleaning and cookies and in-laws.

'Will you get any Christmas presents?' she asked.

'Maybe some socks,' Erlendur said. 'Hopefully.'

He hesitated before saying: 'Don't upset yourself about the boy's father. These things always happen. We feel certain, convinced even, then something always comes along that erodes it.'

Elínborg nodded.

Erlendur followed her through the lobby and they exchanged farewells. He planned to go up to his room to pack. He'd had enough of the hotel. He was seriously beginning to miss his 'hole with nothing in it', his books, his armchair and even Eva Lind lying on the sofa.

He was standing waiting for the lift when Ösp surprised him.

'I've found him,' she said.

'Who?' Erlendur said. 'Your brother?'

'Come with me,' Ösp said, heading for the stairs to the basement. Erlendur hesitated. The lift doors opened and he looked inside. He was on the trail of the murderer. Perhaps Ösp's brother had come to turn himself in at her urging: the lad with the chewing tobacco. Erlendur felt no excitement about it. None of the expectation or sense of triumph that accompanied solving a case. All he felt was fatigue and sadness because the case had stirred up all manner of associations with his own childhood, and he knew he had so much left to come to terms with in his own life that he had no idea where to begin. Most of all he wanted to forget about work and go home. Be with Eva Lind. Help her to get over the troubles she was dealing with. He wanted to stop thinking about others and start thinking about himself and his own people.

'Are you coming?' Ösp said in a low voice, standing on the stairs and waiting.

'I'm coming,' Erlendur said.

He followed her down the stairs and into the staff coffee room where he had first spoken to her. It was as squalid as ever. She locked the door behind them. Her brother was sitting at one of the tables and leaped to his feet when Erlendur walked in.

'I didn't do anything,' he said in a high-pitched voice. 'Ösp says you think I did it, but I didn't do anything. I didn't do anything to him!'

He was wearing a dirty blue anorak with a rip on one shoulder that revealed the white lining. His jeans were black with grime and he was wearing scruffy black boots that could be laced up to the calves, but Erlendur saw no laces in them. His fingers were long and filthy, clutching a cigarette. He inhaled the smoke and blew it back out. His voice was agitated and he paced back and forth in the corner of the kitchen like a caged animal, cornered by a policeman who was poised to arrest him.

Erlendur looked over his shoulder at Ösp, who was standing by the door, then back at her brother.

'You must trust your sister to come here like this.'

'I didn't do anything,' he said. 'She told me you were cool and just wanted some information.'

'I need to know about your relationship with Gudlaugur,' Erlendur said.

'I didn't stab him,' he said.

Erlendur sized him up. He was halfway between adolescence and adulthood, peculiarly childlike but with a hardened expression that displayed anger and bitterness towards something that Erlendur could not even begin to imagine.

'No one is suggesting you did,' Erlendur said reassuringly, trying to calm him down. 'How did you know Gudlaugur? What relationship did you have?'

He looked at his sister but Ösp just stood by the door and said nothing.

'I did him favours sometimes and he paid me for it,' he said.

'And how did you know each other? Have you known him for a long time?'

'He knew I was Ösp's brother. He thought it was funny that we're brother and sister, like everyone does.'

'Why?'

'My name's Reynir.'

'So? What's funny about that?'

'Ösp and Reynir. Aspen and Rowan. Brother and sister. Mum and Dad's little joke. Like they're into forestry.'

'What about Gudlaugur?'

'I first saw him here when I came to meet Ösp. About half a year ago.'

'And?'

'He knew who I was. Ösp had told him a bit about me. She sometimes let me sleep at the hotel. On his corridor.'

Erlendur turned to Ösp.

'You cleaned that alcove very carefully,' he said.

Ösp gave him a blank look and did not reply. He turned back to Reynir.

'He knew who you were. You slept on the corridor in front of his room. What then?'

'He owed me money. Said he would pay.'

'Why did he owe you money?'

'Because I did him favours sometimes and—'

'Did you know he was gay?'

'Isn't that obvious?'

'And the condom?'

'We always used condoms. He was paranoid. He said he didn't take chances. Said he didn't know if I was infected or not. I'm not infected,' he said emphatically and looked at his sister.

'And you chew tobacco.'

He looked at Erlendur in surprise.

'What's that got to do with it?'

'That's not the point. Do you chew tobacco?'

'Yes.'

'Were you with him the day he was stabbed?'

'Yes. He asked me to see him because he was going to pay me.'

'How did he get hold of you?'

Reynir took a mobile phone out of his pocket and showed it to Erlendur.

'When I arrived he was putting on his Santa suit,' he said. 'He said he had to rush off to the Christmas party, paid me what he owed, looked at his watch and saw he had time for a quickie.'

'Did he have a lot of money in his room?'

'Not that I knew of. I just saw what he paid me. But he said he was expecting a load of money.'

'Where from?'

'I don't know. He said he was sitting on a goldmine.'

'What did he mean by that?'

'It was something he was going to sell. I don't know what it was. He didn't tell me. Just said he was expecting loads of money, or a lot of money, he never said loads. He never talked like that. Always spoke polite and used classy words. He was always really courteous. A good bloke. Never did me any harm. Always paid. I know loads of worse people than him. Sometimes he just wanted to talk to me. He was lonely, or at least he said he was. Told me I was his only friend.'

'Did he tell you anything about his past?'

'No.'

'Nothing about being a child star once?'

'No. A child star? At what?'

'Did you see a knife in his room that could have come from the hotel kitchen?'

'Yes, I saw a knife in there but I don't know where it came from.

When I went to see him he was picking away at his Santa suit. He said he had to get a new one for next Christmas.'

'And he didn't have any money besides what he paid you?'

'No, I don't think so.'

'Did you rob him?'

'No.'

'Did you take half a million that was in his room?'

'Half a million? Did he have half a million?!'

'I'm told you always need money. It's obvious how you get it. There are people you owe money. They've threatened your family ...'

Reynir glared at his sister.

'Don't look at her, look at me. Gudlaugur had money in his room. More than he owed you. Maybe he'd sold part of his goldmine. You saw the money. You wanted more. You did things for him that you thought you ought to be paid more for. He refused, you argued, you grabbed the knife and tried to stab him, but he held you off until you managed to sink the knife into his chest and kill him. You took the money ...'

'You tosser,' Reynir hissed. 'What fucking bollocks!'

' ... and since then you've been smoking hash and shooting up or whatever it is you—'

'You fucking creep!' Reynir shouted.

'Go on with the story,' Ösp called out. 'Tell him what you told me. Tell him everything!'

'Everything about what?' Erlendur said.

'He asked me if I'd give him one before he went up to the Christmas party,' Reynir said. 'He said he didn't have much time but had money and he'd pay me well. But when we were starting that woman burst in on us.'

'That woman?'

'Yes.'

'What woman?'

'The one who caught us.'

'Tell him,' Erlendur heard Ösp say behind his back. 'Tell him who it was!'

'What woman are you talking about?'

'We forgot to lock the door and suddenly the door opened and she burst in on us.'

'Who?'

'I don't know who it was. Some woman.'

'And what happened?'

'I don't know. I buggered off. She shouted something at him and I legged it.'

'Why didn't you give us this information straight away?'

'I avoid the cops. There's all kinds of people after me and if they know I'm talking to the cops they'll think I'm grassing and they'll get me for it.'

'Who was this woman who caught you? What did she look like?'

'I didn't really notice. I buggered off. He was mortified. Pushed me away and shouted and totally lost it. He seemed to be terrified of her. Scared shitless.'

'What did he shout?' Erlendur asked.

'Steffí.'

'What?'

'Steffí. That was all I heard. Steffí. He called her Steffí and he was scared shitless of her.'

32

She was standing outside the door to his room with her back to him. Erlendur stopped and watched her for a moment, and saw how she had changed since the first time he saw her, storming into the hotel with her father. Now she was just a tired and weary middle-aged woman who still lived with her crippled father in the house that had always been her home. For reasons unknown to him, this woman had come to the hotel and murdered her brother.

It was as if she sensed his presence in the corridor, because suddenly she turned round and looked at him. He could not decipher her thoughts from the expression on her face. All he knew was that she was the person he had been looking for since he first went to the hotel and saw Santa sitting in a pool of his own blood.

She stood still by the door and said nothing until he was standing right next to her.

'There's something I have to tell you,' she said. 'If it makes any difference.'

Erlendur thought she had come to see him concerning the lie about her friend and felt the time had come to tell him the truth. He opened the door and she walked in ahead of him, went to the window and watched the snow.

'They forecast it wouldn't snow this Christmas,' she said.

'Are you ever called Steffi for short?' he asked.

'When I was small,' she said, still looking out of the window.

'Did you brother call you Steffí?'

'Yes, he did,' she said. 'Always. And I always called him Gulli. Why do you ask?'

'Why were you at this hotel five days before your brother's death?'

Stefanía gave a deep sigh.

'I know I shouldn't have lied to you.'

'Why did you come?'

'It was to do with his records. We thought we were entitled to some of them. We knew he had quite a few copies, probably all the ones that didn't sell when they came out, and we wanted a share if he was planning to sell.'

'How did he acquire the copies?'

'Dad had them and kept them at home in Hafnarfjördur, and when Gudlaugur moved out he took the boxes with him. He said they belonged to him. To him alone.'

'How did you know he was planning to sell them?'

Stefanía hesitated.

'I also lied about Henry Wapshott,' she said. 'I do know him. Not very well, but I should have told you about him. Didn't he tell you he met us?'

'No,' Erlendur said. 'He has a number of problems. Is anything true that you've told me up to now?'

She did not answer him.

'Why should I believe what you're telling me now?'

Stefanía watched the snow falling to earth and was remote, as if she had vanished back into a life she led long ago when she knew no lies and everything was the truth, fresh and pure.

'Stefanía?' Erlendur said.

'They didn't argue about his singing,' she said suddenly. 'When Dad fell down the stairs. It wasn't about singing. That's the last and the biggest lie.'

'You mean when they had a fight on the landing?'

'Do you know what the kids called him at school?'

'I believe I do,' Erlendur said.

'They called him The Little Princess.'

'Because he sang in the choir and was a sissy and—'

'Because they caught him wearing one of Mum's dresses,' Stefanía interrupted him.

She turned away from the window.

'It was after she died. He missed her terribly, especially when he wasn't a choirboy any more but just a normal boy with a normal voice. Dad didn't know, but I did. When Dad was out he sometimes put on Mum's jewellery and sometimes he tried on her dresses, stood in front of the mirror, even put on make-up. And once, it was in the summer, some boys walked past the house and saw him. Some were in his class. They peeped in through the living-room window. They used to do that sometimes because we were considered odd. They started to laugh and jeer, mercilessly. After that he was considered an absolute freak at school. The kids started calling him The Little Princess.'

Stefanía paused.

'I thought he just missed Mum,' she continued. 'That it was his way of getting close to her, wearing her clothes and putting on her jewellery. I didn't think he had unnatural urges. But it turned out otherwise.'

'Unnatural urges?' Erlendur said. 'Is that how you regard it? Your brother was a homosexual. Haven't you been able to forgive him for that? Is that why you had no contact with him for all those years?'

'He was very young when our father caught him with a boy. I knew he had his friend in his room, I thought they were doing their home-work together. Dad came home unexpectedly to look for something and when he walked into Gudlaugur's room he saw them doing something abominable. He wouldn't tell me what it was. When I came out the other boy was running down the stairs, Dad and Gulli were on the landing shouting at each other, and I saw Gulli give him a shove. He lost his balance, fell down the stairs and never stood up again.'

Stefanía turned back to the window and watched the Christmas snow gliding to earth. Erlendur said nothing, wondering what she thought about when she disappeared within herself like now, but he could not imagine it. He thought he gained some kind of answer when she broke the silence.

'I never mattered,' she said. 'Everything I did was a secondary consideration. I'm not saying that from self-pity, I think I stopped that ages ago. More to try to understand and explain why I never had any contact with him after that awful day. Sometimes I think I gloated over the way everything turned out. Can you imagine that?'

Erlendur shook his head.

'When he left, I was the one who mattered. Not him. Never again him. And in some strange way I was pleased, pleased that he never became the great child star he was supposed to become. I expect I envied him the whole time, much more than I realised, for all the attention he got and the voice he had. It was divine. It was as if he'd been blessed with all those talents but I had none; I thumped away at the piano like a horse. That was what Dad called it when he tried to teach me. Said I was totally devoid of talent. Yet I worshipped him because I thought he was always right. Usually he was kind to me and when he became unable to look after himself my talent became looking after him. I was indispensable to him then. And the years went by without anything changing. Gulli left home, Dad was in a wheelchair and I took care of him. Never thought about myself at all, what it was that I wanted. The years can pass like that without you doing anything except living in the rut you create for yourself. Year after year after year.'

She paused and watched the snow.

'When you begin to perceive that that is all you have, you start to hate it and try to find the culprit, and I felt my brother was to blame for everything. Over time I began to despise him and the perversion that ruined our lives.'

Erlendur was about to add something, but she went on.

'I don't know if I can describe this better. How you lock yourself up inside your own monotonous life because of something that, decades later, turns out to be so unimportant. Actually turns out to be unimportant and harmless.'

'We understand that he thought he had been robbed of his childhood,' Erlendur said. 'That he wasn't allowed to be what he wanted to be, but was forced to be something completely different, a singer, a child star, and he paid the price when he was bullied at school. Then it all came to nothing and those "unnatural urges", as you call them, compound the picture. I don't think he can have been very happy. Maybe he didn't want all that attention you clearly longed for.'

'Robbed of his childhood,' Stefanía said. 'Could well be.'

'Did your brother ever try to discuss his homosexuality with your father or you?' Erlendur asked.

'No, but we might have seen it coming. I don't know if he even realised what was happening to him. I have no idea about it. I don't think he knew why he wore Mum's dresses. I don't know how or when those people discover they're different.'

'But he was fond of the nickname in some perverse way,' Erlendur said. 'He's got this poster and we know that …' Erlendur stopped mid-sentence. He didn't know whether to tell her that Gudlaugur had asked his lover to call him Little Princess.

'I don't know anything about that,' Stefanía said. 'He could have been tormenting himself with the memory of what happened. Maybe there was something inside him that we'll never understand.'

'How did you get to know Henry Wapshott?'

'He came to our house one day and wanted to talk about Gudlaugur's records. He wanted to know whether we had any copies. It was last Christmas. He had obtained information about Gudlaugur and his family through some collector and told me that his records were incredibly valuable abroad. He had talked to my brother, who refused to sell him any, but that changed somehow and he was prepared to let Wapshott have what he wanted.'

'And you wanted your share of the profits.'

'We didn't think that was unreasonable. It didn't belong to him any more or less than to my father. At least, that was how we saw it. Our father paid for the recordings out of his own pocket.'

'Was a substantial sum involved? That Wapshott offered for the records?'

Stefanía nodded. 'Millions.'

'That corresponds with what we know.'

'He has plenty of money, that Wapshott man. I believe he wanted to avoid the records going into the collectors' market. If I understood him correctly, he wanted to acquire all the existing copies of the records and prevent them from flooding the market. He was very straightforward about it and was prepared to pay an incredible sum. I think he finally talked Gudlaugur round just before this Christmas. Something must have changed for him to attack him like that.'

'Attack him like that? What do you mean?'

'Well, haven't you got him in custody?'

'Yes,' Erlendur said, 'but we have no proof that he attacked your brother. What do you mean by "something must have changed"?'

'Wapshott visited us in Hafnarfjördur and said he had persuaded Gudlaugur to sell him all the copies, and I expect he was making sure that there were no others around. We told him there weren't, Gudlaugur had taken them all when he left home.'

'That's why you went to the hotel to meet him,' Erlendur said. 'To get your cut of the sale.'

'He was wearing his doorman's uniform,' Stefanía said. 'He was in the lobby carrying suitcases out to a car for some tourists. I watched him for a while and then he saw me. I said I had to talk to him about the records. He asked about Dad ...'

'Did your father send you to see Gudlaugur?'

'No, he would never have done that. After the accident he never wanted to hear his name mentioned.'

'But he was the first thing Gudlaugur asked about when he saw you at the hotel.'

'Yes. We went down to his room and I asked where the records were.'

*

'They're in a safe place,' Gudlaugur said, smiling at his sister. 'Henry told me he'd talked to you.'

'He told us you were planning to sell him the records. Dad said half of them are his and we want half of the proceeds.'

'I've changed my mind,' Gudlaugur said. 'I'm not going to sell them.'

'What did Wapshott say to that?'

'He wasn't pleased.'

'He's offering a very good price for them.'

'I can get more for them if I sell them myself, one at a time. Collectors are very interested in them. I think Wapshott's going to do the same even if he told me he wants to buy them to keep them out of circulation. I expect he's lying. He's planning to sell them and make money out of me. Everyone was going to make money out of me in the old days, especially Dad, and that hasn't changed. Not in the least.'

They stared at each other.

'Come home and talk to Dad,' she said. 'He doesn't have much time left.'

'Did Wapshott talk to him?'

'No, he wasn't there when Wapshott came. I told Dad about him.'

'And what did he say?'

'Nothing. Only that he wanted his share.'

'What about you?'

'What about me?'

'Why have you never left him? Why haven't you got married and had a family of your own? It's not your life that you're living, it's his life. Where's your life?'

'I suppose it's in the wheelchair you put him in,' Stefanía snorted, 'and don't you dare ask about my life.'

'He has the same power over you that he had over me in the old days.'

Stefanía exploded with rage.

'Someone had to look after him! His favourite, his star, turned into a voiceless queer who pushed him down the stairs and hasn't dared talk to him since. Prefers sitting in his house at night and creeping out before he wakes up. What power does he have over you? You think you got rid of him for once and for all, but just look at you! Look at yourself! What are you? Tell me that! You're nothing. You're scum.'

She stopped.

'Sorry,' he said. 'I shouldn't have said that.'

She didn't answer him.

'Does he ask about me?'

'No.'

'He never talks about me?'

'No, never.'

'He hates the way I live. He hates the way I am. He hates me. After all these years.'

*

'Why didn't you tell me this before?' Erlendur said. 'Why this game of hide-and-seek?'

'Hide-and-seek? Well, you can imagine. I didn't want to talk about family matters. I thought I could protect us, our privacy.'

'Was this the last time you saw your brother?'

'Yes.'

'Are you quite sure?'

'Yes.' Stefanía looked at him. 'What are you implying?'

'Didn't you catch him with a young man just as your father did, and throw a fit? That recalled the root of the unhappiness in your life and so you decided to put an end to it.'

'No, what ...?'

'We have a witness.'

'A witness?'

'The lad who was with him. A young man who did your brother favours for money. You caught them in the basement, the lad ran away and you attacked your brother. Saw a knife on his desk and attacked him.'

'That's all wrong!' Stefanía said, sensing that Erlendur meant what he was saying, sensing the noose genuinely closing on her. She stared at Erlendur, unable to believe her own ears.

'There's a witness—' Erlendur began, but didn't manage to finish the sentence.

'What witness? What witness are you talking about?'

'Do you deny having caused your brother's death?'

The hotel telephone began ringing and before Erlendur could answer his mobile began ringing in his jacket pocket as well. He cast an apologetic look at Stefanía, who glared back at him.

'I must take this call,' Erlendur said.

Stefanía backed off and he saw her take one of Gudlaugur's records, which was on the desk, out of its cover. When Erlendur answered the hotel telephone she was scrutinising the record. It was Sigurdur Óli. Erlendur answered his mobile and asked the caller there to hold.

'A man got in touch with me just now about the murder at the hotel and I gave him your mobile number,' Sigurdur Óli said. 'Has he called you?'

'There's someone on the other line right now,' Erlendur said.

'It looks as though we've solved this case. Talk to him and call me. I sent three cars over. Elínborg's with them.'

Erlendur put the receiver down and picked up his mobile again. He didn't recognise the voice, but the man introduced himself and started his account. He had barely begun before Erlendur's suspicions were confirmed and he figured it all out. They had a long talk and at the end of the conversation Erlendur asked the caller to go down to the police station and give a statement to Sigurdur Óli. He called Elínborg and gave her instructions. Then he put his mobile away and turned to Stefanía, who had put Gudlaugur's record on the turntable and switched it on.

'Sometimes, in the old days,' she said, 'when records like this were being made, there was all kinds of background noise that got onto the recordings, maybe because people didn't take much care about making them, the technology was primitive and the recording facilities were poor too. You can even hear passing traffic on them. Did you know that?'

'No,' Erlendur said, not grasping the point.

'You can hear it on this song, for example, if you listen carefully. I don't think anyone would notice unless they knew it was there.'

She turned up the volume. Erlendur pricked up his ears and noticed a background sound in the middle of the song.

'What is that?' he asked.

'It's Dad,' Stefanía said.

She played the part of the song again and Erlendur could hear it clearly, although he couldn't make out what was being said.

'That's your father?' Erlendur said.

'He's telling him he's wonderful,' Stefanía said remotely. 'He was standing near the microphone and couldn't contain himself.'

She looked at Erlendur.

'My father died yesterday,' she said. 'He lay down on the sofa after dinner and fell asleep as he sometimes did, and never woke up again. As soon as I entered the room I could tell he was gone. I sensed it before I touched him. The doctor said he had had a heart attack. That's why I came to the hotel to see you, to make a clean sweep. It doesn't matter any more. Not for him and not for me either. None of this matters any more.'

She played the snatch of song a third time and on this occasion Erlendur thought he could make out what was said. A single word attached to the song like a footnote.

Wonderful.

'I went down to Gudlaugur's room the day he was murdered to tell him that Dad wanted a reconciliation. By then I'd told Dad that Gudlaugur kept a key to the house and had sneaked inside, sat in the living room and crept back out without our noticing. I didn't know how Gudlaugur would react, whether he wanted to see Dad again or whether it was hopeless to try to reconcile them, but I wanted to try. The door to his room was open ...'

Her voice quavered.

' ... and there he lay in his own blood ...'

She paused.

' ... in that costume ... with his trousers down ... covered in blood ...'

Erlendur went over to her.

'My God,' she groaned. 'I'd never in my life ... it was too appalling for words. I don't know what I thought. I was terrified. I think my only thought was to get out and try to forget it. Like all the rest. I convinced myself it was none of my business. That it didn't matter whether I was there or not, it was over and done with and was none of my business. I pushed it away, acted like a child. I didn't want to know about it and I didn't tell my father what I saw. Didn't tell a soul.'

She looked at Erlendur.

'I should have called for help. Of course I should have called the police ... but ... it ... it was so disgusting, so unnatural ... that I ran away. That was the only thing I thought of. Getting away. To escape from that terrible place and not let a single person see me.'

She paused.

'I think I've always been fleeing him. Somehow I've always been running away from him. All the time. And there ...'

She sobbed gently.

'We should have tried to patch things up much earlier. I should have arranged that long before. That's my crime. Dad wanted that too, in the end. Before he died.'

They fell silent and Erlendur looked out of the window, and noticed that it was snowing less.

'The most terrifying thing was ...'

She stopped, as if the thought was unbearable.

'He wasn't dead, was he?'

She shook her head.

'He said one word, then he died. He saw me in the doorway and groaned my name. That he used to call me. When we were little. He always called me Steffi.'

'And they heard him say your name before he died. Steffi.'

She looked at him in surprise.

'They who?'

Suddenly Eva Lind was standing in the open doorway. She stared at Stefanía and at Erlendur, then at Stefanía again and shook her head.

'How many women have you got on the go anyway?' she said, with an accusatory look at her father.

33

He couldn't discern any change in Ösp. Erlendur stood watching her working, wondering if she would ever show remorse or guilt for what she had done.

'Have you found her, that Steffí?' she asked when she saw him in the corridor. She dumped a pile of towels into the laundry bin, took some fresh ones and put them in the room. Erlendur walked closer and stopped in the doorway, his thoughts elsewhere.

He was thinking about his daughter. He had managed to convince her who Stefanía actually was, and when Stefanía left he asked Eva Lind to wait for him. Eva sat down on the bed and he could tell at once that she was altered, she was back to her old ways. She launched into a tirade against him for everything that had gone wrong in her life and he stood and listened without saying a word, without objecting or enraging her even further. He knew why she was angry. She was not angry with him but with herself, because she had crashed. She could control herself no longer.

He didn't know what drug she was using. He looked at his watch.

'Are you in a hurry to go somewhere?' she said. 'Rushing off to save the world?'

'Can you wait for me here?' he said.

'Piss off,' she said, her voice hoarse and ugly.

'Why do you do this to yourself?'

'Shut up.'

'Will you wait for me? I won't be long and then we'll go home. Would you like that?'

She didn't answer. Sat with bowed head, looking out of the window at nothing.

'I won't be a minute,' he said.

'Don't go,' she pleaded, her voice less harsh now. 'Where are you going?'

'What's wrong?' he asked.

'What's wrong!' she barked. 'Everything's wrong. Everything! This fucking bloody life. That's what's wrong, life. Everything's wrong in this life! I don't know what it's for. I don't know why we live it. Why! Why??'

'Eva, it'll be—'

'God, how I regret not having her,' she groaned.

He put his arm around her.

'Every day. When I wake up in the morning and when I fall asleep at night. I think about her every single day and what I did to her.'

'That's good,' Erlendur said. 'You ought to think about her every day.'

'But it's so hard and you never break out of it. Never. What am I supposed to do? What can I do?'

'Don't forget her. Think about her. Always. She helps you that way.'

'How I wish I'd had her. What kind of a person am I? What kind of person does something like that? To her own child.'

'Eva.' He put his arm around her, she huddled up to him and they sat like that on the edge of the bed while the snow quietly settled over the city.

When they had been sitting for some time Erlendur whispered to her to wait for him in the room. He was going to take her home and celebrate Christmas with her. They looked at each other. Calmer now, she gave a nod.

But now he was standing at the door of a room on the floor below watching Ösp at work. He couldn't stop thinking about Eva. He knew he had to hurry back to her, take her home, be with her and spend Christmas with her.

'We talked to Steffi,' he called into the room. 'Her proper name's Stefanía and she was Gudlaugur's sister.'

Ösp came out of the bathroom.

'And what, does she deny everything, or …?'

'No, she doesn't deny anything,' Erlendur said. 'She knows where her fault lies and she's wondering what went wrong, when it happened and why. She's feeling bad but is beginning to come to terms with it. It's tough for her because it's too late for her to make amends.'

'Did she confess?'

'Yes,' Erlendur said. 'Most of it. In effect. She didn't confess in so many words but she knows the part she played.'

'Most of it? What's that supposed to mean?'

Ösp walked through the doorway past him to fetch detergent and a cloth, then went back into the bathroom. Erlendur walked inside and watched her cleaning as he had done before when the case was still open and she was a kind of friend of his.

'Everything, really,' he said. 'Except the murder. That's the only thing she's not going to own up to.'

Ösp sprayed cleaner onto the bathroom mirror, unmoved.

'But my brother saw her,' she said. 'He saw her stab her brother. She can't deny that. She can't deny being there.'

'No,' Erlendur said. 'She was down in the basement when he died. It just wasn't her who stabbed him.'

'Yes, Reynir saw it,' she said. 'She can't deny it.'

'How much do you owe them?'

'Owe them?'

'How much is it?'

'Owe who? What are you talking about?'

Ösp rubbed the mirror like her life depended on it, like it would all be over if she stopped, the mask would drop and she would have to give up. She went on spraying and polishing, and avoided looking herself in the eye.

Erlendur watched her and a phrase from a book he once read about paupers in times of old crossed his mind: she was a bastard child of the world.

'Elínborg is a colleague of mine who just checked your record at the crisis centre. The rape crisis centre. It was about six months ago. There were three of them. It took place in a hut by Lake Raudavatn. That was all you said. You claimed not to know who they were. They snatched you one Friday night when you were in town, took you to that hut and raped you one after the other.'

Ösp went on polishing the mirror and Erlendur couldn't see whether what he said had the slightest effect on her.

'In the end you refused to identify them and refused to press charges.'

Ösp did not say a word.

'You work at this hotel but you don't earn enough to clear your debts and you don't earn enough to cover your habit. You've managed to keep them at bay with small payments and they give you more stuff, but they've been threatening you and you know they follow through with their threats.'

Ösp did not look at him.

'There's no pilfering at this hotel, is there?' Erlendur said. 'You said that to hoodwink us, lead us on a wild goose chase.'

Erlendur heard a noise in the corridor and saw Elínborg and four police officers in front of the door. He gestured to her to wait.

'Your brother is in the same position as you. Maybe you have the same account with them, I don't know. He's been beaten up. He's been threatened. Your parents have been threatened. You don't dare to name these people. The police can't act because they are only threats, and when these people do do something, seize you and rape you in a hut, you don't give their names. Nor does your brother.'

Erlendur paused and watched her.

'A man phoned me just now. He works for the police, the drug squad. He sometimes gets calls from informants who tell him what they hear on the streets and on the drug scene. He received a call late last night, this morning really, from a man who said he had heard a story about a young girl who was raped six months ago and had trouble paying her dealers, until she settled her debt a couple of days ago. Both for herself and for her brother. Does that sound familiar?'

Ösp shook her head.

'It doesn't sound familiar?' Erlendur asked again. 'The informant knew the girl's name and that she worked at the hotel where Santa Claus was killed.'

Ösp went on shaking her head.

'We know that Gudlaugur had half a million in his room,' Erlendur said.

She stopped wiping the mirror, dropped her hands to her sides and stared at herself.

'I've been trying to stop.'

'Drugs?'

'It's pointless. They're merciless if you owe them.'

'Will you tell me who they are?'

'I didn't mean to kill him. He was always nice to me. And then ...'

'You saw the money?'

'I needed the money.'

'Was it because of the money? That you attacked him?'

She didn't answer.

'Was it the money? Or was it because of your brother?'

'A bit of both,' Ösp said in a low voice.

'You wanted the money.'

'Yes.'

'And he was taking advantage of your brother.'

'Yes.'

*

Out of the corner of her eye she saw her brother on his knees, a pile of money on the bed and the knife, and without a moment's thought she grabbed the knife and tried to stab Gudlauger. He parried her with his arms but she lurched at him again and again until he stopped thrashing around and slumped against the wall. Blood spurted out of a wound in his chest, his heart.

The knife was bloodstained, her hands were bloody and blood had spilled onto her coat. Her brother had got up from the floor and run out into the corridor, heading for the stairs.

Gudlaugur gave a heavy groan.

A deathly silence descended in the little room. She stared at Gudlaugur and at the knife in her hands. Suddenly Reynir reappeared.

'Someone's coming down the stairs,' he whispered.

He took the money, grabbed his sister who was glued to the spot, and dragged her out of the room and into the alcove at the end of the corridor. They hardly dared to breathe as the woman approached. She peered into the darkness but did not see them.

When she reached Gudlaugur's door she let out a muffled scream and they could hear Gudlaugur.

'Steffí,' he groaned.

Then they heard nothing more.

The woman went into the room but they saw her come straight back out. She backed away all the way up against the corridor wall, then suddenly turned away from the room and walked off quickly without so much as a backward glance.

*

'I threw the coat away and found another one. Reynir got out. I had to go on working. Otherwise you'd have sussed it all out at once, or I thought so anyway. Then I was asked to fetch him for the Christmas party. I couldn't refuse. I couldn't do anything that would draw attention to myself. I went down and waited in the corridor. His door was still open but I didn't go inside. I went back up and said I found him in his room and I thought he was dead.'

Ösp looked down at the floor.

'The worst thing is he was never anything but kind to me. Maybe that's why I got so mad. Because he was one of the few people who treated me decently here, and then my brother ... I went mental. After everything that ...'

'After everything they did to you?' Erlendur said.

'There's no point in bringing charges against those bastards. For the most brutal and bloodiest rapes they maybe get a year, a year and a half inside. Then they come back out. You lot can't do anything. There's nowhere to go for help. You just have to pay up. No matter how you go about it. I took the money and I paid. Maybe I killed him for the money. Maybe because of Reynir. I don't know. I don't know ...'

She paused.

'I went mental,' she repeated. 'I've never felt like that before. Never flown into such a rage. I relived every second in that hut. Saw them. Saw it all happening again. I took the knife and tried to stab him everywhere I could. Tried to slash him and he tried to defend himself but I just stabbed and stabbed and stabbed until he stopped moving.'

She looked at Erlendur.

'I didn't realise it was that hard. That hard to kill someone.'

Elínborg appeared in the doorway and gestured to Erlendur that she couldn't understand why they didn't arrest the girl.

'Where's the knife?' Erlendur asked.

'The knife?' Ösp said, walking over to him.

'The one you used.'

She paused for a moment.

'I put it back where it belongs,' she said eventually. 'I cleaned it as well as I could in the staff coffee room, then got rid of it before you came.'

'And where is it?'

'I put it back where it belongs.'

'In the kitchen, where the cutlery's kept?'

'Yes.'

'The hotel must own five hundred knives like that,' Erlendur said in desperation. 'How are we supposed to find it?'

'You could start in the buffet.'

'The buffet?'

'Someone's sure to be using it.'

34

Erlendur handed over Ösp to Elínborg and the officers and hurried up to his room where Eva Lind was waiting for him. He put his card in the slot and threw the door open to find that she had opened the big window completely and was sitting on the windowsill, looking down at the snow falling to the ground several floors below.

'Eva,' he said calmly.

Eva said something he couldn't make out.

'Come on, dear,' he said, approaching her cautiously.

'It looks so easy,' Eva Lind said.

'Eva, come on,' Erlendur said in a low voice. 'Home.'

She turned around. She took a long look at him, and then nodded.

'Let's go,' she said quietly, stepped down onto the floor and closed the window.

He walked over to her and kissed her on the forehead.

'Did I rob you of your childhood, Eva?' he said in a low voice.

'Eh?' she said.

'Nothing,' he said.

Erlendur took a long look into her eyes. Sometimes he could see white swans in them.

Now they were black.

Erlendur's mobile rang in the lift on the way down to the lobby. He recognised the voice at once.

'I just wanted to wish you a merry Christmas,' Valgerdur said, and she seemed to be whispering down the phone.

'You too,' Erlendur said. 'Merry Christmas.'

In the lobby, Erlendur glanced into the dining room packed with tourists gorging themselves on the Christmas Eve buffet and chattering away in all imaginable languages, their joyful murmuring spreading all over the ground floor. He couldn't help thinking that one of them was holding a murder weapon in his hands.

He told the head of reception that Rósant may well have been responsible for sending the woman who slept with him that night and who demanded payment afterwards. The man replied that he was beginning to suspect something of the sort. He had already informed the owners of the hotel about what manager and head waiter were up to, but did not know how they would tackle the matter.

Erlendur caught a glimpse of the hotel manager looking in astonishment at Eva Lind. He was going to pretend he hadn't noticed him, but the manager darted into his path.

'I just wanted to thank you, and of course you don't need to pay for your stay!'

'I've already settled,' Erlendur said. 'Goodbye.'

'What about Henry Wapshott?' the manager asked, blocking Erlendur's way. 'What are you going to do with him?'

Erlendur stopped. He was holding Eva Lind by the hand and she looked at the manager with drowsy eyes.

'We're sending him home. Was there anything else?'

The manager dithered.

'Are you going to do anything about those lies the girl told you about the conference guests?'

Erlendur smiled to himself.

'Are you worried about that?'

'It's all lies.'

Erlendur put his arm around Eva Lind and they set off towards the front door.

'We'll see,' he said.

When they crossed the lobby Erlendur noticed people stopping all about and looking around. The sentimental Christmas songs were no longer jingling through the speakers, and Erlendur smiled to himself when he heard that the reception manager had agreed to his request and changed the music on the sound system. He thought about the records. He had asked Stefanía where she thought they might be, but she didn't know. Had no idea where her brother kept them, and was uncertain whether they would ever be found.

Gradually the murmuring in the dining room died down. The guests exchanged astonished looks and peered up at the ceiling in search of the wondrously beautiful song that reached their ears. The staff stopped in their tracks to listen. Time seemed to stand still.

They left the hotel and in his mind Erlendur sang the beautiful hymn in chorus with the young Gudlaugur, and sensed once again the deep yearning in the boy's voice.

O Father, turn me into a light for all my life's short stay . . .

Read on for an excerpt from
the next Inspector Erlendur thriller

The Draining Lake

Now Available

1

She stood motionless for a long time, staring at the bones as if it should not be possible for them to be there. Any more than for her.

At first she thought it was another sheep that had drowned in the lake, until she moved closer and saw the skull half-buried in the lake bed and the shape of a human skeleton. The ribs protruded from the sand and beneath them could be seen the outlines of the pelvis and thigh bones. The skeleton was lying on its left side so she could see the right side of the skull, the empty eye sockets and three teeth in the upper jaw. One had a large silver filling. There was a wide hole in the skull itself, about the size of a matchbox, which she instinctively thought could have been made by a hammer. She bent down and stared at the skull. With some hesitation she explored the hole with her finger. The skull was full of sand.

The thought of a hammer crossed her mind again and she shuddered at the idea of someone being struck over the head with one. But the hole was too large to have been left by a hammer. She decided not to touch the skeleton again. Instead, she took out her mobile and dialled emergency services.

She wondered what to say. Somehow this was so completely unreal. A skeleton so far out in the lake, buried on its sandy bed. Nor was she on her best form. Visions of hammers and matchboxes. She found it difficult to concentrate. Her thoughts were roaming all over the place and she had great trouble rounding them up again.

It was probably because she was hung-over. After planning to spend the day at home she had changed her mind and gone to the lake. She had persuaded herself that she must check the instruments. She was a scientist. She had always wanted to be a scientist and knew that the measurements had to be monitored carefully. But she had a splitting headache and her thoughts were far from logical. The National Energy Authority had held its annual dinner dance the night before and, as was sometimes the way, she had had too much to drink.

She thought about the man lying in her bed at home and knew that it was on his account that she had hauled herself off to the lake. She did not want to be there when he woke up and hoped that he would be gone when she returned. He had come back to her flat after the dance but was not very exciting. No more than the others she had met since her divorce. He hardly talked about anything except his CD collection and carried on long after she had given up feigning any interest. Then she fell asleep in a living-room chair. When she woke up she saw that he had got into her bed, where he was sleeping with his mouth open, wearing tiny underpants and black socks.

'Emergency services,' a voice said over the line.

'Hello – I'd like to report that I've found some bones,' she said. 'There's a skull with a hole in it.'

She grimaced. Bloody hangover! Who says that sort of thing? A skull with a hole in it. She remembered a phrase from a children's rhyme about a penny with a hole in it. Or was it a shilling?

'Your name, please,' said the neutral emergency-services voice.

She straightened out her jumbled thoughts and stated her name.

'Where is it?'

'Lake Kleifarvatn. North side.'

'Did you pull it up in a fishing net?'

'No. It's buried on the bed of the lake.'

'Are you a diver?'

'No, it's standing up out of the bed. Ribs and the skull.'

'It's on the bottom of the lake?'

'Yes.'

'So how can you see it?'

'I'm standing here looking at it.'

'Did you bring it to dry land?'

'No, I haven't touched it,' she lied instinctively.

The voice on the telephone paused.

'What kind of crap is this?' the voice said at last, angrily. 'Is this a hoax? You know what you can get for wasting our time?'

'It's not a hoax. I'm standing here looking at it.'

'So you can walk on water, I suppose?'

'The lake's gone,' she said. 'There's no water any more. Just the bed. Where the skeleton is.'

'What do you mean, the lake's gone?'

'It hasn't all gone, but it's dry now where I'm standing. I'm a hydrologist with the Energy Authority. I was recording the water level when I discovered this skeleton. There's a hole in the skull and most of the bones are buried in the sand on the bottom. I thought it was a sheep at first.'

'A sheep?'

'We found one the other day that had drowned years ago. When the lake was bigger.'

There was another pause.

'Wait there,' said the voice reluctantly. 'I'll send a patrol car.'

She stood still by the skeleton for a while, then walked over to the shore and measured the distance. She was certain the bones had not surfaced when she was taking measurements at the same place a fortnight earlier. Otherwise she would have seen them. The water level had dropped by more than a metre since then.

The scientists from the Energy Authority had been puzzling over this conundrum ever since they'd noticed that the water level in Lake Kleifarvatn was falling rapidly. The authority had set up its first automatic surface-level monitor in 1964 and one of the hydrologists' tasks was to check the measurements. In the summer of 2000 the monitor seemed to have broken. An incredible amount of water was draining from the lake every day, twice the normal volume.

She walked back to the skeleton. She was itching to take a better look, dig it up and brush off the sand, but imagined that the police would be none too pleased at that. She wondered whether it was male or female and vaguely recalled having read somewhere, probably in a detective story, that their skeletons were almost identical: only the pelvises were different. Then she remembered someone telling her not to believe anything she read in detective stories. Since the skeleton was buried in the sand she couldn't see the pelvis, and it struck her that she would not have known the difference anyway.

Her hangover intensified and she sat down on the sand beside the bones. It was a Sunday morning and the occasional car drove past the lake. She imagined they were families out for a Sunday drive to Herdísarvík and on to Selvogur. That was a popular and scenic route, across the lava field and hills and past the lake down to the sea. She thought about the families in the cars. Her own husband had left her when the doctors ruled out their ever having children together. He remarried shortly afterwards and now had two lovely children. He had found happiness.

All that she had found was a man she barely knew, lying in her bed in his socks. Decent men became harder to find as the years went by. Most of them were either divorced like her or, even worse, had never been in a relationship at all.

She looked woefully at the bones, half-buried in the sand, and was close to tears.

About an hour later a police car approached from Hafnarfjördur. It was in no hurry, lazily threading its way along the road towards the lake. This was May and the sun was high in the sky, reflecting off the smooth surface of the water. She sat on the sand watching the road and when she waved to the car it pulled over. Two police officers got out, looked in her direction and walked towards her.

They stood over the skeleton in silence for a long time until one of them poked a rib with his foot.

'Do you reckon he was fishing?' he said to his colleague.

'On a boat, you mean?'

'Or waded here.'

'There's a hole,' she said, looking at each of them in turn. 'In the skull.'

One officer bent down.

'Well,' he said.

'He could have fallen over in the boat and broken his skull,' his colleague said.

'It's full of sand,' said the first one.

'Shouldn't we notify CID?' the other asked.

'Aren't most of them in America?' his colleague said, looking up into the sky. 'At a crime conference?'

The other officer nodded. Then they stood quietly over the bones for a while until one of them turned to her.

'Where's all the water gone?' he asked.

'There are various theories,' she said. 'What are you going to do? Can I go home now?'

After exchanging glances they took down her name and thanked her, without apologising for having kept her waiting. She didn't care. She wasn't in a hurry. It was a beautiful day by the lake and she would have enjoyed it even more in the company of her hangover if she had not chanced upon the skeleton. She wondered whether the man in the black socks had left her flat and certainly hoped so. Looked forward to renting a video that evening and snuggling up under a blanket in front of the television.

She looked down at the bones and at the hole in the skull.

Maybe she would rent a good detective film.